Murder Under The Pier

ALSO BY MAX MANNING

DETECTIVES KANE & GRANGER
Book 1: A Body On The Flats
Book 2: Murder Under The Pier

STANDALONE
The Killer In Me

MURDER
Under the
PIER

MAX MANNING

Detectives Kane & Granger Book 2

JOFFE BOOKS

Joffe Books, London
www.joffebooks.com

First published in Great Britain in 2025

© Max Manning

This book is a work of fiction. Names, characters, businesses, organisations, places and events are either the product of the author's imagination or are used fictitiously. Any resemblance to actual persons, living or dead, events or locales is entirely coincidental. The spelling used is British English except where fidelity to the author's rendering of accent or dialect supersedes this. The right of Max Manning to be identified as author of this work has been asserted in accordance with the Copyright, Designs and Patents Act 1988.

No part of this book may be used or reproduced in any manner for the purpose of training artificial intelligence technologies or systems. In accordance with Article 4(3) of the Digital Single Market Directive 2019/790, Joffe Books expressly reserves this work from the text and data mining exception.

Cover art by Dee Dee Book Covers

ISBN: 978-1-80573-045-3

For my wife, Valerie.

CHAPTER 1

Murder is a cold-blooded business. Edison Kane knows that better than most.

He takes a deep breath and gazes across the estuary. The vast sky wears an ominous pre-dawn glow. With a shiver, he pulls the collar of his coat up against the spiteful wind and treads swiftly through the mud. He ducks beneath the blue-and-white tape and steps under the pier.

The Detective Inspector's eyes photograph the scene. The victim is in his mid-forties, his hair short and sandy. He's wearing a pale blue shirt, the sleeves rolled up neatly to his elbows, and black jeans.

He's staring dead-eyed at Kane. An expression of confusion mixed with terror on his pale, clean-shaven face. The noose around his neck is fashioned from a length of what looks like blue nylon rope tied to a rusty horizontal beam. Kane shivers again. This time it isn't the wind. He's seen countless bodies in his time but something about this one chills him to the bone.

He looks across at the lone police constable standing guard with his back to the encroaching water. The man's shoulders are hunched, his hands tucked in the pockets of his jacket.

"Get the pathologist to message me when he gets here. And make sure he knows the tide is coming in. I'll be waiting in the café across the road."

The uniform gives him a withering stare, followed by an almost imperceptible nod. Kane turns and walks away, a sympathetic smile tugging at his lips. He remembers well what it's like to be at the bottom of the pile. At the beck and call of the higher ranks. The officer's attitude could be better but who can blame him? He looks bored rigid, in need of a good feed and several degrees colder than the corpse he's guarding.

Kane retraces his route across the mud and climbs the concrete steps up to the promenade, his breath curling like wisps of smoke in the cold air. The yellow glow from the café's steam-fogged windows looks warm and inviting.

He opens the door and sits at the nearest vacant table. The place is busy considering the early hour. Kane orders a black coffee. A couple of years ago, when the sight of a dead body had zero effect on his appetite, he would have happily tucked into a greasy fry-up. Things are different now.

Since the murder of his wife, every killing feels personal. A fresh bleed from an unhealed wound.

The door swings open and Kane greets the new arrival with a nod. Detective Sergeant Bailey Granger sits down and smiles at him.

"Why the hell are these seaside resorts always so bloody miserable in the winter?"

Kane doesn't answer this. He knows Granger is not expecting him to. "I wasn't sure you'd want to come back to this town. You know, after what happened to you."

"Didn't have much choice, did I? I was told you were desperate for me to be assigned to this case. I guess you must be missing me."

Kane nods. Narrowly escaping with your life after being kidnapped by a serial killer is enough to make anyone rethink the risks they're taking. Stepping away from the murder team turned out to be a good career move for Granger too.

It's true. He's missed working with her. Missed her youthful energy, her quick mind and ability to rein him in when necessary. But the main reason he wants her back on his team is that she's a good detective. Very good. "Congratulations on your promotion, by the way. I suppose you'll be after my job next. I'd better watch my back."

Granger doesn't deny it. "So, what are we looking at? Fill me in."

Kane smiles, remembering how Granger likes to get straight to business. "An as-yet unidentified male, mid-forties, found dead under the pier. Suspended by his neck. Simple noose arrangement. Blue braided nylon rope."

Granger frowns. "Any chance this is suicide?"

"No chance. Not the way the rope is set up."

Kane's phone vibrates. He digs it out of his pocket and checks the screen: Carter has arrived.

"Come on, follow me. You can see for yourself."

Walking down the shingle beach, Kane can see that someone has been busy in his absence. Wooden timber boards stretch across the estuary mud providing a safe, clean walkway. Powerful spotlights illuminate the crime scene as four hunched figures in white forensic suits, hooded and masked, move slowly around the victim, scooping mud into shallow plastic boxes.

The tall, gaunt figure of Martin Carter stands just outside the taped area, waving his hands as he directs a police photographer snapping pictures of the suspended body. As Kane and Granger approach, the pathologist turns and pulls down his face mask. "Whose bright idea was it to drag me out of my warm bed? There isn't time for me to do anything useful here."

Kane has known Carter for years and has never seen him this ruffled. "Lovely to see you too, Martin. What's the problem?"

"What the hell does it look like? I get here to be told the crime scene is about to be flooded. We have thirty minutes at the most before seawater is swirling around our knees. Forensics are doing their best to remove the surface before any evidence is swept away. Then it's going to have to be sifted and that will take days."

Kane doesn't say what he's thinking, which is that maybe the pathologist should stop complaining and concentrate on the job in hand.

"Have you had the chance to take a look at the victim?"

Carter gives him a scornful look. "Well, he's hanging by his neck right in front of me. He's pretty difficult not to look at. I'm sure you can see for yourself that there is no chance that this is suicide."

Kane nods and Carter turns to Granger, inviting her to explain. She doesn't hesitate.

"There is no way the victim could have put the noose around his neck and tied the rope to the metal strut himself. It's too high and there is no sign of a step ladder."

Carter smiles. "Spot on, Detective. You passed the test."

Kane cringes. He knows what's coming, and before he can ask another question to steer the conversation, Granger takes a quick step closer to the pathologist and lifts her chin.

"Sorry," she says, in a way that makes it clear that she isn't, "but I don't need to pass any tests. I'm a detective sergeant and a good one. I'm not your student and you are not my teacher. Anyway, it doesn't take a genius to work it out."

Carter takes a step back and raises both hands in apology. "Whoa, wait. I wasn't trying to suggest anything of the sort. I didn't mean to offend you."

"You may not have meant to but that doesn't mean you didn't," Granger says with a disarming smile.

The exchange reminds Kane of some of the reasons he lobbied so hard to get Granger back on his team — her sharpness at assessing a crime scene and her ability to speak her mind without causing offence.

"I remember you now," Carter says. "Of course. You're the detective who was almost killed by the See No Evil killer."

"That's right," Granger says. "We got him. We put another murderer behind bars. It's done. It's in the past, and I'm only interested in catching the next one."

Kane decides to move the conversation on. "Any idea how long the victim has been here? Time of death?"

Carter shakes his head. "I'm not a miracle worker. You'll have to wait until I carry out the autopsy. First, I've got to get the body cut down before the tide swamps us."

Kane scans the crime scene and the deserted beach to his right. Even in the icy grip of winter, the promenade and the streets around the pier can be busy during the day and late into the evening. The victim must have been strung up in the early hours.

"Let's go," he says to Granger. "There's nothing for us here."

Carter lifts a hand and waves his forefinger. "I didn't say that, Detective Inspector. There is something you need to hear before you leave."

Kane has worked with the pathologist enough to know that he loves a dramatic moment. It pisses him off every time but he's learned to put up with it. If Carter's excited, it means he's found something significant.

"Come on then, Martin. For God's sake, get on with it."

Carter grins. "I was able to get close enough to examine the neck and face. There's damage to the neck caused by the tightening of the noose but very little bruising. Nowhere near as much as I would expect. There's also a marked absence of what we call petechial haemorrhages around the neck and face. Tiny purple or black spots caused by capillary rupture."

"Get to the point. This means what?"

"This means that I'm fairly sure our victim was already dead before he was hanged. He'd probably been dead for a while. No heart pumping means no blood circulating, no proper bruising, no strangulation marks."

"You're suggesting that he was murdered, then later strung up under the pier, the body put on show for all to see?"

"Exactly."

"Why would anybody do that?"

"You tell me. You're the detective. It's up to you to work that one out."

CHAPTER 2

"Who found the body?" Kane sits down behind the desk in the office the locals always assign to Major Investigation Team detectives. Small, shabby and cold, it's one way of showing the 'big shot' outsiders that they're not welcome.

Granger puts both hands on the back of the chair opposite him and leans forward. "Actually, it was one of the uniforms. A Police Constable Mark Weaver. I'm told he was out for his regular early morning run along the seafront before starting his shift."

Kane knows he's let himself go since he lost Lizzy more than a year ago. He's always promising himself that he's going to shape up, organise a programme of regular exercise, but without her by his side it's hard to find the motivation. His inability to get more than a few hours' sleep means he needs to preserve his energy to do his job. At least, that's his excuse. There's another reason he's thought about exercising more. It might help him nod off at night. Whenever he does manage to fall asleep, he doesn't feel sad, guilty or lonely. For that short time, he doesn't miss Lizzy, because he doesn't know she's gone. And if he could just sleep long enough to dream, it's possible he could see her, even talk to her again.

"I need to speak to this PC Weaver. Is he around?"

Granger nods. "His sergeant told him to forget about working his shift today and go home but he says he's fine. I believe he's in the canteen right now."

This is one of the many reasons Kane was determined to get Granger back. She's been on the case for a couple of hours and already knows everything that's going on.

Kane gets up. "No point in wasting time then."

"He's probably still a bit shaken up. Be gentle with him."

* * *

Kane makes his way to the ground floor canteen. He attracts several curious glances, even a few hostile ones, as he navigates the busy corridors. Not a single "good morning" greeting, even though they all know who he is. He's the Brentwood MIT man drafted in last year to catch the See No Evil killer. He's the outsider who solved the case, but not before the psycho took the life of Detective Constable Linda Finch, one of their own.

The four-storey station has benefited from a taxpayer-funded refurbishment since his last visit. The fresh decor and shiny new fixtures fail to hide the utilitarian dullness of the building.

Kane pushes open the canteen door and steps inside. The room is hot, smells of coffee and chip fat and is bustling with uniforms and plainclothes officers at the end of their night duty or about to start the day tour.

He spots a police constable sitting alone at a corner table, staring into a steaming mug. The officer looks up and stands as Kane approaches. In his late twenties, he's as tall as Kane, broad-shouldered and pale, with jet-black hair.

Kane nods, pulls back a chair and they both sit down. "I take it you're Mark Weaver?"

The uniform nods nervously. Says nothing.

"I'm Detective Inspector Kane. I'm leading the investigation into the murder of the man you found hanged this morning."

"I know who you are."

Kane wonders whether Weaver is suffering from shock.

"Is this your first dead body?"

Weaver shrugs. "No. Seen a couple. An old guy who died in his armchair. A motorcyclist who hit a tree. Broke his neck."

Kane knows from experience that dead bodies aren't equal when it comes to emotional impact. Weaver needs to find a way of coping if he wants a long career in policing.

"This one was different. I know. I get it."

"I thought it was a dummy at first. Then I saw the face. The eyes. His swollen tongue . . ." Weaver falters, drops his head and covers his face with his hands.

Kane feels for the young uniform. Despite what people may think, police officers don't have their emotions surgically removed when they join up. But when it comes to murder investigations, time is of the essence. He needs to hear Weaver's account now.

"I understand you were running along the seafront?"

Weaver removes his hands from his face. Red-eyed, he sits back in his chair and sighs. "I always go for an early run if I'm not on night duty. The earlier the better. It's peaceful. Nobody around."

"Exactly what did you see and at what time?"

Weaver takes a sip of his coffee. "I ran from my flat in Shoeburyness along the seafront to the pier and back. Four miles. As I approached the pier, I dropped down from the promenade to the beach. I remember I checked my watch because I was halfway and it was 6 a.m. I'm usually a bit faster than that."

Kane isn't interested in Weaver's sporting prowess. He wants to know what he saw or didn't see.

"Do you always run past the pier?"

"Not always. The seafront is a regular route though. I saw something hanging from one of the horizontal struts. It was still quite dark. When I realised what it was, I called it in straight away."

"You phoned from under the pier?"

"No, I went back to the promenade because the phone signal was better."

Kane is impressed that Weaver was out running on a freezing February morning before working a long day shift. He definitely needs to get back into shape.

"Did you see anyone or anything suspicious?"

Weaver takes a moment to think, then shakes his head. "Not really. The beach was as deserted as usual at that time. A couple of cars passed by while I was calling the station."

"Any vehicles parked on the seafront?"

Weaver takes a longer sip of coffee. "Actually, I think I passed a white van before dropping down onto the beach."

"You think you passed it?"

"No, I did see it. It was parked. The engine was off. No lights. But, I . . ."

"But what?"

"Well, I remember now. It wasn't there when I came back to call the station."

Kane's brain buzzes. This could be an early breakthrough and early breakthroughs solve cases. He wonders what Weaver's gut is telling him.

"You think the white van could be important?"

The constable takes a moment to think before answering. When he speaks he sounds confident and almost as excited as Kane feels.

"I think the killer would have needed to get the victim as close to the crime scene as possible. A body, dead or alive, is notoriously difficult to carry."

Kane nods. Weaver has had a shock but he's still thinking logically. Maybe he could be a useful addition to the team.

He tries to remember what he was like when he was a young police constable. It's difficult. He knows he was ambitious and had his sights set on making detective right from the start. If Weaver has the same ambitions this could be his big chance.

"How would you like to be part of this murder investigation? I think you could be useful and it would be valuable experience for you."

Weaver sits up straight. "Are you serious?"

"I'm always serious. If you want, I'll request that you be assigned to my team. Be warned though, it won't be an easy ride."

Weaver nods enthusiastically. "If you think I can be of use, then I'll give it a go. I'm not afraid of hard work."

Kane is reassured by the young constable's reaction. A healthy mixture of confidence and caution.

"Right then, PC Weaver. I will sort it."

CHAPTER 3

Granger opens her front door as quietly as she can. She steps inside and closes it behind her, wincing as the lock clicks loudly into place. The short, narrow hallway is lined with neatly stacked cardboard boxes, each box labelled with the name of the room their contents need to be unpacked in.

She edges her way along the hall, determined not to wake her daughter, who she hopes is fast asleep upstairs. The living room door is ajar, and through the gap she can see her mother slumped in an armchair, head back, snoring noisily.

Her first day back on the murder squad was never going to be a good day to move house. It couldn't be helped and it's such a relief to be in a new place in a new town. She feels a pang of guilt that she left her mother to walk Daisy to school, take the bus to their new home to oversee the removal company's delivery of their belongings, then pick Daisy up, feed her and put her to bed in her new room.

What would she do without her mother? She certainly wouldn't be able to do the job she loves, not to the level she's capable of. Without her recent promotion, they would never have been able to afford moving away from the crime-ridden housing estate where she grew up in Harlow. Their new home is a smaller terraced property but it's on a quiet cul-de-sac on the outskirts of the town of Brentwood, where her Major Investigations Team is based.

Her mother stirs, gasps and her head flops to one side. She falls still, the room suddenly silent. Granger walks quickly to the armchair, kneels and touches her mother's hand. The skin is cold and clammy.

"Wake up, Mum. Come on. Mum, Mum!"

Her mother's head turns slowly and her eyes open wide. "What you doing? Why you shouting, Bailey?"

Granger let's go of her mother's hand and stands up. "Sorry, Mum. Are you all right?"

"There's nothing wrong with me, girl. Don't worry yourself. Just tired. Been a long and busy day."

Granger's heart has stopped thumping. She looks at her mother, who's now smiling up at her. She's always seemed younger than her years, her brown face free of wrinkles. She'll be sixty-six in a few months and is suddenly showing signs of ageing.

Granger wonders whether it is her fault. Maybe she's asking too much of her. She suspects that's the case. The problem is there is nothing she can do about it. Not if she wants to keep doing what she's doing.

Her mother lifts herself out of the armchair with a groan. "I suppose your working days are going to be even longer now you are back investigating murders. I still don't understand why you've chosen to go back to that after what happened to you last year."

Granger sighs. She doesn't need to be reminded how close she came to death the last time she worked with Kane. That's why she asked to be transferred to the human trafficking unit. She had made a success of that, earned her promotion to detective sergeant, and it gave her time to realise what she really wanted to do.

"I know you don't like it, Mum, and we are never going to agree on it. But I want you to know that I appreciate everything you do for me, and for Daisy."

Her mother heads for the door. "I'm going to bed. You should get some sleep too."

Granger follows her. "I'm going to get myself a hot drink then do some unpacking before I go up. I can't leave it all to you."

Her mother starts to climb the stairs, hesitating on the first step. "Do you want to tell me about your new case? I'll listen if it'll help you."

"No, Mum. Thanks for the offer but I don't think you will really want to hear the gory details."

"Actually, you're probably right. I don't want to know. It'll only make me worry more and I won't be able to sleep. I am proud of you though, darling. You do know that, don't you?"

Granger watches her mother climb the stairs slowly, her right hand gripping the banister, then walks into the kitchen. As she waits for the kettle to boil, she closes her eyes, recalling the crime scene. The victim murdered first, then strung up, left hanging like a slab of meat. What sort of mind could contemplate doing that to another human being? A monstrous one.

Why does she want to spend her life hunting monsters? To win justice for murder victims and their loved ones. To protect her family, especially her beautiful, innocent daughter.

Granger remembers the night she told Daisy, who was struggling to get back to sleep after a nightmare, that monsters don't really exist and are just pretend. Made up to make storybooks more fun.

It was a big, fat lie. Granger had seen with her own eyes that monsters live and walk among us. Every time she helps take a killer off the streets, she makes the world a safer place for her little girl.

CHAPTER 4

First thing the next morning, Kane summons his team for a briefing. The moment he walks through the door, the incident room falls silent. Granger is standing by a large whiteboard, marker pen at the ready.

In front of her are three desks occupied by the detectives who make up the initial murder squad. Kane recognises two DCs assigned from his Major Investigations Team in Brentwood. DC Meera Kush is, as usual, dressed immaculately in a dark trouser suit, her dark hair tied back in a short ponytail. She greets Kane with an almost imperceptible nod and he reminds himself that her delicate appearance belies a steely core.

Beside her sits DC Dec Brown, unshaven, his bright blue jacket clashing with his yellow tie. He flashes a toothy smile and Kane recalls that some of his colleagues refer to him on the sly as DC Dick Brain. In Kane's mind they're bullies who don't realise that the joke is on them. Brown is a lot smarter than those who like to snigger behind his back.

He strides briskly past the desks and stands beside Granger. "Good morning. Most of you have worked with me before. As usual, I'll be leading this investigation. Together we're going to catch this killer. Have no doubt about that."

He turns to Granger, who nods in the direction of the third detective. He's perched on the edge of a desk, his arms folded across his chest, his legs crossed at the ankles.

"This is Detective Sergeant Alex Scott. He's been based here in Southend for seven years and has been assigned to the team."

Heavily built, with greying, slightly receding hair, Scott acknowledges the introduction with a lazy tilt of his head but says nothing.

"It's good to have you join us," Kane says, aware that local detectives can sometimes harbour resentment toward outsiders brought in above their heads. He hopes this one won't give him trouble. "It's always handy to have a detective on the team with detailed knowledge of the area and good local contacts."

Kane points to the only uniformed officer in the room. Weaver is sitting at a desk further back, looking out of place, slightly overawed to be in the company of experienced detectives.

"This is PC Mark Weaver. He was out on an early morning run along the seafront when he found our murder victim suspended by the neck under Southend's famous leisure pier. I suggested getting him assigned to the team and he has agreed to join us. Of course, we will be able to call on some of his uniformed colleagues as and when we need to."

He steps aside and gives Granger a nod. She writes the word "VICTIM" in capital letters at the top of the whiteboard and puts a question mark underneath it.

"We still haven't identified the victim. That's got to be our priority. I'm told he had nothing on him — no wallet, no credit cards. It looks like the killer removed them, possibly to drain the victim's bank accounts." She glances at Scott. "Any progress on the missing persons reports?"

The detective shakes his head. "Nothing so far. We've got two reports filed at the moment — two or three a day is pretty normal here. A girl of fifteen who hasn't been home for three days and an old dear in her eighties who's done a runner from a care home on the seafront."

"What about DNA?" Kush asks.

Granger shrugs. "That will be taken later this morning at the autopsy and we'll run it through all our databases. The chances of a match are low unless our victim has been arrested or convicted of a crime."

"I suppose it's possible that the dead man lives alone and has no friends, so there is no one to notice that he's not around," says Brown.

Scott shakes his head and gives a snort of derision. "Someone will report him missing soon. The man's bound to have family, neighbours, possibly workmates — someone he deals with on a daily basis."

Granger turns back to the whiteboard and writes "witnesses" and "white van".

"Someone living in the area around the pier may have seen or heard something suspicious. We need to knock on doors. I know it takes a lot of time, but it often turns up something important. Mark, you can help out, and we'll need a few more uniforms. Meera, can you organise that?"

"Sure, I can do that," Kush replies, with a distinct lack of enthusiasm.

"We need to trace the white van PC Weaver saw parked near the scene," Granger continues. "Alex and Dec, you two get on to the CCTV footage. There must be plenty of cameras along the seafront. Find that van."

It can take a while for a new team to gel, Kane knows that, but a murder investigation is always a race against time and the early stages can make or break a case. It's his job to make sure his detectives are energised from the start. He steps forward. "We owe this victim justice. As murder squad detectives, we work relentlessly — we trace, we hunt, we interview and, most of all, we speak up for the dead. I expect us all to bring maximum effort, focus and commitment to solving this case. Now, let's get cracking."

CHAPTER 5

Kane is surprised to find Martin Carter asleep in his office. He's sitting back in the chair, his long legs raised, the heels of his shiny black shoes resting on the edge of the desk.

Kane slams the door shut. Carter opens his eyes, mumbles a string of obscenities and closes them again. In the past, Kane has put up with the man's quirks because he's never worked with a better pathologist. Since losing Lizzy, he's less tolerant than he used to be. He guesses it's down to the anger still burning like acid deep inside.

"Come on, Martin. I haven't got time for this bullshit. It's not funny."

Carter slides his feet off the desk and sits up straight. "You think you're busy? I've three autopsies scheduled today. Your man found hanging under the pier, and then I've got to travel to London to do two more. A few years ago it would be one autopsy a week. It seems murder is all the rage nowadays and it's exhausting."

Kane believes him but right now there is only one dead body he's interested in.

"I know you're busy, so why are you wasting time? I was expecting you to examine our man this morning."

"Keep calm, Inspector Kane. It's all done. I sacrificed a couple of hours of sleep to start early. No, no, there's no need to thank me."

Kane sits on the edge of his desk and leans toward Carter. The pathologist wouldn't be here in person unless he had found something of particular interest. He never misses the opportunity to bask in his own brilliance. Kane suppresses an urge to tell him to stop messing around and get on with his job. As much as it irks him, he decides to play along.

"I take it you were right about the victim already being dead when he was strung up?"

"Of course," Carter says with a grin. "And I'm happy to report that I now know how he was murdered. Although it still needs to be confirmed with more specialist blood tests, I'm confident I'm right about this too. Toxicology reports can take several weeks, as you know, but I'll send you my initial findings report later today."

Kane sighs. "Just get to the point and tell me now."

Carter holds up a hand. "Calm down. There were no obvious signs of injury on the victim's body, apart from the damage to the neck done by the noose. For someone who I'd say was in his forties, he seemed to be robust and in good health. However, I did find a subcutaneous puncture wound on the left side of his abdomen. I did some preliminary blood tests and I'm confident he died after someone injected him with insulin. But, like I said, Toxicology will confirm that."

Kane's mind races. He has a hundred questions and needs to prioritise the important ones.

"An insulin injection would kill you?"

"If the dose is large enough, then yes, it most certainly would. You'd fall into a coma and brain cells would start dying off rapidly."

"A subcutaneous injection is a jab into the fat beneath the skin?"

"Correct. Well done you."

"Is that a tricky procedure? Would you need some medical training?"

"Not particularly, but it would help."

Kane pauses to think. This is unexpected. Murder by insulin injection is not something he's come across before. There are so many simpler ways to snuff out a life. The killer must have a reason for choosing this method. It shows premeditation and would need meticulous planning.

"I assume it's not easy to get hold of insulin unless you are prescribed it because you're diabetic, or you work in a hospital or a pharmacy?"

"You assume correctly."

The office door opens and Granger leans in. She pauses to catch her breath. "Sorry to interrupt but a woman has just called to report that her husband has been missing for three days. The description matches our victim."

CHAPTER 6

While the drive from the station to the caller's address would normally take no more than ten minutes, a sudden cloudburst slows the traffic to a crawl. Fat raindrops pummel the car and overwhelm the windscreen wipers, blurring Kane's view as he turns right to head west along Royal Terrace.

In the passenger seat, Granger tuts and shakes her head. "I told you, didn't I? These seaside towns seem gloomier than anywhere else in the winter. The rain is heavier, the wind icier and the clouds always look menacing. It's not yet noon and you can barely see the road."

As suddenly as it started, the downpour stops. As they pass a monumental statue of Queen Victoria, the road rises sharply and to their left they catch sight of the swirling waters of the Thames Estuary. Out on the horizon, the clouds part, revealing a sliver of sky the colour of denim.

Kane gives Granger a quick glance. "You know that Southend-on-Sea is a bit of a misnomer?"

"I do, yes. Because the seafront actually looks across the estuary, not out to sea. But it's where the Thames flows into the North Sea, so I think it's fair enough. Southend-on-Estuary doesn't have a great holiday vibe, does it?"

Kane grins. He should have known better than to try to catch Granger out. "Good. Just checking that you've done your research."

He feels lucky to have Granger back by his side for this case. She's as sharp as a razor and driven to keep proving what a good detective she is. One day, she'll have his job. If she wants it.

"Do you think this missing man is likely to be our victim?" Granger asks.

"It's looking that way. The age and description fits. Did you ask someone to do a background check?"

"I did it myself. Before we left."

"Of course you did. What do we know about this Adam Golding?"

"He is interesting. He owned a couple of amusement arcades and a pub in the centre of town. A family business inherited from his father. He sold the company, Pure Gold Ltd, a year ago for three million."

"Is that so? That is interesting. I don't suppose he's had time to spend all that cash."

"Why would the wife wait three days before reporting him missing?"

"We'll find out soon. You can ask her if she killed her husband for the money."

"I might just do that," says Granger. "Insulin is a strange murder weapon."

Kane agrees. "I understand it can be tricky to inject if you haven't done it before. There's got to be a good chance the killer is a diabetic and used to injecting themselves, or a medical professional with access to insulin. It also must be near on impossible to inject someone if they're in a position to resist."

He turns into Westcliff Parade and Granger waits for him to park and switch off the engine before she speaks again. "The victim would have had to be immobilised — either tied up or unconscious — to enable the killer to inject him?"

"It's the only scenario that makes sense. What I can't figure out is why the killer would then go to the trouble of hanging the dead man by the neck for all to see. It would have to be carefully planned. You'd need a ladder of some kind and probably a winch to haul the body up."

Granger unfastens her seat belt and turns to Kane. "I think the hanging is almost more important to the killer than the murder itself. The man is dead, yes, but death is not enough. The killer wants the world to see what he's done. He's put the victim on display. It's a punishment. An act of humiliation."

Kane nods. He'd been thinking along similar lines. A high-profile murder for a high-profile victim.

The detectives get out of the car and climb the white stone steps to the entrance of Clifton House, a five-storey block of luxury flats. Granger presses the penthouse video intercom and Kane holds his warrant card up to the camera. "DI Kane and DS Granger for Ruth Golding."

The speaker crackles for a few seconds before they are buzzed in.

On the way up in the lift, Granger runs her fingers over the expensive walnut panelling. "These flats probably go for at least a million each. The penthouse a million and a half."

The lift comes to a halt and they step out. On the other side of the corridor, the polished oak door to the penthouse has been left open for them. Granger leads the way in and they walk slowly down a short, narrow hall, which flows into a wide open-plan space. The flat is expensively decorated in a modern style. Wide-planked oak floors, a large leather sofa and matching armchairs. On the south side of the room, a wall of glass offers an uninterrupted view of the sea.

A door at the far end opens and Ruth Golding enters. Her high heels click-clack as she walks to the sofa and smooths her skirt with her palms as she sits. Kane thinks she looks dressed for a night out. Her dark hair is tied back into a sleek ponytail, her full Cupid's bow lips are painted a deep cherry red. She eyes Kane expectantly, then looks across at Granger. "Have you found Adam? Is he all right? I've been going out of my mind with worry."

The detectives move a couple of steps closer to the sofa and exchange glances.

"We believe he's been found," Granger says. "But I'm afraid the news isn't good."

"What do you mean? What's happened? Is he hurt?"

"I'm sorry to have to tell you that the description you gave us matches a body found on the seafront."

Golding drops her head and covers her face. Her shoulders shake as she sobs silently into her hands. When she looks up, her make-up is smudged where tears have rolled down her cheeks.

"There must be some mistake. Adam can't be dead."

Kane walks to the sofa and sits beside her. He cradles her hand softly between his. "When you're ready I'll need you to identify the body. Is there family or a friend who can come to sit with you?"

Golding shakes her head and sniffs. "What happened? Adam has never been ill in his life. This isn't right. It doesn't make sense."

Her hand is trembling. Kane gives it a gentle squeeze. "I'm afraid it appears that your husband was murdered."

Golding pulls her hand away. "What do you mean? No, not Adam. I don't believe you. You've got this all wrong."

Kane would like to offer her hope, at least give her space to take the news in. He can't do either. Each hour that passes reduces his chances of catching the killer.

"Are you sure you don't want to call someone?"

Golding gives him a confused stare. Kane knows the look well. He's seen the same expression dozens of times. He also knows exactly how she's feeling. Disbelief, panic, denial. The moment he heard about Lizzy will haunt him for ever.

He lets go of Golding's hand and stands up. There are some difficult questions he needs to ask and there's no easy way to go about it.

"Did your husband have any enemies, Mrs Golding? Can you think of anyone who might want to harm him?"

She stares up at him. Blankly this time. She shakes her head. "Why would anyone want to kill Adam? He's a successful businessman. There are always going to be some people upset by decisions he makes. But murder? No. It can't be true. Can it?"

"I know this is hard to take in," Granger says. "But can you tell us why you took three days to report that your husband was missing."

Golding covers her face with her hands and groans. "We had a row. He lied to me. He's always been a good liar."

"What did you row about?"

"He had to go away for a couple of days for an investment conference in London. At least, that's what he told me."

Golding pauses and drops her head again. When she looks up, her eyes are wet. "The night before he was due to come back, I called him. He didn't answer, so I phoned the hotel he said he'd booked."

"You did that because?"

"Because I don't trust him. He's cheated before. More than once. The hotel said they didn't have an Adam Golding booked in."

"You thought he was with another woman?"

"I knew he was."

"What did you do?"

"I called his mobile again and left a voicemail message telling him not to bother coming home. That he was a lying bastard and that I wanted a divorce."

Granger flashes a look at Kane. "That's why you took so long to report him missing?"

Golding nods and dabs her eyes with the back of her hand. "We've been married ten years, but I know he doesn't care about me. Not really. He'll never admit what he's done, and he hates confrontation. We own a cottage overlooking the River Crouch. I just thought he'd gone there to keep out of the way until I'd cooled off. He'd done that before."

Granger stands. "Okay, Mrs Golding. Thank you. Now point me in the direction of the kitchen and I'll make you a cup of tea."

When Granger leaves, Kane sits back down on the sofa. "I know this is going to be distressing but do you think you are up to formally identifying the body today?"

Golding's jaw drops and her eyes widen. "The dead body? It won't be Adam. It can't be. How was this person killed exactly?"

"We're still investigating." Kane doesn't want to give her too much detail right now. He wants the identity of the victim confirmed as soon as possible and, considering the state of the marriage, she needs to be ruled out as a suspect.

"We can drive you to the morgue right now. It'll take no more than twenty minutes. If your identification is positive, then we'll need to ask you a few more questions."

After a moment's silence, Golding gets up and walks quickly over to a shelf inset below the huge wall-mounted television. She grabs a silver photograph frame and hurries back to Kane, holding it out for him to see.

"Look, that's Adam. That's him. It's not your corpse, is it? This is a big mistake."

The picture shows a short, wiry, fair-haired man sitting in a deckchair on a beach, holding a full champagne glass up to the camera. He's tanned, smiling broadly and clearly loving life. Kane recalls the victim's pale, swollen, contorted face and lifeless eyes. The features are the same but death changes everything.

He'd like to spare her the ordeal, at least give her more time to come to terms with the news. He understands her fear. Her denial. But time is a luxury he doesn't have.

"I'm sorry to have to ask you to do this, Mrs Golding. I can't make an identification. I've never met your husband."

Granger returns carrying a mug of steaming tea. She offers it to Golding, who takes it and simultaneously hands her the photograph.

"It's not Adam, is it? The body you found. It can't be him."

Granger glances briefly at the picture and hands it back. "I can't say. You are the only one who can tell us that. Maybe we could give you some time but wouldn't it be better for you to get this over with? Then at least you'll know for sure. One way or the other."

Golding sits back down on the sofa, placing the photograph gently on the cushion beside her. "All right. We should go. It won't be Adam but let's do it now."

CHAPTER 7

Kane opens the morgue door and steps back to usher Ruth Golding inside. She hesitates, reluctant to enter the house of the dead. She turns to Granger. "What do I have to do?"

"A medical attendant will take you to a room with an internal window. On the other side of the glass will be the body covered by a sheet. When you are ready, the attendant will pull the sheet back a little for you to make identification."

"What will I see?"

"You'll see the face of the man we think is your husband. You won't need more than a second or two to be sure. Don't worry, I'll be with you."

Kane decides not to tell her that although the morgue attendant will have done his best, the face of the corpse will be distorted and discoloured. The mouth will appear unnatural because it will have been sewn closed and the eyes glued shut. Whether she was involved in her husband's murder or not, the image will haunt her. He knows that all too well.

Golding reaches out and touches Granger's forearm lightly with her fingers. "I'd like you to come in with me. Please."

"If that's what you want."

Kane watches Golding take a deep breath. Her face sets as she steels herself for what she's about to do and see.

They go inside and find an attendant waiting for them. Tall, thin and youthful, wearing a knee-length white coat and thick, black-framed glasses. He helps Golding fill out a form, leads them into the identification room and hurries out.

On the other side of the glass window, a crisp white sheet covers the contours of a body. The attendant enters, walks across to the body and looks up at Golding, waiting for her to nod that she's ready.

Kane is watching her carefully. Instead of nodding, she shuts her eyes tightly. After a few seconds, they flutter open and the attendant pulls the sheet back.

Golding lifts a trembling hand to her lips. Her face pales. She looks as if she might faint.

"Adam," she says softly.

* * *

Back at the station, they settle Golding down in an interview room with a cup of milky, sweet tea before taking a five-minute break in Kane's office.

"If they divorced, she'd be entitled to half of everything," Granger says. "I'm guessing that would be enough to keep her pretty comfortable for the rest of her life. Now that he's dead, she's likely to get the lot."

Kane takes a sip of his coffee and puts it back down on his desk. She's right. Cynicism is negative when it comes to investigating. Suspicion is crucial. Ruth Golding will have to be considered a possible suspect for now. Jealousy and financial greed are both common motives for murder.

She looked genuinely distraught at the morgue. Kane's gut feeling is that she isn't involved in the murder of her husband. There's no need for him to voice this thought. Gut feelings are often plain wrong.

"She's either completely innocent or a great actor. There's no way she could have carried out the killing by herself. She's not strong enough to hoist a body up."

Granger shrugs. "She could just be a brilliant liar. And anyway, if she'd hired someone to murder her husband, it would still be distressing to see him lying on a mortuary slab after ten years of marriage."

The office door swings open and a stocky man neither of them has seen before steps in. A smile that doesn't reach his eyes spreads across his jowly face as he introduces himself. "Detective Inspector Mick Munro. Wanted to drop in to say hello and wish you good luck in your investigation. If there's anything you need, come to me. I know everything there is to know about the villains on this patch."

Kane nods his thanks. "That's good to know. It's important to have access to local knowledge."

Munro lifts a hand and brushes his greying fringe to one side. "True. I've worked this patch for fifteen years. That's why I can't understand why you glory hunters from the murder squad have been drafted in here without me being assigned to your team. Well, I suppose you know what you're doing."

Kane sighs. The last thing he needs is a hostile local stirring up trouble. Especially a high-ranking officer.

"I can assure you we do. Thanks for the offer though."

Munro's mouth contorts into an ugly sneer and he turns to Granger, his eyes widening as if noticing her for the first time.

"Ah, it's you. You almost managed to get yourself killed the last time you were in town. I suggest you try to be a bit more careful this time, love."

Granger doesn't reply. Instead, she offers him a soft smile, which riles him more than anything she could have said.

"I hear you've already been promoted to DS. I think it's great that youngsters like you are being fast-blacked."

Kane jumps to his feet. "What did you say?"

Munro holds up both hands. "Calm down, pal. I said it's good that people like Granger are being fast-tracked. We obviously need young female officers telling our experienced detectives how to do their jobs."

Kane moves closer to Munro, his heart beating hard. "That's not what I heard. Take that smirk off your face and be very careful what you say next."

Granger steps between the two men. "Hold on, hold on. Everything is cool. I'm just grateful that officers like DI Munro are taking an interest in people like me. Younger detectives, I mean. We need all the support we can get."

Munro gives her a puzzled glare and marches out the room. Granger shuts the door behind him and turns to Kane. "You didn't need to do that, you know."

Kane knows full well that Granger can stand up for herself. The point is she shouldn't have to. She's the best detective on his team and, as far as he's concerned, a friend.

"I can't believe you let him get away with that shit. He's a bully."

"He hasn't got away with anything and he knows it. I've heard it all before, you know. It gets boring after a while. Apparently, I'm being fast-tracked through the ranks because I'm a woman or because I'm not white, or both. Dinosaurs like Munro are heading for extinction. His days are numbered and he knows it. The best way I can speed that process up is by showing everybody that I can do this job as well as anybody. So, let's get on with solving this case."

***

When Kane and Granger return to the interview room, they find Ruth Golding slumped over the table, head in her hands. She looks up, her eyes red and puffy. "Can I go home now? I'm tired."

Kane sits on the chair facing her. "I'm sorry but not yet. We need to ask you a few more questions."

"Am I under arrest now?"

"No. You've agreed to help us with our inquiries. Even though this is a voluntary interview, it will be recorded on video and can be used in evidence. Do you want me to arrange for a duty lawyer to sit with you?"

Golding glances up at a camera mounted high on the wall and shakes her head. "I don't need a lawyer. I've not done anything wrong. How long will this take? When can I go home?"

Kane doesn't want to promise anything. A lot will depend on her answers. If they feel she's lying they can formally arrest her and hold her for up to twenty-four hours without charging her. If they suspect she's involved in the murder and need to question her further, they can apply for more time.

"How long have you and Adam been having marriage troubles?"

Golding sniffs loudly and sits up straight. "I first found out he was cheating on me two years after we married."

"And you've been married for ten years?" Granger asks.

Golding pauses. "It would have been our ten-year anniversary next month." The tone of her voice suggests she can't believe she put up with him for so long. "The stupid girl worked for him. Half his age, she was. Can you believe he tried to justify what happened by saying she looked like me? Thought I'd be flattered. I relented and agreed to give him a chance to make it up to me. He can be very persuasive when he needs to be." She sniffs again, brushing her nose with the back of her hand. "Could be, I mean."

Kane gives her a sympathetic nod. He doesn't say anything. The silence encourages her to carry on.

"Since then, I've never really felt that I could trust him. There were many occasions when I was sure he was up to no good again but I turned a blind eye to it. Things got worse after he sold the businesses. I guess he had more time on his hands."

Granger moves forward and sits next to Kane. She smiles across the table. "Can you tell us why he sold up?"

Golding shrugs. "I guess he'd had enough. Running a business on your own isn't easy. He said he wanted to enjoy the benefits of his hard work."

"With you?"

"I think so. What are you getting at?"

Granger ignores the question. She waits a few seconds before dropping her own. "Do you know how much your husband sold his company Pure Gold Ltd for?"

"Er, yes. Of course. Three million pounds. It wasn't a secret. Details of the sale were reported in the local newspaper. What has this got to do with Adam's death?"

"Are you the sole beneficiary of Adam's will?"

Kane gives Granger a sideways glance. She never wastes words and gets to the point quickly. He usually likes that, but maybe this time, considering Golding has come straight from identifying her dead husband, a softer approach would be better.

Golding eyes them both warily. "I believe I am. And he's the sole beneficiary in my will. What has this got to do with anything? Am I a suspect? Maybe I do want a lawyer involved now. This is getting scary."

Granger shrugs. "Look, I'm sorry. I understand this is a difficult time for you. You've declined legal representation but you are entitled to change your mind at any time. If you feel you need a lawyer present now then that can be arranged."

Golding takes a moment to think, shakes her head and bursts into tears. "This is ridiculous. I didn't do anything. I wouldn't hurt Adam. Despite everything, I actually loved him, and deep down he loved me too."

"You were going to divorce him for cheating on you. Your relationship was in a bad way."

"He was selfish and weak. Yes, I told him I'd had enough. That doesn't mean I wanted him dead. That's crazy." Covering her face with her hands, she gushes in between sobs. "I've never seen a dead body before. He doesn't look like my Adam. I wish it wasn't him."

Granger pulls a tissue from her jacket pocket and hands it across the table.

Golding takes it and dabs her eyes. "You haven't told me yet — where was he found? How was he killed?"

Granger looks at Kane, who shakes his head. "We're still waiting for the full autopsy report. We'll be assigning a family liaison officer to you for the next few weeks and he or she will fill you in on the details."

Why does anybody kill anybody? Kane knows that if they can find the reason for Adam Golding's murder, they'll find the killer. Lust, love, loathing, jealousy, secrets, money, revenge. The seven deadly motives.

Ruth Golding's grief is convincing, her emotional distress believable. But this early in an investigation, you must suspect everybody and believe no one.

"What I will tell you, because some of this will come out in the press in the next few days, is that someone went to a lot of trouble to plan and then carry out the murder. Can you think of any reason someone would want Adam dead?"

"Not really. He liked to keep people at arm's length. Unless they were attractive young women. He didn't really have close friends, or real enemies."

That's unlikely, Kane thinks. *You don't accrue the kind of wealth Golding did without being ruthless, at least in business.*

"What about your husband's family?" Granger asks. "Is there someone you'd like us to contact?"

Golding sniffs and wipes her nose with the tissue. "Adam's father died of a heart attack when he was at university. His mother ran the businesses herself until she had a fatal stroke just before we got married. There's only his older brother left. Tony. They haven't spoken for years. Never will now."

Granger's eyes light up as she leans eagerly across the desk. "What happened?"

Golding sighs. "When their mother died, she left everything to Adam. She decided he was the best person to keep the family businesses going. Adam felt bad about it all. Even though he would have preferred to have shared everything equally with his brother, he told me he felt he had to honour his mother's wishes. Tony wasn't a happy bunny."

"I bet he wasn't. Do you know where he lives?"

"Not his exact address. I remember Adam told me a while ago that his brother had ended up moving into a flat on one of the big local housing estates."

Granger glances at Kane. He agrees with a nod that they're done and stands up. "Thank you for your patience and cooperation."

Golding sighs loudly. "Is that it?"

"For the moment, yes. One of our constables will drive you home."

Once Golding has left, Kane sits back down beside Granger.

"She's definitely still in the frame. Three million is a lot of money. I thought it was interesting how she casually slipped us the information about the feud with his brother. As if she had no idea it makes him another person of interest. We need to track him down quickly."

Granger nods. "It shouldn't be difficult. I'll also get a full background check done. He's not going to get a penny of the fortune he must believe he deserves but he's certainly got a motive."

Kane agrees. He also understands. Revenge is powered by passion. Sometimes, the mere thought of it is enough to ease your pain.

CHAPTER 8

Kane paces back and forth across the waiting area outside Rebecca Baxter's consulting room. The inexplicable fluttering in his stomach makes him wonder why he ever thought it would be a good idea to do this again.

The door opens and the psychologist stands on the threshold. "I'm ready if you are."

Kane scans the room, which has been redecorated and refurnished, the walls given a fresh coat of pale blue paint. Baxter sits behind a curved glass desk and waves Kane into a small Scandinavian-style armchair with wooden armrests.

"I wasn't expecting to see you here again," she says. "It's been a while."

Kane knows exactly when he had his last therapy session. Twelve months and three days ago. "I didn't think I'd be back here either. Thanks for agreeing to see me so early this morning. How are things with you?"

Kane senses that Baxter is fighting back a smile as she tries to keep her expression professionally stern.

"We are not here to talk about me. Why have you felt the need to return to therapy? The last time I saw you I thought you seemed well. Are you struggling again?"

Kane takes a moment to consider his response. He knows Baxter isn't going to like what he's about to say. It wouldn't surprise him if she threw him out.

"I'm not here for a therapy session. The honest answer is that, thanks to you, I'm much better. I'm back in control of my life. I still have bad days. Days when all I can think about is the black hole in my life and how I failed to catch the man who murdered my wife. Most of the time though, I'm good. Most importantly, I can do my job to the level it needs to be done."

Baxter is listening intently. She shifts in her seat and frowns. Kane guesses she's waiting for him to carry on. To explain.

"I'm here because I need to, well, I want to talk to you . . . to ask for some advice about visiting Jack Newman."

Baxter stays silent. Kane imagines he can hear her mind whirring electronically as she gathers her thoughts and decides how to react.

"You must know I can't talk about him. I was one of the psychologists who assessed him and drew up a psychiatric report for the court. You have access to that report. He was convicted and sent to Broadmoor, the country's most notorious high-security psychiatric hospital. That case is closed. What are you doing even thinking about it?"

Kane knew this was going to be difficult. At least she hasn't asked him to leave. Not yet.

"He's written to me, asking me to pay him a visit. I've refused and I've resisted up until now. I'm back in Southend investigating another murder and it's made me think about my wife's killer still walking the streets."

Baxter stands, smooths the wrinkles on her skirt and walks around to the front of the desk.

"I know this is a weird thing for a psychologist to say, but are you out of your mind? How do you think the See No Evil killer is going to help you. You need to keep away from that man. He murdered three people in cold blood and you caught him. Job done. You and Detective Granger made the world a much safer place. Now focus on solving your new case."

Baxter is talking sense. Kane has been telling himself to move on for months. He wishes it was that simple.

"I've not told anyone else this. The last time I spoke to him, just before he was locked up, he told me that he had information that would help me find the person who murdered Lizzy."

"You believe him? A psychopathic triple killer."

"What if he does know something? He sounded convincing. I don't know what to believe."

"Believe me, that man is a pathological liar. He's a natural manipulator and this is a way he can wield some kind of power over the detective who caught him."

Kane looks down at his hands. His palms are sweaty. "I know what you're saying is right. I agree with everything you're telling me. No matter how hard I try, I can't block out the voice in my head that keeps repeating the same question. What if? What if? What if?"

Baxter moves back to her chair and sits. She puts her elbows on the desk, steeples her fingers and stares intently at Kane. He remembers that she did that a lot during his therapy sessions and wonders whether the prolonged eye contact is meant to make him feel so uncomfortable he's forced to speak.

"I suppose I'd better leave then," he says, shifting his gaze and conceding the staring contest.

Baxter sits backs and sighs. "I think you'd better. The work I do here is separate from the work I do for the Prison Service and the police. These sessions are solely for clients needing therapy, for me to help them resolve psychological issues, not for me to advise you how to conduct your life."

Kane stands up, angry at himself for wasting time when he should be concentrating on the case. Granger will already be at the station, raring to pay Tony Golding a visit.

"You're right. I apologise. My mistake. I just thought that ... well, I'm not sure what I thought. I've a murder investigation to be getting on with. I'd better get going."

As he moves to leave, Baxter holds up a hand. "Wait a minute. I haven't finished yet. I meant what I said, but if you don't need therapy then you're not a client. That means that if want to chat, about anything, there's no reason why we can't do that as acquaintances, or even friends, is there?"

Kane fails to hide his surprise as he steps hesitantly toward the door. "I guess not."

"I understand you're going to be working flat out on this new case of yours. Still, if you need a break, if you feel like it, we could talk sometime, over a coffee or something."

Kane walks to the door, opens it and turns back. "Okay, thanks."

CHAPTER 9

Granger navigates the car through the maze of narrow roads toward Tony Golding's flat in a tower block on Southend's notorious Kingsbury Estate.

She's not expecting a warm reception. According to the local drug unit, the brother of the murder victim has been earning himself a reputation as a dealer of cannabis and cocaine.

She turns to Kane, who's studying the screen of his mobile. "It seems that after he was robbed of his inheritance, Golding decided crime was the best way to refill his pockets. Word is he's not averse to violence and is smart enough to get minions to do his dirty work for him."

Kane looks up. "Sounds to me like he'd have no qualms about ordering the murder of his brother." He jabs a finger at his mobile. "I've just been reading about this estate. It says the place is a hotbed of gang-related crime. Drug dealing, stabbings, acid attacks and sexual assaults. Never a dull moment." He pockets the phone and scans the streets. "So where the hell is everybody? It's the middle of the afternoon and there's nobody in sight."

Granger shakes her head. She grew up on an estate like the Kingsbury. It's a case of knowing where to look. The back alleys, the dark corners, the dead ends. "There are plenty of people about. I can assure you we're being watched by dozens of pairs of eyes right now. This may be an unmarked car but all of those watching will probably already know we're police."

"I'll take your word for it."

They pass a deserted and run-down children's play park opposite a row of three graffiti-covered lock-up garages before Granger pulls up at the foot of the tower block.

As they enter the foyer, Kane coughs and gags. "God," he says, covering his nose with a hand in a futile attempt to block the stench of urine and cannabis. He heads for the lift and presses the button. Granger walks to the stairwell and waves him over.

"You must be joking. It's the tenth floor."

Granger shrugs. "I'm taking the stairs. If you want to risk the lift, it's up to you. It'll smell even worse than here and there's a good chance it'll break down, trapping you between floors."

She starts to ascend the stairs and Kane follows reluctantly. By the time she reaches the seventh floor, his breathing is ragged. She pauses to allow him to catch up.

He holds up a hand. "You don't have to say it. I know, I've got to find the time to go to the gym."

"You know, you actually look as though you're in pretty good shape but you're very obviously not at all."

Kane scowls. "I'll take that as a back-handed compliment, shall I?"

The walls of the stairway over the last three floors are sprayed with zigzags of bright red paint designed to look like dripping blood.

"Interesting artwork," Kane says. "Very effective. Good to see socio-economic deprivation doesn't kill creativity."

Granger hopes that Kane is joking. She knows that poverty on estates like this one can smother every aspect of a child's life, and that the dripping blood graffiti is almost certainly a warning from one gang to another. Growing up will be less of a struggle for her girl.

They enter the lobby on the tenth floor and Granger leads the way to flat 78. She knocks twice, waits ten seconds and knocks again.

The door is opened by a shaven-headed man who Granger reckons is in his late forties. Beneath his baggy tracksuit trousers and stained T-shirt, he's tall and lean.

"What do you want? No, don't bother, I don't want to know," he says.

Before he can shut the door, Granger places a foot across the threshold and holds up her warrant card. Golding's chin is squarer than his dead brother's. His eyes set deeper.

"We're looking for Tony Golding."

The man makes no effort to look at the card. "You've found him. Well done. Now you can fuck off."

Kane steps forward. "We're here to talk to you about your brother. Adam."

Golding shrinks back at the mention of his brother's name. "What's the bastard done now?"

"Let's go inside."

The living area is small, clean and uncluttered. A television, a coffee table and mini fridge plugged in beside a single armchair. Golding sits, lifts his long legs and rests his bare feet on the table.

"What's this about? I'm a busy man. Doing nothing all day's a lot harder than it looks."

He appears irritated rather than nervous about the presence of detectives in his home. Granger wonders whether that's because he has nothing to hide, or because he's confident he's the smartest person in the room.

"I'm afraid we're here to give you some news. I'm very sorry, but your brother Adam, he's dead," she says. "He's been murdered."

"He's what? You're kidding me. This is a joke, right?"

"We don't joke about murder."

Golding's face breaks into a smile full of malice. He leans over the arm of the chair, opens the fridge and pulls out a can of lager. He yanks the ring pull and takes a long swig. "Wow. This must be what winning the lottery feels like. That news is worthy of several drinks. Sorry I can't offer you two a can but I've only got twelve left."

Kane steps forward. "You don't seem very upset by the death of your only sibling," he says. "Celebrating because your brother has died isn't a normal reaction. I take it you and Adam didn't get on?"

Golding snorts, chokes on a mouthful of beer and spits it out on to the front of his T-shirt. He wipes his mouth with the back of his hand. "We've not spoken for years. I despise the guy. This news has made my day."

Granger is studying Golding. He looks nothing like his brother. He's taller, beefier, his hair is darker and his face more masculine. He turns his head and catches her staring, a hint of menace in his grey eyes.

"Is it right that you two fell out over money?" Kane asks.

"It wasn't just about money. He took everything from me. Destroyed my life. I'm the older brother but our mother left him everything. The family amusement arcades, the properties. The lot. I didn't get a penny."

"She must have had her reasons. She wouldn't do something like that just to spite you."

"She was old and frail. Her memory was going, her mind was fragile. Adam turned her against me. He dripped poison into her ear every chance he got."

"Why would he do that to you?"

"Because he could. Because he always was a cunning, conniving, evil little bastard."

Granger exchanges a glance with Kane. She knows he's thinking the same. A festering sibling rivalry can turn deadly, which is a strong motive, putting him in the frame as a potential suspect.

"I take it there wasn't a lot of brotherly love around even before you found out he'd been left everything."

"I couldn't stand the little creep. He always had to be the centre of attention. We kept it civil at family gatherings, but

I avoided being in the same room as him whenever possible. I knew the feeling was mutual but I didn't realise that all the time he was plotting to steal from me."

"I still don't get how he was able to persuade your mother to cut you out."

Golding clenches his jaw and looks around the room as if trying to find someone or something to punch.

"The little snake told her I was incompetent when it came to business. That I'd ruin everything the family had built up. That all I was interested in was spending money on women and drugs."

"Were you doing drugs?"

Golding smirks. "Yeah. Women too. A bit of coke on nights out. Everyone was doing it. It didn't do me no harm. Adam made out I was some kind of addict. He lied to steal everything that belonged to me. You know what? He even had the nerve to offer me a job. Manager of one of the arcades. Tried to make out that he cared. Said he'd look after me. I told him exactly where he could stick his job. He stole my life and I'm glad he got what was coming to him."

Granger listens to Golding making no effort to hide the extent of his hatred for his brother. She has a feeling that he's trying too hard and wonders what he's hiding. She catches Kane's eye for a second, covers her mouth with a hand and coughs. "Sorry, but can I use your bathroom?"

Golding points to a door. "Through there to the right."

She walks across the tiny kitchen and finds the bathroom. She flushes the toilet and leaves, crossing the kitchen to what she guesses must be the bedroom door. She grabs the handle, twists it slowly, taking care not to make a noise, and goes inside.

The single bed is unmade and the room smells of sweat. Lying side by side on the bedside table are three mobile phones and a set of car keys. Granger suspects that if the local drug unit could get their hands on just one of those phones they'd have enough evidence to put him away for a long time. Without a proper warrant, she has no legal right to search the flat and anything she might find could be argued as inadmissible in court. That's why she's being careful not to search. She's just taking a look.

She backs out of the room, closing the door carefully. Back in the living area, Kane is quizzing Golding about his whereabouts on the days leading up to his brother's murder.

"I was here. In this flat. I don't work, don't get out much at all. Sometimes I go to the convenience store a couple of minutes' walk away. I might have gone to the Painted Lady, the pub around the corner. I prefer to buy cans and drink them here. It's cheaper."

Kane acknowledges Granger's return with a curious look before turning back to Golding. "Your brother's wife can't think of anybody who might want him dead. From what you've said you have a good reason to hate him."

Golding crushes the empty beer can and lets it fall on to the carpet. "His wife's a lying bitch. Don't believe a word she tells you. If you want to find his killer, I'd take a good look at her."

"What makes you say that?"

"She's a gold-digger. Only after his money. I told him as much. He didn't like it and married her anyway."

"She told us Adam didn't really have any enemies."

"She lied. Everyone hated him, eventually. We were never close. Even as a kid he was an evil little worm. Always out for himself. I couldn't stand him and the feeling was mutual. We played at happy families when we had to, for our mum's sake. When he — when he betrayed me, when he stood smirking in the solicitor's office as the will was read out, I wanted to kill him there and then. If you find out who did this, let me know. I'd love to buy them a drink and shake their hand."

He opens the fridge door and pulls out another can. "I'd like you to go now. I've got some serious celebrating to do. Show yourself out."

"We'll need you to attend the station to make a formal statement, preferably tomorrow."

"And if I don't want to?"

"We'll arrest you. Also, we're probably going to have more questions for you, so don't think about taking any exotic holidays soon."

Golding grunts, takes another swig of lager and gives him the finger.

Kane turns to go but Granger stalls him with a wave. "One last question, Mr Golding. Do you drive a white van?"

Golding leers as his gaze moves down slowly from her face to her ankle boots and back up again. "As you asked so nicely, Detective, I don't drive a white van. I don't drive anything. Can't afford it."

The detectives step outside into a freezing February drizzle. They run to the car. Granger starts the engine and turns up the heater. "What do you think?"

"I think the man's got serious anger issues."

Granger drives off, accelerating gradually for a couple of hundred yards before pulling up beside the children's playground.

"What are you doing?" Kane asks.

"We know Tony Golding's a drug dealer. He's got three mobiles on his bedside table and car keys. He said he doesn't drive."

"I knew you weren't checking out the colour of his bathroom tiles. We don't have a search warrant."

"I wasn't searching. I didn't touch anything. Honest. I wanted to see if he'd made his bed. It says a lot about a man's character."

Kane gives a sigh of exasperation and shakes his head. "What are we doing here?"

"Keeping an eye on those lock-up garages across the road. I reckon our visit has shaken him up a bit. Made him restless. Give it ten minutes or so."

The drizzle turns into a cloudburst, fat raindrops pummelling the roof of the car like a frenetic drumroll. As suddenly as it started, the downpour eases back to a miserable drizzle.

Just before the ten minutes is up, Granger lifts a hand and points into the murk. A tall figure in tracksuit trousers and a hooded jacket jogs into sight. Shoulders hunched and head bowed, Tony Golding unlocks the middle garage, heaves up the door and slips inside. After a few minutes, a shiny black BMW saloon emerges. Golding gets out and closes the garage door before accelerating away.

The detectives exchange glances. "That's an expensive motor," Granger says.

"He lied to us about not having money. He lied to us about not having a car. What else is he lying about?"

CHAPTER 10

Kane perches on the edge of a desk, watching Granger conduct the Thursday morning briefing. On the whiteboard she has added the names of their two suspects. The wife and the brother.

"We know that both Ruth Golding and Tony Golding have possible motives for wanting our victim dead. As yet, we have no evidence linking either of them to the murder. The door-to-door inquiries drew a blank and there's no sign of the white van seen near the pier just before the body was found."

As usual, Granger's delivery is energetic and authoritative. Kane's lucky to have her by his side. He can depend on her to step up when he needs her to. When he needs time to get his head together.

He scans the room, studying his team. Meera and Dec sit at adjacent desks, Alex, the local detective sergeant, stands behind them. Mark, the uniform who found the victim under the pier, leans against the wall next to the window. Kane notes that they are all listening intently to Granger's summary, their expressions determined.

Kane takes a sip of his third coffee of the morning. It's from the machine outside his cubbyhole of an office and tastes like shit. Regardless, he needs the caffeine almost as much as he needs a breakthrough in this case.

Since Lizzy's murder, he's rarely managed more than a few hours' sleep. Last night his mind whirled with questions about the interview with Tony Golding, the burner phones in his bedroom and the BMW in the lock-up. When he managed to stop thinking about the case, he agonised over whether it was time to sell up and leave the home he'd built with Lizzy. Nothing reminded him more of his loss; nothing stabbed the knife of grief deeper than the cold, silent empty rooms.

Prior to the briefing, Kane spent thirty minutes on the phone with former Major Investigation Team friend and colleague, now his boss, Detective Chief Superintendent Helen Dean. Adam Golding was a high-profile local businessman and now it's time to make details of his murder public.

Kane must face the media at a press conference tomorrow, with Ruth Golding making an appeal for information. Dealing with journalists is his least favourite part of the job. In his mind, they're a necessary evil, like root canal work, or having a colonoscopy. The press will lap Ruth Golding up. They love a glamorous grieving widow. She's still a suspect and he's going to be watching her carefully. The pressure of facing the media can crack even the most convincing liars.

Kane also knows from experience that the journalists will want more than the tears of a murder victim's wife. Crime reporters are the same the world over. They like nothing more than a horrible murder, preferably with lots of blood. He desperately needs something positive, something meaty to feed the news-hungry wolf pack and keep them off his back.

Kane focuses his attention back on Granger as she outlines the plan of action for the day. Without appearing to try, she projects enthusiasm, optimism and authority.

He can do authority and experience, no problem. Neither he nor Granger are perfect detectives. But together they make a perfect combination.

"We will be dividing into two teams today," Granger declares, "to carry out two important operations.

"We've decided to move quickly on Tony Golding. We've applied for a warrant to arrest him on suspicion of drug dealing. That will give us time to hold him while we search his flat and lock-up garage. Of course, we'll also be looking for any evidence that ties him to his brother's murder.

"As soon as the paperwork arrives, Meera, Alex and Mark will head out to the estate with DI Kane. You'll need to take a few more uniforms in case some of the tower block residents object and kick off.

"Dec, you're coming with me to the Goldings' cottage in the country. It's where Ruth Golding says she assumed her husband had run off to after she told him she wanted a divorce. It's in a place called Canewdon, a tiny village in the middle of nowhere, once famous for a coven of witches.

"So, Dec, please try not to piss off the locals."

CHAPTER 11

Kane raps his knuckles on the door of Tony Golding's flat and takes a step back. Beside him stands Meera Kush. The detectives are flanked by two stern-faced police constables.

Golding doesn't have a record of violence but that's not a reason to be complacent. Maybe he just hasn't been caught.

The door opens and Golding appears, shaking his head. He's wearing the same stained T-shirt and tracksuit trousers as yesterday. He moves forward, his broad-shouldered frame filling the doorway. "What now? Don't tell me my sister's been murdered as well? That'd be weird, because I don't have one."

Kane holds up his warrant card. "I'm Detective Inspector—"

"I know who you are. What you want now?"

"Tony Golding, I am arresting you on suspicion of dealing drugs. I also have a warrant to search your flat and your lock-up garage."

Golding glares at Kane, his jaw clenching. "Tell me you're joking."

"We've a car waiting to take you to the station, unless you'd prefer to drive yourself there in your shiny, very expensive BMW saloon. You lied about owning a car. What else are you lying about?"

Golding eyes the two uniformed officers nervously.

"What if I choose not to go with you?"

Kane smiles. "That's not how this works. You don't have a choice."

Golding rolls his shoulders back and lifts his chin. "I'm not agreeing to an interview without my lawyer present."

"You've got your own lawyer, have you? Very fancy. We usually call in the duty solicitor."

Being able to afford expensive legal representation shows Kane that Golding is more than a small-time dealer. It's also going to make the interrogation a lot trickier.

Downstairs a dozen or so local youths, all wearing jeans and dark hoodies, mill around the entrance to the tower block. When Golding emerges alongside Kane, followed by Kush and the two uniforms, the youths crowd around them, blocking the way to the parked police cars.

Kane holds up a hand. "Obstructing police officers in the course of their duty is a serious crime. You have ten seconds to move away or you'll all be joining Mr Golding here down at the station."

The youths don't budge. Kane is regretting sending the other uniforms to help Weaver and Scott search the garage. He turns to Kush. "Call for backup. This mob are getting arrested."

Golding steps forward and catches the eye of the tallest youth. "Move it," he snarls. "Go on, get out of here."

The kid slips his hands into the pockets of his hoodie, shrugs and leads the gang into the tower block.

Kane watches the two uniforms escort Golding to one of the cars and put him in the back seat. He wonders whether to stay around until the flat and lock-up garage have been searched but decides to get DC Kush to drive him back to prepare for the press conference.

By the time they arrive, Golding is handing his watch and mobile phone over to the custody sergeant, who places them carefully in sealed plastic bags. When he spots Kane watching, he twists his head and glares at him. "What's going on? I'm supposed be here to answer questions. Why am I being put in a cell?"

Kane takes a step closer. Golding is rattled. A little less cocksure. The prospect of a night in a police cell can have that affect. "You've been told you're under arrest. That means we can hold you for up to twenty-four hours before deciding whether to charge you or release you."

Golding's eyes narrow and he tries to close in on Kane but one of the uniforms steps between them. "I'm ready to answer your questions as soon as my lawyer's here. I want to get on with it."

Kane shrugs. "That's nice to know but we're not ready yet. We're entitled to carry on gathering evidence while you're still in custody, so you're going to have to wait. Take him to his cell."

He turns and walks away before Golding can say anything else. As he passes the squad room on his way to his office, his phone rings. He checks the screen. It's DC Scott.

"Alex, tell me you are about to make my day."

"I'm about to make your day."

"You found something? Burner phones in the flat?"

"No. In the lock-up. It was in the boot of the BMW, under the spare wheel. A length of nylon rope. It looks to me like it matches the rope used to string Adam Golding up."

CHAPTER 12

Dec Brown twists in the passenger seat, peers out of the window and points to the grey tower of Canewdon's ancient church. "Slow down, would yer? This is a fascinating old building."

Granger keeps her foot on the accelerator. Brown is a jovial guy, good company, but he hasn't stopped talking since they headed north out of town thirty minutes ago. She's starting to wish she'd paired up with Kush or Weaver.

"I don't doubt it. This isn't a day out. We've got work to do. Anyway, the place looks as if it's likely to collapse any day now."

Brown gives a grunt of disappointment. "That's what's so interesting, you see. I looked it up on the internet. It was built in the fourteenth century. Legend has it that as long as the church tower stands, there will be six witches in the village."

Granger slows the car, turning sharply into a narrow lane overhung with leafless trees that seem to claw at the roof. "You believe in all that rubbish, do you?"

Brown flashes her a sideways grin. "Not all of it. 'Course I don't. But it still scares me."

Five minutes later, Granger pulls up on the large shingle drive of Sea Creek Cottage. Set in the centre of wide plot, the Goldings' country retreat has whitewashed walls and a thatched roof.

The detectives walk up to the front door and Granger slips the key into the lock. Initially, Ruth Golding had been reluctant to hand it over, insisting that she should go with them. She'd changed her mind when told that the search warrant gave them authority to force entry if necessary.

"What exactly are we looking for?" Brown asks.

"Anything that suggests that Adam Golding came here after his wife found out he lied about attending an investment conference. She said he was driving his Ranger Rover. No sign of that."

Granger pushes the door open and they go in. The inside of the cottage is a shock. A complete contrast to the chocolate-box exterior. Ultra-modern and open-plan, the floor is a pristine expanse of limestone tiles. Granger crosses into the living area. The furniture is a mix of dark leather and chrome, matching the kitchen's blend of black marble and stainless steel.

Brown whistles. "There's certainly been a helluva lot of cash spent on this place. My second home is a one-man tent."

Granger isn't that impressed. She prefers cosy to flashy. "You take a look around here. I'm going to check out the bedrooms and bathroom."

The main bedroom is what estate agents would describe as "compact" — just enough room for a double bed and one table and lamp. It doesn't look as if anyone has slept there for a while and smells strongly of some kind of cleaning fluid. Either the Goldings are clean freaks, or someone has been doing their best to get rid of forensic evidence.

Granger opens the curtains to let the daylight in. The view stretches across open fields down to marshland south of the River Crouch. The second bedroom is smaller still and doesn't even have a bed. The wardrobes are full of clothes and Granger guesses the Goldings use it as a dressing room.

The bathroom is equipped with a shower and a sink and smells of bleach. The shower head is dripping and the tiles directly outside the cubicle are damp. Granger's pulse quickens. She squats, swipes a finger across a wet tile. As she rises, she spots a blue toothbrush lying on the sink near the hot tap. The bristles are topped with a dab of toothpaste.

Granger doesn't touch it. Someone standing at the sink put the brush down and never picked it up again. She visualises Adam Golding bent over about to brush his teeth. He hears a suspicious noise or an unexpected knock on the front door and goes to investigate. She gets up and uses her elbow to lever the door open, careful not to touch the handle.

She finds Brown in the kitchen, peering into the stainless-steel fridge. "Good job I'm not hungry. Just half an avocado and a carton of milk. Actually, I reckon it's safe to say the avocado hasn't been in here that long because it's only just starting to discolour. You know, if you squeeze lemon juice on it, the flesh doesn't oxidise and stays green."

Granger walks to the fridge and checks out the contents herself. Brown's decision to throw in a useful culinary hack might be a little irritating but she reckons he's got a good point.

She picks up the milk carton and checks the expiry date. "You're right. The milk's fresh too. We need to get a forensics team out. It's looking very likely that Adam Golding did stay here shortly before he was murdered. It's even possible that he was killed right here, because he was already dead when his body was hung up under the pier."

Brown shuts the fridge door and waves a finger at Granger. "You know what? I was saying earlier that there must have been an awful lot of money spent on this place. Well, it would be surprising to me if there weren't some strategically placed security cameras. Rich people are pretty good at protecting their assets. That's how they stay rich. Also this is their country retreat and would be lefty empty for long periods."

Granger runs to the front door. "You check the back."

Once outside she walks a few steps away from the cottage, turns around and scans the building. Nothing over the front door. Her eyes travel to the left, toward a line of conifer trees to the side of the cottage. That's when she sees it. A small white orb with a black lens, attached by a bracket screwed into the white side wall of the cottage. It would capture side-on footage of anyone approaching the front door.

Granger's excitement is short-lived. As she gets closer, she sees the lens is shattered. Probably battered with a rock or a stick. She turns to check the other side wall to the right. Nothing.

Brown steps out, shaking his head slowly. She knows what he's going to say before he says it. "There are two security cameras covering the rear of the cottage, both of them pretty smashed up."

Granger motions toward the camera above her. "Same." She digs her phone out of her coat pocket. She needs to alert Forensics and report to Kane. There's no doubt in her mind now that Adam Golding was here and that his murderer disabled the security cameras. There should be footage of the killer approaching the cameras before smashing them but she'd bet the face would be hidden.

The sky suddenly darkens and Granger pulls her collar up. A spiteful wind whips up out of nowhere, swirling yellow leaves around her feet. Brown sprints back to the cottage as the clouds start spitting rain and Granger follows.

She pauses on the doorstep, sheltered by the eaves. She lifts her phone to her ear, ready to call Kane, when a single raindrop slides down the nape of her neck. She twists around, looks up and that's when she sees what the murderer missed. A security camera hidden under the eaves and angled to cover the front door.

CHAPTER 13

"Are you ready for this?" Granger asks, her dark eyes bright with anticipation.

"I've not had time to view any of this myself. I'm hoping we're going to strike lucky."

Kane is less optimistic. Yes, the killer made a big mistake. A blunder that could change everything. But the range of the camera will be limited. Apart from that, he doesn't believe in luck.

He drags a chair up to the desk and sits beside Granger. "Come on then. Let's do it."

She takes a sharp breath and clicks play. "Here we go. First, we've got the footage from the cameras on the side of the cottage before the lenses were smashed."

The laptop screen flickers for a moment before a figure appears at the entrance to the gravel drive. The man, tall and slender, glances furtively to his left and then to the right. He then walks quickly toward the camera. In his right hand he's carrying what looks like a wooden broom handle.

Kane and Granger both lean closer to the screen as he approaches the camera. He's wearing tracksuit bottoms, trainers and a dark zip-up hoodie. The hood is down. He's also wearing gloves and a black balaclava. Only his eyes and the bridge of his nose are visible. Kane notes the care the killer has taken to conceal his face. A premeditated, meticulously planned murder by a killer who knew his victim, or at least knew where he was staying and that he was alone.

He swaps a glance with Granger. It could be Tony Golding — the physique and height look right. They'd expected that the face would be covered. Their hope is that the killer gets careless once he believes he's put all the security cameras out of action. They watch the figure raise the broom handle and jab it hard into the lens.

Granger sits back in her chair and lets out a long breath. "The footage from the camera on the other of side of the cottage will be the same. We don't see a car pulling up. Maybe he parked in the lane away from the cottage and walked the rest of the way."

Kane agrees. "The balaclava doesn't mean the video is useless. Far from it. We can get a body language expert to make a good guess on age by the way he moves and holds himself. The tech team should be able to calculate his height. It may not be worth making the footage public though."

Granger selects another video file. "This is from the hidden camera he missed."

They both lean in again as the footage rolls. They can hear feet crunching on the gravel as the killer nears the door but he's not yet visible because he's approaching from the side. He steps up to the door, sinister eyes staring out of the balaclava. He raises a gloved fist and knocks hard.

Kane looks at Granger. She's holding her breath. He wonders whether she's thinking the same thing. If only Adam Golding had been more cautious about opening the door.

The killer knocks again. As soon as the door opens a fraction, he launches at it with his shoulder. They hear a frantic scuffle and Golding's cry of fear as the killer bundles his way in, slamming the door behind him.

The footage stops. A heavy silence fills the room.

"Move on," Kane says, and Granger clicks on fast forward. They watch the footage roll for what feels like several minutes until a head emerges from the door.

"Look, the time stamp says this is an hour and a half later," Granger says, "he's taken the balaclava off but pulled his hood up."

The killer backs slowly out of the cottage. His face is hidden because he's bent over and dragging Adam Golding's limp body over the threshold.

"It looks to me like he's already been injected with a lethal dose of insulin and is either sinking into a coma or is already dead," Kane says.

Once Golding's feet are clear, the killer releases his grip on the wrists, letting the arms flop lifelessly on to the gravel, and walks back to pull the door shut. As he turns, he looks briefly up to his left, exposing an ear, the tip of his nose and part of his jawline to the camera. He bends and grabs Golding's wrists again and after a couple of backward steps they are out of range of the camera.

"Can you go back to when he looks up and freeze it?" Kane says.

Granger nods and they both study the image for a moment before Kane claps his hands together in frustration.

"It's a partial profile and it's at strange angle. I'm not sure it's going to be of any help."

"Could it be Tony Golding? The build is similar."

Kane takes a moment to study the image again. "You're right about the build. But the truth is it could be anybody. I don't think there's any point in making any of the footage public. We're not going to get an ID from it and I don't want it put out just to titillate the media."

He has no doubt that the press would kill for the gruesome images of the killer dragging Adam Golding's lifeless body over the threshold. But the dead deserve as much respect as the living.

Granger closes the video file and leans back in her chair.

"That's disappointing. I was hoping we were going to hit the jackpot there."

Kane walks to the whiteboard, puts his hands on his hips and studies the headshot of Adam Golding. He tries to imagine what their victim could have possibly done for someone to believe he deserved to be killed then strung up like a carcass of meat.

"I think we can assume that Golding was already dead, which means the killer would have had to drag the body to his car or van where he kept whatever he needed to hang the body under the pier."

Granger swivels in her chair. "How did the killer know where Golding would be and that he'd be alone? As far as we are aware, his wife is the only person who knew that he used that place as a bolthole."

Kane turns back to the whiteboard to look at the photographs of the victim's wife and drug dealing brother. It certainly seems the killer knew a lot about the victim.

"I don't know," he says. "But we're going to find out. I promise you that. We're making good progress now. I reckon if we keep pushing, keep doing the right things and asking the right questions, we have a good chance of cracking this case pretty swiftly."

CHAPTER 14

Kane checks his press conference notes for the umpteenth time. He won't use them but likes to have them with him just in case.

It's three days into the investigation and a media circus is the last thing he wants to have to deal with.

He edges up to the conference room door and looks through the glass. He guesses there are half a dozen journalists and he can see a man at the back adjusting a portable TV camera.

Tony Golding has been in a holding cell overnight while they wait for Forensics to reach a verdict on the rope found in his garage. They won't be able to keep him in custody much longer unless they get something from an interview.

Kane hears a murmuring behind him and turns around. Ruth Golding's head is down as she studies her script, while a silver-haired press officer in a pinstriped suit advises her to take a deep breath before speaking and not to be tempted to answer questions. He's clearly more nervous than she is.

Kane has lost count of the number of press conferences he's been involved in. It's the one part of running a murder investigation that he hates. According to the force's media team, only local journalists are attending this one. Kane hopes he can get this case sewn up before the national newspapers judge the story juicy enough to unleash their reporters on Southend. Glory-hunting national newspaper hacks are always harder to deal with.

If they can't get what they want, they have no qualms about turning on the detectives running the investigation, digging up personal dirt and questioning the competence of the officer leading the hunt.

A nod from the press officer is Kane's cue to go. He opens the door and strides in. The journalists stop chattering and an air of expectancy fills the room. Kane waits for Golding to take her seat behind a long oak-effect table and sits beside her. He puts his notes down and looks straight at his audience, making a point of not speaking until the barrage of camera flashes stops.

"Thank you all for joining us today. You know how much we value the support of the media when it comes to a murder investigation."

This is the part that really irks him. Having to play the game and spout nonsense to reporters he's pretty sure don't give a damn about justice. Most of them are interested in one thing. The chance to bathe in the glory of a big news story. Still, he knows the big benefit of press coverage is that appeals to the public for information and for witnesses to come forward often provide a crucial breakthrough.

"Before we get started, I'll explain the rules to you. Mrs Golding is going to make her appeal for information. That's it. She will not be answering questions. When she's finished, I will fill you in on how the investigation is going and will respond to questions if I feel they are appropriate."

Some of the reporters shift restlessly in their seats, a few muttering discontentedly under their breath. Journalists hate being told what they can and can't do.

Kane looks across at Ruth Golding and gives her a nod. She picks up her script, her hands already shaking, and puts it back down.

"My husband Adam Golding left our house at around 6 p.m. on the evening of the second of February. I understood he was going to attend a conference in London. He drove off in our black Ranger Rover. That was the last time I saw him alive."

Kane detects a quiver in her voice, the blood draining from her face as her initial composure melts away.

"My Adam was a kind and loving husband, and I don't know how I'm going to go on without him. But I will do my best to find a way. Before that, I need to know why he was murdered, and I want to see his killer brought to justice."

She has the full attention of the whole room, with the journalists hanging on her every word. In Kane's mind the brother is now their prime suspect but Ruth Golding is not yet in the clear. She has two strong motives — revenge for his cheating, and the money she will now inherit. There's definitely more to her than meets the eye. She certainly knows how to play the gallery. And how to lie. This loving marriage story sounds convincing but will fall apart if one of these reporters decides to sniff around and uncovers the truth about the couple's relationship.

Golding pauses to wipe a tear from her cheek. "Adam didn't deserve to die like he did. Nobody does. I don't know why this happened to him. He's the innocent victim of a killer who is still out there walking the streets. Please, everybody watching or listening to this, I beg you. If you saw Adam or his Range Rover on that night, or if anyone suspects they know who did this terrible thing to him, please contact the police. Please help us."

She buries her head in her hands and sobs, her shoulders heaving until she loses all control and collapses face down on the table. The silver-haired press officer dashes to her side, helps her up from her seat and leads her away.

The room is buzzing with the drama of Golding's breakdown and Kane motions with a hand for the reporters to settle down. He'd like to get this over with as quickly as possible but it's a game that has to be played.

"You already know that the murder victim was found hanging by the neck under the pier. We now have new information about his death."

The murmuring stops and Kane feels the weight of every pair of eyes in the room.

"We can now say for certain that Adam Golding was dead before the killer chose to place a noose around his neck and hang him in a public place. This was a cold-blooded and barbaric act. We have yet to establish a motive for this murder and I want to assure the public that we are doing everything in our power to find the killer. A white transit-type van was seen parked close to the pier shortly before the body was found and we are busy trying to trace that vehicle. As Mrs Golding has just said, anybody who might know anything they believe might help our inquiry should contact us by ringing our murder information helpline, or through the Essex Police dedicated online information portal as soon as possible. They can do so anonymously if they wish. There's nothing to fear."

Kane shifts his seat back as if he's about to stand up and go. As much as he wants to exit now and avoid the inevitable salvo of questions, he knows that's not going to happen.

A short, chubby reporter wearing an ill-fitting, crumpled linen jacket dives in. "If Adam Golding's cause of death wasn't hanging, what was it? And why would anyone bother hanging a dead person?"

Kane knew this was coming. "You are?"

"Tom Young of the *Essex Recorder*."

Kane is sure he hasn't seen the reporter before but the *Recorder* was one of the local papers that questioned his mental state during the Jack Newman investigation. The paper won't hesitate to go after him again if it gets the chance.

"Well, Mr Young, I'm afraid I'm not in a position to release that information yet."

"Why not?"

Kane takes a deep breath. Even though over the years he's become adept at playing the media game, being asked to explain his decisions to someone who hasn't a clue about solving murders still gets under his skin.

"Now isn't the right time to make this particular detail public."

Everyone can hear the irritation in Kane's voice. A smirk slides across the reporter's face. "Why not?"

"Because I say so and I'm in charge of this investigation."

A woman with a short blonde crop jumps in to fill the silence. "Ingrid Grey, from the *Leigh Standard*. Adam Golding recently sold off all his businesses, probably banking millions of pounds in the process. Are you looking at the possibility that there could be a financial motive to his murder?"

For God's sake, Kane thinks. *Does she really believe that we're too stupid to work that one out ourselves?*

"We are considering and looking into all possibilities. As I said earlier, we're doing everything within our power to solve this case. I'm sure we can depend on you, the ladies and gentlemen of the press, to support us in our efforts to take Adam Golding's killer off the streets."

Kane checks the clock on opposite wall, high above the journalists' heads. "I'll take one more question," he announces.

Several of the journalists start talking over one another, desperate to make themselves heard, but one jumps out of her chair and launches straight into her question. "I am aware that your team carried out a search of a flat and made an arrest at a tower block on the Kingsbury Estate yesterday afternoon. Does this mean you already have a suspect in custody?"

Kane takes a moment to study the reporter. Compared to the others, she's fresh-faced and informally dressed in jeans, a brown leather jacket and a tartan scarf. He's sure he's never seen her at a press conference before.

"I can confirm that there has been a development in the case and an arrest has been made. That's all I'm prepared to say at this stage. As soon as I feel able to give you more detail I will. Our priority right now is to focus on gathering evidence. Now, I have work to be getting on with, thank you."

He leaves the room, ignoring other journalists as they shout out their questions. In the adjoining room, Ruth Golding is sitting at a table sipping a cup of tea. She appears remarkably composed considering the emotional distress she displayed during the press conference.

Kane wonders how much of it was for show. She'll need to be questioned again once his team have delved deep into her background. For now he's eager to get on with questioning her brother-in-law.

She looks up as he passes. "I'm sorry I broke down in there," she says with a sniff. "I thought I'd be able to hold it together. Once I let myself think about what happened to Adam and what he must have gone through, it just became impossible. Did I do all right?"

"Don't worry, you did fine. You made the appeal to the public for information and as far as helping us with the investigation goes, that's the important bit."

Kane strides on before she can speak again. He passes the lift and takes the stairs to the ground floor. He's in desperate need of some fresh air. Once outside the station, he gives Granger a call. She answers straight away.

"Hi. How did it go with the press?"

"As well as could be expected."

"Oh right, that good?"

Kane isn't in the mood to go into detail. She'll see it all on the TV later. "Anything back from Forensics on the nylon rope?"

"Not yet. Expecting to hear in the next hour or so."

Kane would rather wait until he can positively connect the rope found in Tony Golding's car to the rope used to hang the victim before starting the interview, but he's worried that Golding's solicitor will be pushing for police bail if they don't charge him soon.

"Arrange for Golding to be brought up to interview room one in half an hour. See you then."

Kane puts his hands in his trouser pockets and heads down toward the seafront. He needs to clear his head. When he reaches the promenade, he leans on the rails, takes a deep breath and stares out to where the vast overcast sky meets the sea.

It's a grey, misty day. Bitterly cold and damp. Despite this, the seafront is busy with people keen to breathe the salty air, walk their dogs or tuck into a greasy fish and chip lunch.

Tony Golding is shady. Kane is sure of that. He's almost certainly dealing drugs and using the estate gangs to sell his product. During the search of his flat the sniffer dog reacted to a sprinkle of white powder on the bathroom floor. It tested positive for cocaine but all Golding has to do is admit he buys small amounts for personal use.

They found no evidence that he supplies drugs. No sign of the burner phones Granger saw on his bedside table. That proves nothing, except that he's smart enough to have realised that the police would return with a search warrant.

That's why, in Kane's mind, leaving a piece of the nylon rope used to hang his brother hidden in the boot of his car makes no sense. Maybe he assumed that the police didn't know about his lock-up garage.

Until the discovery of the rope, Kane wouldn't have put Tony Golding down as his brother's murderer. A person capable of lashing out in a rage and causing serious harm or even death, yes. But not a cold-blooded killer.

Dark clouds swirl ominously on the horizon. Kane decides to return to the station before they sweep inland and spit their stinging rain. He turns abruptly, almost bumping into a young woman.

He's about to apologise when he recognises the smiling face and tartan scarf. "What the hell are you doing? Are you following me?"

The reporter looks horrified. "God no. 'Course not. I wanted to introduce myself properly. I didn't get the chance before. I'm the *Southend Herald*'s crime reporter. In the spirit of local cooperation, I'm hoping that we can, maybe we can, er, help each other out."

Kane sighs. "Go on then."

"What?"

"Introduce yourself properly."

"Oh, right. Yeah." She holds out a slender hand. "I'm Sam Hunter. I've been on the crime beat for the *Herald* for nearly six months now and I'm loving every minute of it."

Kane ignores her offer of a handshake. He wonders whether she landed the job straight out of university. She looks young enough.

"Good to meet you, Sam. I'm always willing to nurture good relations with local journalists. Any questions about the Adam Golding case should be directed to our media office, not to me. Now, I must get back to the station."

"To interview Tony Golding?"

Kane stops in his tracks. "What did you say? You know we've arrested him?"

Hunter's smile widens. "Of course. I've not been doing this job for long but I've made a lot of contacts pretty quickly. I didn't mention his name in the press conference because I guessed you might not want it made public."

Kane doubts that's the real reason. It's more likely that she didn't want to tip off her rivals. Maybe this reporter is a lot tougher than she looks. "Okay, I appreciate that. Thank you. Is there anything you can tell me about Tony Golding that might be useful?"

Hunter hesitates. "Nothing you don't already know. From what I hear around town, he's definitely selling drugs and is a lot smarter, and scarier, than the average dealer. Cocaine mainly. Some cannabis. No evidence for you. Yet."

Kane considers warning her that nosing around in a drug dealer's business can be extremely dangerous. He holds back. Even though she's young and inexperienced, she has a job to do and from what he's just heard, she seems to be doing it well.

"Listen," he says. "Maybe we can cooperate to some extent. If you give me reason to trust that you can act responsibly and are genuinely interested in helping us solve crimes, then perhaps we can work something out."

"I don't think that's going to be a problem."

"Good. Then maybe we can sometimes share information as long as it won't jeopardise an ongoing investigation. But I guess you probably understand why I might be a bit wary of the press."

Hunter gives him a wide, disarming grin.

"I can assure you that you don't need to be wary of me."

CHAPTER 15

On arriving back at the station, Kane makes a fleeting visit to the canteen to pick up a couple of coffees. As he approaches his office, he checks his watch. It's nearly noon. They haven't long to prepare for the Tony Golding interview.

He enters his office to find Granger sitting at his desk making notes. She looks up, a frown of concentration on her face.

"I've started without you. You can have your seat back now."

Kane puts her coffee down on the desk in front of her.

"You stay where you are. I'm good. I just needed some fresh air after the press conference. I never enjoy them."

Granger puts her pen down and sits back. "You know what you're doing. You handled it well."

"You think so?"

"I think you should stop fishing for compliments so we can get on with this interview prep."

Kane grins, crosses the room, and leans back against the pale blue wall.

"We have no more than a couple of hours before we hit the twenty-four-hour deadline and have to decide to charge or release him, which means we don't have the time to pussyfoot around.

"I think it's a good idea if you lead the questioning and go in hard on the murder from the beginning."

Granger raises her eyebrows in surprise. "He's been arrested on suspicion of drug dealing."

"That's right. We can ask him anything we want to, can't we?"

"His lawyer won't like it. He'll probably advise him not to say anything."

Kane shrugs. "That's his right. But I have a feeling Tony Golding is the type of man who won't like being pushed, especially by a woman. Also, he's spent a long night in a police cell so I suspect he's going to be on edge. Susceptible to a little goading. We're still waiting for Forensics to come back with a verdict on the rope but we can still use it to squeeze him. Catch him off guard."

Granger picks up her coffee and takes a sip while she thinks for a moment. "It's worth a try. What about the drug dealing?"

"Well, that's where I come in. At the right moment, hopefully, when Golding is starting to struggle. Are you up for it?"

Granger grabs her pen and scribbles furiously. When she finishes, she flips her notepad shut and flashes Kane a smile.

He walks to the door and grabs the handle. His sergeant's passion for the job constantly reminds him why he loves detective work.

"Come on then. Let's do it."

* * *

Tony Golding's lawyer is an expensively dressed, smug-looking man in his forties, his face as tight as the skin on a snare drum.

He's waiting for Kane outside the interview room and offers him a business card before introducing himself.

"Delighted to meet you, Detective Inspector. I don't think our paths have crossed before. I'm James Pope. I've spoken to my client and he's hoping it won't take long to sort out this unfortunate misunderstanding."

Kane dismisses the proffered business card with a wave. "There's no misunderstanding as far as I'm concerned. We need to question your client on some extremely serious matters. Now that you've had time to consult with him, we need to get started."

Pope is taken aback by Kane's abruptness. He tries to show his displeasure with a frown but his forehead won't crease.

Kane steps past him into the interview followed swiftly by Granger. Tony Golding is sitting upright, both his hands gripping the edge of the table in front of him. He glares at the detectives as they take their seats, ignoring Pope completely.

To Kane he looks like a caged animal. Full of pent-up energy and emotion. He clearly didn't enjoy his night in a police cell.

Granger flips her notepad open but doesn't bother to look at it. As agreed, she gets straight to the point. "Did you kill your brother, Adam, in an act of revenge for what you've already told us he did to you regarding your rightful inheritance?"

Golding lifts a hand and rubs furiously at his unshaven chin. "No. This is ridiculous."

"When we first came to your flat to tell you Adam was dead, far from being upset, you seemed delighted."

"The bastard got what he deserved."

Pope darts a nervous glance at Golding.

"I'd like to remind my client that he doesn't need to respond to any questions if he doesn't want to. 'No comment' will suffice."

Golding turns to Pope and fixes him with a fierce stare until the lawyer looks away. While Pope will be being paid a lot of money for his legal expertise, the man living in a council estate tower block has shown him who's boss.

Granger presses on. Keen to capitalise on the tension, she sharpens her tone. "Can you remember what you were doing and where you were on the day your younger brother went missing, the second of February?"

"No I can't. Shit, I can't remember what I did yesterday. But I was probably at home in the flat the whole day."

"Can you prove it?"

"Can you prove I wasn't?"

Pope shakes his head in despair. "I think we should break here. I need to consult further with my client."

The last thing Kane wants is to stop the interview now. Golding's decision to ignore his lawyer's advice means he's more likely to slip up. A break would give Pope a chance to smooth-talk Golding back into line.

"We've just started and have a lot to get through," he says. "You've had plenty of time to sort things out between you."

"My client is obviously confused about some of these questions and I insist I'm given the opportunity to advise him further."

"What about you?" Kane asks, turning to Golding. "Do you want this break?"

Golding shrugs. "If one of you will make me a coffee, yeah."

Kane stands up. "We'll give you ten minutes. That's it. And no coffee."

DS Scott is waiting for them in the corridor. Kane knows by the look on his face that the news isn't good.

"Forensics have called. The rope found in Golding's car is the same type of rope used by his brother's killer but that is as far as they are willing to go. It's impossible to prove that it's an actual piece of the rope used to make the noose. It's a common type of nylon rope that is sold in DIY superstores and hardware shops all over the country."

Kane nods. It's what he feared. It's not conclusive enough to charge Golding with murder. Still, the rope can be used to pile the pressure on.

Granger has been listening intently and, as usual, she's on the same page. "Golding doesn't have to know the detail, does he? We can tell him that we know for a fact that it's the same type of rope. That's true. It's definitely going to make him nervous, give him something to worry about."

Back in the interview room, Kane notices that Golding is still and looking more focused. His lawyer's pep talk has clearly paid dividends.

Granger switches on the recording but before she can continue, Golding speaks. "What about my coffee? I'd like a coffee."

Granger pauses and glances at Kane. He shakes his head. "I said no coffee. Maybe we can get you something when this interview ends."

"That's not good enough. This a breach of my human rights, isn't it?" Golding turns to his lawyer for confirmation.

Pope stares back at him in confusion.

"Your rights were read to you earlier, remember?" Kane says. "Let me remind you: You do not have to say anything, but it may harm your defence if you do not mention when questioned something which you later rely on in court. Anything you say may be given in evidence. Now, there's no mention of you being able to order a coffee whenever you feel like it, is there? If you insist on playing the fool you can go back into a cell and we'll carry this on later."

Golding smiles, slumps back in his chair and waves at Granger. "Please continue."

Granger obliges. "While searching your car one of our officers found a length of rope in the boot. Do you remember when you bought it and what you use it for?"

Golding frowns. "I haven't a clue what you're on about, lady."

"I'm not a lady, or a dame, or a baroness. I'm a detective sergeant."

"Good for you, lady."

Granger takes a slow breath, determined not to rise to his goading. "The blue nylon rope found in your car is the same kind of rope used to fashion a noose and hang your brother under the pier. Can you explain that?"

For the first time, Golding appears anxious. He looks at Pope for help.

"My client doesn't have to explain anything if he chooses not to."

Granger makes a point of ignoring the lawyer and locks eyes with Golding. "What was the rope doing in your car, Tony?"

"No comment."

"Did you forget about it? After killing Adam? A bit careless to stuff it in your boot."

"No comment."

Kane can see that Pope is smiling now, delighted that his client has at last decided to play safe and follow instructions.

It's time to take over the questioning and switch tactics.

"During our search of your flat we found traces of cocaine on the bathroom floor."

"So what?"

"Possession of a Class A drug is a serious offence."

"I don't know anything about it. I've never been in possession of cocaine. Traces, you say? Maybe the previous tenant was a user. Nothing to do with me. You know if I admit to having a small amount in my flat for personal use, I'll get a fine. That's all. It's not worth your trouble."

"Dealing cocaine is a different matter though. Serious jail time."

"I don't deal any kind of drug. I'm not stupid. You took my phone. Didn't find anything on it, did you?"

Kane doesn't answer. The search of Golding's flat failed to find the burner phones Granger saw in the bedroom. All that proves is that Golding is smart. Smart enough to have moved them after their visit.

Kane looks up at the clock on the wall opposite. They're running out of time and still haven't got enough to charge him with anything other than possibly possession for personal use.

"This is outrageous," Pope says. "You have no evidence to justify holding my client any longer. As his legal representative, I insist you either charge him or let him go."

Kane looks at Granger. They both know that the lawyer is right. Kane stands and aims his response at Golding. "I'll speak to the custody sergeant and arrange for you to be released on police bail. Make no mistake, you are still under investigation. We're not finished with you yet."

The detectives leave the room. Neither of them speak until they're back in Kane's office.

"Golding's a slippery customer," Kane says. "But we'll get him. For dealing drugs if nothing else."

Granger doesn't respond. She's fiddling with her phone, a worried frown on her face.

"Is everything okay?"

"I've seven missed calls since I put my phone on silent for the interview. I don't recognise the number. Give me a minute, will you, I need to call it back."

Kane sits behind his desk and considers their next move. Ruth and Tony Golding are still the main suspects. Both have strong motives. The wife would have had to be working with someone else. She's not strong enough to have been able to hang her husband's dead body under the pier. Tony is physically capable. He would also have plenty of criminal associates who'd be happy to kill for money.

Granger bursts into the office. "I'm sorry. I've got to go." Her eyes are red as if she's been crying.

"What's happened? Are you all right?"

"It's Mum. She's in hospital. She collapsed in the kitchen while cooking. Daisy found her unconscious on the floor. They've been trying to get hold of me for ages but I had my phone on silent because of the interview. I'm so stupid. I've got to go. Daisy's at the hospital waiting for me. I'm sorry."

Granger's common-sense approach to life always belies her age. The tears now rolling down her face emphasise her youth and vulnerability.

"You've nothing to be sorry for," Kane says. "I'll drive you to the hospital. Drop you off."

Granger sniffs and shakes her head. "Thanks for the offer, but you don't need to. You've got too much to do."

"I can get a uniform to take you."

"I'm all right to drive myself. I'm okay."

Kane watches her as she runs, still sobbing, to the lift. She isn't okay.

CHAPTER 16

Granger hurries down the wide, windowless corridor, weaving her way through the steady stream of medics and visitors heading the other way.

A red sign on the white-painted wall tells her to take a sharp left turn to find Ward 27. She presses the entry button and pushes her way inside the instant the grey double doors are buzzed open.

The ward is narrow and gloomy. It smells of a mixture of pine cleaning fluid and hope.

As she nears the nursing station, she spots Daisy sitting nearby. Her head is bowed, her stick-thin legs swinging. Granger breaks into a run, crouches, wraps her arms around her daughter and hugs her tight. "It's all right. I'm here now."

The little girl slides off the chair and buries her head in her mother's chest.

"I was scared, Mummy. I didn't know what to do."

Granger hugs her again, kissing her gently on the cheek. "Don't you worry, my darling. Mummy's here now and we'll see Grandma soon. You did such a good job dialling 999 and asking for an ambulance. Just like we practised. Grandma's got doctors and nurses taking care of her now. Everything's going to be fine."

She's saying what her five-year-old needs to hear, but she fears the worst. If anything happens to her mother, she'll never forgive herself. She has asked so much of her. Long days caring for Daisy, combined with the stress of being estranged from her sons because of her daughter's decision to ignore their disapproval and forge a career as a police officer.

Hundreds of people, Granger guesses, must have sat on this ward waiting to hear whether their loved ones will live or die. Their hearts hammering just like hers, their throats tight, their stomachs churning.

A woman in pale blue scrubs approaches, and Granger stands up quickly, cradling Daisy in her arms like a baby. The woman is short and black-haired, fatigue etched on her face.

"I take it you're Daisy's mum?"

"That's right. Bailey Granger. What's happened to my mother?"

"I'm Doctor Malik. Naomi is conscious and keen to see you."

Granger's knees almost buckle with relief. "Thank God. Thank you, Doctor. What's wrong with her? Why did she fall? Is she going to be all right?"

The medic summons up a half-smile. "I'm afraid I can't answer all of those questions right now. She is doing well, considering. Mentally, she seems a strong woman and that counts for a lot. Her blood pressure is dangerously high and that's almost certainly the reason she fainted. Unfortunately, she hit her head on the floor when she fell and has a painful swelling on her forehead."

"What's causing her blood pressure to be so high? Is it serious?"

"We don't know yet. We will be keeping her in overnight, just to be safe. We've already started her on medication that will get her blood pressure down and she'll probably have to stay on it permanently. She should be able to go home tomorrow, once we've done some tests to determine her heart health."

Granger doesn't like the sound of that. "I'd like to see her now, if that's all right."

She puts Daisy down, takes her hand and they follow Dr Malik along a cold corridor, fluorescent strip lights flickering ominously overhead.

They turn into a bustling general ward and Dr Malik leads them to the first bed, drawing back the blue plastic curtain.

Naomi is lying on her back, her eyes closed, her grey hair splayed on the pillow. As Granger steps nearer, her mother's eyes open. A smile spreads across her face. "Well, my girl, there you are. At last. What took you so long?"

She looks old and frail. Not like herself at all. Granger wants to throw her arms around her and weep. She holds back. She doesn't want Daisy to see how worried she is.

"Oh, Mum, that swelling is nasty. Does it hurt bad?"

Naomi shakes her head and waves a hand at her. "Don't you worry, girl, this is nothing. I've had worse scrapes than this. I'm on strong painkillers and they're working. I'm in the best place and they're looking after me, you know. Making sure I have everything I need. The nurses here are wonderful. They work so hard."

Despite the bravado, Granger can tell that her mother is shaken and more than a little frightened.

"Me and Daisy will be staying the night here in one of the family rooms. I can check on you and get you anything you need."

"No, no, no. Don't be silly, girl. That's not necessary. Daisy needs her own bed. Poor girl must have been so scared. I dropped the pan and scattered her fish fingers over the floor. Are you hungry, darling? You both go home. I will sleep better knowing that my girls are comfortable. That's the truth."

Granger opens her mouth to argue but stops herself. She knows how stubborn her mother is and that what she's saying makes sense.

She lifts Daisy and perches her on the edge of the bed, takes her mother's hand and gives it a gentle squeeze. The skin is cool and papery. Granger has always considered her mother to be robust. Indestructible, even. It's clear she hasn't been paying attention. The years have crept up on her.

"We'll stay with you a little longer, maybe ten minutes, then let you rest. We'll both be back in the morning. Daisy won't be in any fit state to go to school."

Her mother nods, closing her eyes for a few seconds before speaking again. "Bailey, I need you to do something for me."

Granger suspects she knows what's coming.

"Of course. What is it?"

Her mother grimaces. "Please don't tell your brothers I'm in hospital. I don't want to worry them. They have their lives to get on with. They'll only make a fuss and, anyway, I'm going to be fine. The doctors say I can probably go home tomorrow."

"Oh, Mum. Sterling and Marcus have to be told. I can't keep this from them. If they found out they'd never speak to me again."

"But they don't speak to you now."

Granger sighs. She fell out with her brothers when she joined the police four years ago. Now, they rarely visit their mother and only when they know Granger and Daisy won't be there. She hates that they don't have a relationship with their niece.

They will blame her too. She's sure of that. It would be so much easier to do as her mother asks.

"I'm sorry, Mum. I can't keep them in the dark about this."

Her mother shakes her head slowly. "I haven't got the strength to argue with you. But make sure they know that they don't have to worry about me. High blood pressure is common at my age."

"They're big boys now, Mum. Don't worry about them. You concentrate on getting better."

Her mother gives her a doubtful look. "If you drop Daisy off at school tomorrow, you can go into work, you know. You have a murder case to solve."

Granger knows that her absence will cause Kane and the team a few problems. But nobody is indispensable. She's been throwing herself into her work since her return to the Major Investigations Team. To prove to everyone, including herself, that she's there on merit. That she's got what it takes. Maybe she needs to put family first. For once.

"Don't worry. They'll just have to cope."

CHAPTER 17

Kane heads for the incident room, sips his takeaway coffee, and walks along the narrow corridor. He passes the squad room where Detective Inspector Mick Munro is holding court at his desk, entertaining a huddle of local officers with stories of his triumphs.

Munro glances across the room at Kane and mutters something to his audience, who follow his gaze and erupt into laughter.

Kane thinks briefly about stopping to discover what they're finding so funny and ask why they're not doing something useful like catching criminals. Instead, he carries on until he reaches his office.

He sits behind his desk and checks his watch. It's 8 a.m. and his team are waiting to be briefed. He grabs his phone from his desk and calls Granger.

She usually always answers by the third ring. This time the call goes to voicemail. He decides not to bother her with a message. As he puts the phone back on the desk she calls back.

"Sorry," she says. "I was in the middle of helping Daisy get dressed. We're off to the hospital as soon as we're ready."

Her voice is shaky. Kane guesses it's worry. "How's she doing?"

"Her blood pressure was so high she fainted. They kept her in overnight to keep an eye on her. She's having some tests today to see if they can find a cause. They're probably going to discharge her later."

"That's good."

"Is it? I'm not sure. Maybe the hospital is the best place for her until they know exactly what's wrong."

"They won't let her out if they think she's in danger."

"I'm sorry. I don't know when I'll be able to come back. I don't feel I can leave Mum on her own. I've nobody else to look after Daisy."

Kane can hear she hates leaving the team short-handed. "Don't you worry yourself about us. You may be good but you're not irreplaceable. You concentrate on your family. Everything is under control here."

Granger falls silent for a moment. Kane can almost hear her brain ticking over. "What about Ruth Golding's appeal for information? Anything useful come from that?"

"Nothing of note yet. I'll keep you in the loop if that changes. Keep me updated on your mum. Got to go now. Can't be late for my own briefing."

* * *

Kane walks into the incident room with his head held high, a spring in his step. He wants to make sure his team aren't given the impression that he thinks losing Granger is a setback. Even though he does.

He turns to face them and waits for the chatter to die down.

"You will have heard by now that Detective Sergeant Granger will be taking some time off to deal with a family matter. This cannot be allowed to affect this investigation in anyway. There will be no easing off. No slowing down. In fact, this is the perfect time for us all to drive ourselves even harder."

A couple of the detectives nod in agreement. The rest keep their expressions neutral. Kane guesses they're not sure it's possible to put in more effort than they already are.

"Tony Golding has been released on police bail. I want you three—" he jabs a finger at DS Scott, DC Brown and PC Weaver — "to dig as deep as you can into Golding's drug connections. Get out there on the streets and try to find out where he gets his supplies from. Let's speak to any local informants to hear if there are any interesting rumours doing the rounds. Golding strikes me as the kind of man who thinks he's too clever to be caught and might well be tempted to boast to his cronies about how he took revenge on his businessman brother."

Kane turns to catch DC Kush's eye. "Meera, you're coming with me to interview Ruth Golding again. How have you got on digging into her background?"

Kush straightens her back and takes a moment to consult notes on her electronic tablet. "Well, she was born and brought up here in Southend. Went to a local comprehensive. Worked in administration for the local council accounts department for five years, then moved on to work for Pure Gold Ltd, the Golding family firm."

"That's where she met Adam?"

"It looks that way. He obviously spotted her talent and they got together. Three years later they married."

Kane does his best to hide his disappointment. "All fairly straightforward then?"

Kush puts her tablet down on the desk. "Not quite. Checking the dates, I noticed a two-year gap between leaving the council and joining the Goldings' company. Ruth Sawyer, as she was then, started studying for a nursing degree at the Essex University campus in Southend. According to university records she dropped out halfway through the second year."

Kane falls silent, his heart beating faster as this news sinks in. Nursing degrees involve a lot of practical work on the wards of local hospitals. Ruth Golding would probably be pretty handy with a syringe.

"Well done, DC Kush. Excellent work."

CHAPTER 18

Kane leads DC Kush out of the walnut-panelled lift, across the lobby area to the penthouse. He presses the video intercom and looks directly at the camera.

He waits a moment, then presses the button again. This time they hear the approach of footsteps and the door swings open.

Ruth Golding stares silently at the detectives for a few seconds, her expression as icy as the wind whipping off the estuary. She's dressed casually but expensively in pale blue sweatpants with a baggy cream top.

"You should have let me know you were coming," she says. "What's this about? Has something happened?"

Kane considers telling her that there's no law that says the police have to make appointments to speak to suspects. "Good morning to you. This is Detective Constable Meera Kush. We have some questions we'd like you to help us with, if it's not too much trouble."

Without a word, Golding turns and walks away. Kane and Kush give each other a look and follow. She leads them into the expansive living area and spreads herself on the large sofa.

Kush hesitates, waiting for an invitation to take a seat. When it doesn't come, she sits down anyway on one of the three leather armchairs. Kane chooses to stay standing.

Golding sighs loudly. "What can I do for you, Detective Inspector? How long is this going to take? I don't like unpleasant surprises."

Kane wonders what's happened to the soft-hearted, grieving widow who bared her soul to the public at the press conference.

"This will take as long as I want it to. This is a murder investigation. We don't cut corners. We're here to inform you about something to do with the way Adam was killed. Something that we haven't made public yet. It's not unusual for certain details to be held back until we feel the investigation will benefit by making them public."

Golding sits up straight. Now she's interested. "What are you talking about? What do you mean?"

"I mean that we know for sure that the murderer killed your husband by injecting him with a lethal overdose of medical insulin. The body would then have been transported to the seafront by car or van and then suspended by the neck under the pier."

Golding throws a bemused look at Kush, then back at Kane. "Adam was injected with insulin, you say?"

"That's right. He was murdered by injection. What do you think about that?"

Golding's naturally fair complexion flushes pink. Shock or guilt? Kane wonders.

"What do I think? I think that's terrible. Why on earth would someone do that?"

"Well, that's a good question. One reason could be that it's not easy to detect insulin in a body, even after a lethal dose. Fortunately, our pathologist is one of the best. Not a lot gets past him."

Golding slumps back on the sofa, shaking her head. "I don't understand what's happening here. Why are you telling me this now?"

Kane glances at Kush and gives her a nod. She digs her tablet out of her jacket pocket, powers it up and studies the screen. "We understand that you spent two years working towards a nursing degree in your mid-twenties."

Golding frowns. "That's right. That was a long time ago. More than ten years ago. I gave up because I decided nursing wasn't for me. I couldn't stand the sight of blood. Still can't. What are you getting at?"

Kush puts the tablet down on to her lap. Kane takes a step closer to the sofa and takes over. "We're saying that the person who killed your husband would probably need to have had some medical experience. Need to be comfortable with injecting drugs like insulin."

Golding stands up slowly. She lifts a trembling arm and points across the room toward the door. "Get out of my home or I'll sue you for trespassing. I mean it. How dare you come here and accuse me of killing Adam? Get out, right now."

Kane doesn't move. "I'm sorry, but that isn't how this works."

Golding takes a deep breath and sits back down on the sofa. Tears roll down her cheeks and Kane is intrigued by how quickly her fury has transformed to weeping.

"I can't believe this," she sobs. "I haven't done anything. Are you going to arrest me?"

"Not right now," Kane says. "But don't think even think about leaving the country. I'm going to need to talk to you again very soon."

* * *

Kane checks his watch as Kush drives along the Thorpe Bay seafront on their way back to the station. It's already one o'clock. He opens the passenger window a fraction, the salt in the air making him lick his lips.

The beach is sandy with patches of shingle. Beyond that, shimmering waves churn where the flow of the Thames mixes with the North Sea.

In the distance Kane spots a couple holding hands as they walk along the waterline. Lizzy loved the seaside on a summer's day. The big skies, the sound of laughter, the sweet smell of fresh doughnuts and candyfloss.

A wave of sadness washes over him. Happy memories can do that to you. Especially when you're trying your best to move on.

Kane straightens up in his seat, a stab of guilt snapping him back to the present. He has a job to do. A killer to catch. Anything less than laser focus won't be good enough.

"Well, how do you think that went?" he asks.

Kush keeps her eyes on the road ahead. The lunchtime traffic is heavy. "She lost it, didn't she? She was physically shaking with anger."

"Do you think that was genuine?"

"Don't you?"

Kane isn't sure. He's never found Ruth Golding easy to read. One moment she's seething with righteous anger, the next she's bawling like a baby. He's missing Granger already. Despite her relative youth, she's a better judge of people than he is. Especially when it comes to women.

"I'm finding it hard to make my mind up about her. She's definitely still a suspect. Her marriage was going down the pan and now she's due to inherit a lot of money. She's also had enough medical training to be capable of injecting insulin."

Kush nods. "But if she was involved, she's got to have had an accomplice. She wouldn't be strong enough to hang the body under the pier on her own."

Kane agrees. Bodies don't weigh more just because they're dead. After death the muscles relax and that makes them feel heavier.

As they pull into the station car park, Kane makes a decision he hopes he won't regret but fears he might.

With Granger by his side instead of Kush, he suspects he'd find the strength to resist.

"I'd like you to keep digging into Ruth Golding's background. Something about her isn't adding up. She's lying about something. See if you can speak to some former colleagues, anybody who knew her before she married Adam Golding. I've got an important appointment and it's a long drive."

CHAPTER 19

By the time Kane nears his destination dusk is falling over Berkshire's Bracknell Forest like a grey shroud. The road taking him to the high-security psychiatric hospital snakes through the darkness. After a couple of miles, the forbidding silhouette of the old Broadmoor Hospital looms on the right, its Victorian facade guarded by a barbed wire fence.

Kane puts his foot down. He's always thought there was something nightmarish about the building that, for more than one-hundred-and-fifty years, has been home to the country's worst serial killers.

Five minutes later, at almost five o'clock, he pulls into the brightly lit entrance of the new Broadmoor. At the barrier he flashes his warrant card and the uniformed security guard checks his name is on the visitor list before directing him to a parking space near reception.

The new hospital complex is low-rise and super modern. It smells like every hospital Kane has been in. A male member of staff, dressed casually in jeans and a green polo shirt, escorts him along a bright corridor, decorated with abstract artwork and black and white photographs, to a visiting room.

Kane steps inside and is instantly reminded that although the new hospital is shiny and welcoming compared to the old one, some of the patients will always radiate an evil that makes your blood run cold.

Jack Newman, the man the papers called the See No Evil killer, looks up from his armchair and smirks. "Well, look who it is. The great Detective Inspector Edison Kane. You took your time, but I knew you wouldn't be able to hold out for ever. I appreciate it, though. It's a long drive from Southend. I'm flattered you could make it. You are my one and only visitor. I don't know why. I can be quite charming when I want to be."

Kane knows he shouldn't be wasting his time and Newman knows it too. He should be concentrating on catching Adam Golding's killer. He has no doubt that if Detective Superintendent Dean finds out about this trip, he'll be hauled off the case.

He walks across the room and sits down, nothing but a glass coffee table between him and a cold-blooded murderer.

"What about this place? Splendid, isn't it? The new Broadmoor Hospital opened four years ago. If it was a hotel, I'd give it four stars. The only thing I don't like about it is a lot of the guests are genuinely certifiable. If you're not crazy when you arrive, you will be when you leave."

Kane can't bring himself to speak yet. He hates himself for letting this monster draw him in, after promising he'd never set eyes on him again.

Newman's dark hair is longer and greasier than it used to be. It covers his ears and hangs level with his jawline. His face looks rounder and Kane guesses he's piled on a few pounds since his incarceration.

"Come on, Kane. Cat got your tongue? Say something interesting, won't you? I've been looking forward to this for a long time. You know, if I'd been sent to a prison instead of this hospital for the criminally insane, we'd be sitting in a grubby little box room separated by a plastic screen. This is so much more civilised, don't you think?"

Kane stays silent. He's certain that this man fooled a bunch of psychologists, psychiatrists as well as a jury into believing that he wasn't of sound mind when he killed three people to satisfy his greed, ambition and bloodlust.

The door opens and the staff member in the green shirt pokes his head in. "Would anyone like a coffee, or a tea?"

"Great idea. The usual for me, Mike, and the same for my friend the detective here."

Newman waits for Mike to leave, then rubs his hands together. "What about that? The service here is excellent. They lay on a good supply of mind-altering drugs too. Medication to control behaviour, therapy to change it. That's the mantra. And I even get to go to art classes. The shrinks love the fact that I'm obsessed with painting eyes."

Kane had forgotten how much being in the same room as this man sickens his stomach.

"Why don't you stop all the bullshit. You know why I'm here."

Newman recoils in mock horror.

"Come on now, detective. No need for that. I'd assumed you'd come for a bit of intellectual stimulation. I can't imagine you get much of that at work. I've had a lot of dealings with police officers and most were a few French fries short of a Happy Meal. No wonder crime is rocketing."

The door opens again and Mike walks in with two steaming mugs of coffee, a small bowl of sugar and a spoon on a wooden tray. He puts it down on the glass table.

"Hope you enjoy," he says cheerfully and exits quickly, humming an unrecognisable tune.

Newman puts three spoonfuls of sugar into his drink and stirs it vigorously. He nods at Kane's mug.

"Go on then, it's good quality stuff. Real coffee. Not that instant rubbish you're used to."

Kane doesn't move. He hasn't come to Broadmoor for a cosy chat with a man who kills and mutilates for fun.

"I'm not here to socialise with you. The idea repulses me and you know it. I'm only here to find out what you can tell me about my wife's murder."

Newman sips his coffee slowly. "Of course you are. You want to know who murdered her. That's natural. You'd love to lock him up. Or even worse. I reckon you wouldn't hesitate to kill your darling Lizzy's murderer if you thought there was a chance you could get away with it? I bet you would. Go on, admit it. I can see it in your eyes."

Kane has often fantasised about what he might do if he got his hands on the man who snuffed out his wife's life. He'd never admit it to this man, never give him the chance to argue that he's not a monster, that human nature is inherently evil.

"I want to bring the perpetrator before a court of law. I want to lock him up and throw away the key. Nothing more."

Newman gives him a disbelieving smirk. "If you say so. If that's how you want to play it, then fine. I know the truth though."

"You know nothing about me. Now, what information do you have about the person who murdered my wife?"

"I know that he's vanished off the radar but he'll be back soon. Because he can't help himself."

Kane's shoulders slump. Baxter warned him not to let himself be played by a psychopath looking for a way to spice up his boring existence.

"That's bullshit and you know it. All you're doing is spouting amateur psychology. You're wasting my time."

Newman responds with a long, cold glare. "Have you forgotten that the last time we spoke I named the two drugs your wife's killer used to spike her drink? Details that have never been made public."

Kane has racked his brains every day for more than a year trying to work out how the reporter could have obtained that information.

"I haven't forgotten. Why don't you just tell me how you know those details?"

Newman picks up his mug, takes another sip, and pulls a face. "This stuff has gone cold already. You haven't even touched yours. What a waste."

"Are you going to tell me or not?"

"I'm thinking not. I can tell you don't really believe me. You're just desperate. Why should I bother? I only mentioned it to be helpful. I can tell how much it would mean to you to catch the guy. But, hey, you're not showing any gratitude, any humility."

Kane stands up. "I've had enough of this. Enough of you and your bullshit."

"You go. I've had enough too. Enough of this disrespect. You've got a lot of work to do. You're going to have a hard time solving your latest case. The killer who leaves his victims hanging."

Kane stops in his tracks. "What did you say?"

The grinning psychopath leans right back in his chair and puts his feet on the coffee table, his legs crossed at the ankles.

"You heard me, Detective. We're allowed to watch the news and read the papers if we want to. I was a top reporter. I'm fascinated by the news. Always have been. That's why I was so thrilled when I started making the headlines. Fair enough, it was for killing people but you know what they say, all publicity is good publicity."

"You said 'victims'."

"Ah, yes. You noticed. I see the mind is as sharp as ever."

"There's only one victim."

"So far, Detective. So far. As well as being an ace journalist, I'm also a talented murderer. I know how the murderous mind works. This killer is going nowhere. He'll do it again. Believe me. I thought I could stop. I couldn't. The pull is too strong. Murder, eat, rest, repeat. Murder, eat, rest, repeat."

He laughs loudly at his own sick joke.

"Mark my words, Detective, you're going to have your work cut out with this one. I'm a cold-blooded bastard but this one is inventive. Putting the body on display like that. Pure genius."

Kane gets to his feet. He's heard enough. He's being played by an evil bastard who loves the sound of his own voice.

"I'm wasting my time," he says.

"Nice to see you too, Edison. You'll be back soon. I know it. You want to get your hands on your Lizzy's killer so badly you'd strangle me with your bare hands if you thought it would help you track him down."

Kane strides out of the room, laughter ringing in his ears.

It's gone ten before he gets back to his home in Brentwood. Roadworks on the M25 caused a tortuous diversion.

He hasn't eaten a morsel since lunch but he's too exhausted to even think about making a meal. He undresses and brushes his teeth in a trance, before crashing into bed.

Unfortunately for him, exhaustion rarely equals sleep. His brain won't stop replaying the words Newman used to describe Adam Golding's killer. *Inventive. Pure genius.*

Kane doesn't want to see another murderer glamorised in the media. He's seen it so many times and it drives him mad. Giving them a catchy name only amplifies the fear and excitement. He wishes they'd go for a moniker closer to the truth. Something like the Cowardly Psychopath Killer.

Kane rolls on to his side and closes his eyes. Every single cell in his body is screaming out for sleep. Still, his mind refuses to switch off. He keeps his eyes shut tight and rolls on to his other side.

He hates that he let himself be taken in by a killer's power play. He knows Lizzy would be disappointed in him and that hurts. He's got to get back on track, focus solely on catching Adam Golding's killer. Nothing else matters. If he leads his team to the best of his ability, they will do what they're meant to do — uncover the truth.

The thought is strangely calming. His limbs feel heavy and his breathing slows as his body relaxes into the mattress. At last, his brain surrenders.

A loud ringing wakes Kane with a start. He sits up slowly, leans across and takes his phone off the bedside table. He checks the screen. It's 6.20 a.m. The caller is Detective Constable Kush.

"Meera. What is it?"

"Can you hear me? The signal is poor out here."

Her voice is faint and slightly distorted. Kane can hardly make out what she's saying. "Where are you? What's going on?"

"Sorry but this can't wait. There's been another."

The signal cuts out for a few seconds and all Kane can hear is a loud crackling.

"Say that again, Meera. I lost you there for a moment."

"Another murder. A second victim. Right in front of me. Hanging from the branch of a tree."

Kane jumps out of bed, adrenaline charging his blood. "I'm on my way. Where the hell are you?"

"Sorry, I didn't get that. Can you hear me now? This is important. The victim's face is distorted by swelling. But there's no mistaking who it is."

CHAPTER 20

By the time Kane drives over the single span bridge linking Two Tree Island with Leigh, the sun is already peeking over the horizon, edging the sky with a blood orange wash.

The narrow lane leads to a car park and concrete slipway on the south shore. Kane pulls up between a marked patrol car and a van with "Forensic Investigation" printed on its sides and back.

Kane inhales a lungful of crisp morning air and breathes out a curling cloud of mist. He walks quickly over to the far end of the car park where Detective Constable Kush is waiting for him.

She's wrapped up against the cold in a long woollen coat and is wearing black gloves. He greets her with a nod and a grim smile. "You're sure it's him?"

"No doubt. Come see for yourself. It's not far."

Kush turns and heads down a narrow gravel path through a thicket of leafless trees and bushes.

Kane walks beside her. "What is this place? I've never heard of Two Tree Island."

"Neither had I. It's a small tidal island, a nature reserve popular with birdwatchers and walkers."

After a couple of hundred yards, they approach an area sealed off by crime scene tape. Three figures in pale blue forensic suits are crawling in the long grass under the bare branches of a small tree.

The feet of the hanged man, in pristine white trainers, dangle a couple of inches above their heads.

Kane steps closer, puts his hands on his hips and studies the victim. He's dressed in muddy grey tracksuit trousers and a navy hoodie. The tight blue noose has squeezed the neck, distorting the soft tissue of his face. But Kush is right. It's definitely Tony Golding.

Kane takes a long deep breath. This changes everything.

His thoughts are interrupted by the sound of Martin Carter barking instructions at a photographer snapping the victim from various angles. He stops when he sees them and walks over.

"Well, hello, Detectives. Lovely crisp morning for a murder."

Kane ignores the pathologist's jollity.

"It's exactly the same as the last one, isn't it?"

Carter nods. "It looks like it. Better location, of course. No mud or tidal water to wade through. I'm guessing that the killer scouted out the area in advance because it would have taken him some time to find a tree tall enough to hang the body without the feet touching the ground. There are a lot more than two trees on this island but they're all very low-level."

Kane visualises the killer prowling through the undergrowth in search of a tree high enough for a hanging, even though his victim is already dead. The hanging has got to be a significant part of the ritual.

"You're always going to get a lot of people visiting a place like this. The killer chose this location to put the victim's body on public display again."

"My thoughts exactly," says Carter. "We can't have people stomping around the crime scene gawping at us. We need to close the whole island off to the public for now."

"I'll have a word with the uniforms," Kush says. "It won't be difficult to organise, because as far as I know, that bridge is the only way onto the island. We should check if there are any CCTV cameras covering the bridge or the roads leading to it."

The detectives watch Carter get back to work, ducking under the crime scene tape before crouching to speak to one of the forensic officers combing the undergrowth.

Kane takes another long look at the body hanging from the tree. Tony Golding is a big man. The killer would have to be strong and fit to have dragged his corpse along the track and suspend it from the branch.

"Who found it?"

"A cyclist. I think the paths and trails on the island are meant for walkers but apparently, they're popular with mountain bikers too. Police Constable Weaver took him to the café on the other side of the bridge."

Kane is glad to hear that Weaver is making himself useful. "How's our young uniform coping?"

"Surprisingly well," Kush says. "I think he's got something about him. Comes across confident when dealing with the public. Possible detective material. But don't tell him I said that."

It takes Kane ten minutes to walk to the bridge. He crosses it and turns left into the café's gravel car park. Inside, he finds Weaver sitting at a table opposite a man with a flop of grey-streaked dark hair, wearing a bright orange cycling top. Small and wiry, he looks more suited to riding a horse than a bicycle.

PC Weaver stands. "This is my boss, Detective Inspector Kane. This is Danny Timbrell. He found the victim while out on his bike and called it in."

Kane sits on the vacant chair. "It must have been a shock for you. I know you've already spoken to Constable Weaver and he'll take a formal statement from you later. Are you feeling up to answering a couple of questions for me now?"

The cyclist smiles nervously. "I'm all right. I am. A bit shaky but your officer's been properly looking after me. Even paid for me tea and toasted teacake."

"That's good. Can you tell me exactly what happened?"

Timbrell picks up his mug, drains the dregs of his tea and licks his lips. "It's like I told your man already. I like to get out on me bike early. Even in the winter when it's dark. The old eyes aren't as good as they used to be but I got lights. I was taking it easy round the island when I saw this dark thing ahead. Looked like it was sort of floating. When I got close, I realised it was . . . you know. A body hanging from a branch. Horrible sight, it was. The legs went a bit jelly like. I rode on to the car park and phoned 999 right away."

"You did well. Did you see anyone else out on the trails? A walker? Or a white van in the car park?"

"No. Sorry. That's why I like to get out early. The peace and quiet."

Weaver's brow creases into a frown. "There's another obvious way on to the island, apart from the bridge, isn't there?"

Kane nods slowly. He'd been thinking the same. "A car or van would be the easiest way to move a body. But a boat or a canoe could do the job and there'd be no surveillance cameras to worry about."

"You didn't ask me that," Timbrell pipes up.

"What do you mean?"

"You didn't say nothing about boats. I did see one. Wasn't light enough to see who was in it, though. It was heading away from the island toward Southend as I rode along the southern shore trail. Before I saw the body, it was. I remember thinking that whoever was rowing weren't much good at it. Hadn't got a clue."

CHAPTER 21

Detective Superintendent Helen Dean sits straight-backed, her hands clasped tightly, her elbows resting on her desk.

"Tell me if I have this right," she says. "Your prime suspect in the hunt for businessman Adam Golding's killer was found murdered early this morning."

Kane shifts uncomfortably in his chair. He admits it sounds a touch embarrassing when put that way.

"Tony Golding was certainly under suspicion because of the bitter feud between him and his brother. We also strongly suspected that he was involved in drug dealing. Adam Golding's wife is still under investigation."

Dean steeples her fingers and fixes Kane with a stare. "And has this Tony Golding been murdered by the same person who killed his brother?"

"We're sure that's the case. According to the pathologist, Martin Carter, he too was killed by a lethal dose of insulin before being strung up."

Dean stays silent. Kane guesses she's waiting for him to convince her that he's still the right man for the job. He has a feeling that might be difficult. He and Dean had been rookie detectives together and friends briefly. She left him behind as she rose through the ranks and Kane wonders if she's happy. Sometimes it's difficult to realise that you're under stress.

"The link between the victims couldn't be more obvious. The killer chose them because they are siblings. I've instructed my team to focus on the Golding family. To trace any other close relatives in the area."

"You think they could be in danger."

"I think it's very possible."

Dean sits back in her padded leather chair. "You do know the national press are going to be all over this like rabid dogs now, don't you?"

"I can handle it."

Dean raises her eyebrows. "Are you sure, Edison? You've lost Granger. She's great at dealing with the media."

"And I'm not?"

"I didn't say that. Let's just say you can rub them up the wrong way sometimes."

Kane can't disagree with that. He understands the value of the press when it comes to appealing to the public for information and for asking witnesses to come forward. But the rest of it — the thirst for a story, whipping the public into a fervour, horrible murder, lots of blood — he can't bear it. He became the target of a media witch hunt during the See No Evil case. They claimed he was psychologically unfit because of Lizzy's murder. He'll never forgive them for that.

"We believe that the killer used a rowing boat to transport the body on to Two Tree Island to avoid CCTV cameras. It's likely that he used a stolen boat."

Dean lifts a hand, rubs her forehead and sighs wearily. "I can find funding to add two civilian works to your team," she says. "I'm also hoping to find you a replacement for Granger."

"I'd rather hold on that. I'm hoping she'll be able to come back to work in a few days."

"Is that likely?"

Kane shrugs. "Probably not but I'd like to give her the chance."

Once Granger is officially replaced the door will be shut. There's nobody he trusts more as a colleague, or respects as a detective.

Dean opens her desk drawer and pulls out an A4 sheet of paper. "I thought you might say that, and it frees up funding we can put to good use. I believe a criminal profiler could be of value. Someone who can draw us a detailed picture of the mind of this killer. How he thinks and behaves. This psychologist, Rebecca Baxter, has been doing a fair bit of work for us recently and she's had good results."

She hands the sheet of paper over. "Here are her details. I'll get her to contact you tomorrow."

Kane is momentarily lost for words. He can't tell Dean that he'd feel uncomfortable working with his former therapist. If he hadn't kept those sessions secret, he'd never have been declared psychologically fit to return to work and lead the See No Evil investigation. Apart from that, he's yet to be convinced that profiling is much more than a psychologist taking a few educated guesses.

Before he can object, Dean holds up a hand. "I know your thoughts on psychological profiling, Edison. But we've been using them for years and I and most of my colleagues believe they can be an important tool for senior investigating officers. I want you to run with this."

Kane knows he's got no chance of getting Dean to back down. He also knows Baxter is excellent in her role as a profiler.

"All right. If you think it will help. I'll go with the flow."

CHAPTER 22

Sam Hunter's fingers flutter swiftly across the keyboard, her mind racing, her heart hammering with excitement she didn't expect to feel on a gloomy Monday morning.

She pauses and breathes in the slightly sweaty air of the *Southend Herald*'s newsroom. Around her reporters are typing, slurping strong coffee or talking furiously on their phones. This moment, the blood-warming thrill of writing a big news story, is the reason she chose to pursue a career as a crime reporter. Nothing compares. Maybe one day her parents will get it.

The police media office sent out this press release at 9 a.m. and speed is of the essence. She's in a race to get the story posted on the *Herald*'s website before their rivals.

Her fingers fly again.

The man found murdered on the Two Tree Island nature reserve yesterday has been identified as Tony Golding.

It has been confirmed that he is the estranged older brother of Adam Golding, the local businessman whose body was found under Southend Pier five days ago.

Both victims were left hanging with nooses around their necks, a grisly echo of medieval public executions. Police believe they were murdered by the same killer. Tony Golding, 46, lived in a tower block flat on the Kingsbury Estate. His brother Adam had recently sold his amusement company, Pure Gold Ltd, for more than £3 million.

Ten minutes later, after reading through the article three times, Sam closes the file and sends it to the news editor's inbox. She picks up her mug. The coffee is cold and bitter but she takes another sip.

The adrenaline rush has subsided and nerves have kicked in. She looks over to the other side of the room, where Dawn Brady sits in her glass box, her eyes fixed on her computer screen. Sam knows her boss will already be reading her copy, searching for clumsy sentences and tired clichés. She's thinking about a trip down the corridor for a fresh coffee when she sees Brady lift her head, scour the room and beckon her over.

Sam makes her way across to Brady's office, weaving between the haphazardly laid out desks. A couple of old hands glance up as she passes, shaking their heads and offering her sympathetic looks.

She walks tentatively into the glass cubicle and Brady gestures for her to sit down next to her.

"You know what?" she says. "This is not a bad effort. Not bad at all. Pretty good in fact. Well done, Miss Hunter."

Sam tries hard not to look too pleased with herself. Smug is not a good look. She can't do anything about the blush warming her cheeks. "Oh, that's good. Thank you."

A smile tugs at Brady's lips. Sam inwardly curses herself for sounding like an overeager schoolgirl. She's got to work on developing a bit of journalistic swagger.

Brady wags a finger at the computer screen. "You've done a good job and you deserve your first front-page byline, but this isn't the time to sit back and admire your work. You still need to prove yourself."

Although Sam is aware of Brady's reputation as a hard taskmaster, the swift change of tone catches her off guard.

"No, of course not. I realise that."

"The follow up to this is vital. All our rivals are going to have this story so I need you to get out there and find me an exclusive. What are you working on?"

Sam hasn't had a moment to think about her next move. She's smart enough not to admit it. No need to disappoint her boss.

"Well, I've put out a few feelers, had a word with a few contacts and, um, I'm thinking I might—"

"Just listen," Brady says, cutting her off mercilessly. "I reckon you need to dive a bit deeper into Tony Golding's drug dealing. I know the brothers were supposedly estranged, but were they really? Maybe Adam Golding was financing his dealer brother. If they were treading on someone's toes these could be drug gang killings. That could be why the bodies were displayed so publicly. As a warning to others. What do you think?"

Sam thinks Brady is an experienced journalist who can teach her a lot about crime reporting. She also thinks that right now she sounds like she's losing the plot. From what she's heard, the Golding brothers haven't set eyes on each other or spoken for years. *Why would Adam Golding bother getting embroiled in the drug world? He was already minted.*

"Yeah, well, that sounds like an interesting theory. It's possible, I suppose. I'll make some calls. Ask around on the Kingsbury Estate. I reckon people will be more willing to say what they know about Tony Golding now that he's dead."

Brady eyes her silently. Sam can't tell whether it's a look of curiosity or judgement.

"I suggest you get on it right away. You've done well since you joined us but your six-month trial period is up soon and you need to keep impressing if you want to land this role permanently."

Sam walks back across the newsroom to her desk, trying not to look as sick as she feels. The thought of losing her dream job tears at her insides. Now she's had a taste, she knows for sure it's everything that she imagined it would be and more. Her family would love it if she was forced to come crawling back and admit they were right all along.

She sits down and covers her face with her hands. Crying isn't an option. Not here, in front of a bunch of hard-nosed reporters. It would only prove that she hasn't got what it takes.

Her desk phone rings. She snatches it up, glad of the distraction. "Sam Hunter, crime reporter."

"Hello, can you hear me? Who's this?" The voice is low and furtive.

"This is Sam Hunter. Can I help you?"

"Dunno. Maybe. I told them I wanted to be put through to the paper's crime man."

"You have been. I mean you're talking to the crime reporter. I'm not a man."

"Oh, yeah. Right. I've got a helluva story for you. I'm gonna need paying. That other guy gave me cash if I had something juicy for him."

Even though Sam knows Brady doesn't approve of her reporters paying for stories, she's not going to rule it out. Not until she knows exactly what's on offer. More than anything else, she wants to secure this job.

"It depends if what you've got for me is worth it. Are you going to give me a clue? I need to know who I'm talking to as well."

The line falls silent except for the sound of the man wheezing with every breath.

"No names yet. I'm not stupid. And no details until I see the colour of your cash. I reckon you'll be desperate to meet if you want some interesting information about that murder. You know. The hanging on Two Tree Island."

CHAPTER 23

Granger tips the omelette out of the pan and stands back to assess whether it's edible. Cooking isn't one of her strong points. She's never been that interested. The truth is she'd rather be on her way to the station for Kane's Monday morning briefing than stuck in the kitchen.

She opens a bag of salad and sprinkles a handful of leaves around the plate, hoping a garnish will make the eggy mess more appetising.

She puts the plate on a tray and climbs the stairs. Her mum is sitting up in bed reading. She's two days out of hospital and gaining strength. She closes her book and grins.

"I hope you're hungry," Granger says, placing the tray carefully on her mum's lap. "Don't expect too much. You know I'm useless at this domestic stuff. I apologise in advance."

"You're not useless; you just never had the time." Naomi examines the omelette and grimaces. "Well, this doesn't look too bad." She picks up a fork and prods it to test its consistency. "Hell, Bailey. I do appreciate that you've made the effort. The problem is that this is as runny as a cold nose. If I eat this, I'm likely going to end up back in hospital."

Granger doesn't bother arguing because she knows she'll lose. Her mother's right. The omelette looks about as appetising as a jellyfish. Before she can come up with a way of accepting defeat gracefully, the doorbell chimes. She turns to leave, pulling her phone out of her pocket to check the time. "You're not expecting anyone are you, Mum?"

Naomi shrugs, a worrying glint in her eye. Granger hurries downstairs to the front door and peers through the peephole. The fish-eye lens distorts the face but there's no mistaking the identity of the tall dark man on her doorstep.

Granger is surprised by the mixture of excitement and apprehension churning her stomach. She opens the door. Her big brother, who she hasn't seen for almost three years, looks down at her. He nods and shuffles awkwardly from foot to foot.

Granger takes in the smart suit and tie, the close-cropped beard. He's as nervous as she is and her first instinct is to hug him. Instead, she gives him a half-smile and says one word. "Marcus."

"Bailey. Thanks for the call."

"You didn't say you were coming. Did Mum arrange this? I bet she phoned you too."

Marcus smiles. "How is she?"

"She's a little better. You look taller."

"I'm not. Can I come in?"

Granger leads him down the hall into the kitchen. "Mum's upstairs. First bedroom on the left. No doubt she's expecting you. Go on up."

Marcus doesn't move. "She told me that the tests didn't find a specific cause for her high blood pressure and that as long as she takes her medication, she'll be fine."

"She keeps saying she'll be fine. She needs a proper rest. The last thing she needs is more stress."

Marcus hesitates. "Are you all right?"

"Why wouldn't I be?"

"You seem a bit cold."

Granger sighs. Her brother is an intelligent, well-educated man. But God, he can be stupid sometimes. He and their younger brother as good as disowned her because she joined the police, and he wonders why she appears a bit pissed off. They spent their childhood on an estate in Harlow where everyone, whether they were criminals or not, considered the police as enemy number one. They've all escaped that place now but her brothers can't let it go.

"I suppose Mum gave you our new address?"

"She did." He takes a long appraising look around the kitchen. "The house is nice, Bailey. It's a pretty good area too. You've done well, girl."

Granger allows herself a smile. It's good to hear him say something positive about her choices.

"Go on. Mum's waiting for you. She should've told me you were coming. I've got to get your niece ready for school."

Her brother sprints up the staircase and disappears into their mother's bedroom. She's angry with herself for being angry with him and not being able to hide it. How can he turn up on her doorstep after all this time and seem so calm?

She makes herself a cup of tea, her hand shaking as she stirs in the milk. Marcus is here because their mother is sick. That's all. She mustn't read anything into it. Hope can be treacherous.

Granger takes her drink into the living room, perches on the edge of the sofa and switches on the television. A tall blond weatherman flashes an expensive-looking smile as he warns there's going to be a risk of ice on the roads this morning.

She picks up the remote and switches to a news channel. The female newsreader glances down at her desk to shuffle some papers before staring back at the camera.

"Police in the seaside resort of Southend are investigating the murders of two brothers. Local businessman Adam Golding's body was found hanging under the town's world-famous pier, and the killer left the corpse of his brother, Tony, hanging from a tree on a local nature reserve."

Granger splutters, almost choking on a mouthful of tea. Even though she's off the case, someone should have let her know that the prime suspect has been murdered. She suspects that Kane doesn't want to put pressure on her to return to work.

She puts her tea down and grabs her phone. Her finger hovers over the call button for a moment before she stops herself. Kane is going to be working all hours trying to solve this case. Why would he want to waste valuable time talking to her? She's no good to him. Not now.

Granger hears footsteps behind her and turns to look. Marcus stands in the doorway, a sheepish look on his face.

"That's the case you were on, isn't it?" He nods at the TV.

"It was. I'm on compassionate leave. I've got Mum and Daisy to look after. They've probably already replaced me."

"How is Daisy doing?"

"Like you care. You haven't seen her for three years."

"Does she ever ask about her Uncle Marcus?"

"What do you think?"

Marcus digs into his pocket and pulls out his car keys. "I've got to . . ."

"You're going already? Short and sweet then."

"I'm nipping out to get a Mum a sandwich. She says the omelette's not fit for human consumption." Marcus walks to the sofa and sits down beside her. "I'll be going soon but I'll be back later this afternoon."

"What do you mean?"

"I've arranged to take a couple of weeks off work, maybe longer if I can, to look after Mum. You know, help her with Daisy and stuff."

Granger looks blankly at her brother, trying work out whether she's heard right. "Why would you do that?"

"Because I want to. If that's okay with you? You can get back on the case. Mum's explained how important it is to you and I'd like to help."

Granger can't believe what she's hearing. She desperately wants to. She wonders if the family can be mended after all. "You hate me being in the police."

Marcus shrugs. "Maybe. A little. But catching murderers is a good thing, right? Mum tells me you've already been promoted to Detective Sergeant. Knowing you, you're going to be top brass in a few years."

Granger shakes her head. "Don't you dare say well done. I don't need a pat on the back. I'm not your little sister anymore. I love what I do and I'm good at it."

Marcus smiles. "I bet you are."

Once her brother has gone, Granger leans back on the sofa, replaying their conversation over and over in her head. She's desperate to get back to work, especially now that the investigation has taken such an unexpected turn.

She shakes her head slowly, disappointed with herself for being so selfish. Her mother, who has done so much for her and Daisy, needs her now. Time to step up.

Her train of thought is broken by a creak on the stairs. Naomi, wrapped in her worn blue dressing gown, descends slowly, her left hand gripping the banister.

Granger jumps up and runs to the staircase. She takes her mother's free hand and helps her carefully down the last step.

"What are you doing down here? The doctor said you need to take things easy."

Her mother ignores the question and leads her across the room back to the sofa.

"Don't you worry yourself, my girl, I'm feeling better every day. Doctors don't know everything. Now, did Marcus speak to you about you getting back to work?"

"He did. I don't understand why he's doing this though. Is this your idea?"

"What if it is? Your brother wouldn't go along with it if he didn't want to make things right between you. Don't you want our family to get back to how it was?"

Granger suspected as much. Her mum is using her health scare to reunite the family. Part of her isn't sure whether she should go along with it, whether she's capable of burying her resentment and carrying on as if nothing happened.

"You have it in you to forgive your brothers," her mum says.

Even as a young child Granger suspected that her mum's superpower was mindreading.

"You have a good heart. They have wronged you but you remember how life was growing up on our estate, don't you?"

Granger remembers all right. She remembers being thirteen and seeing one of her brothers' friends being stabbed in the stomach by a shark-eyed sociopath in a hoodie. Everyone thought he was going to die but nobody called the police.

"What about Sterling?"

"What about him? The boy's too busy studying and going to parties to think about anything else. He'll come round too. I know it. Now listen to me. The best thing for you, for Daisy, for all of us, is for you to take Marcus up on his offer. After you've walked Daisy to school, you get back to your murder investigation. I reckon they need you if they want to crack this case. Go on, my girl. Catch the bad guy and make us all proud. Anyway, your cooking is so bad it's going to make me sicker, not better."

Blinking back tears, Granger puts her arms around her mum's thin shoulders and hugs her gently.

"Thank you," she whispers. "For everything."

CHAPTER 24

"Believe nothing, question everything. Challenge yourself to do everything necessary to find this killer."

Kane pauses to let his words sink in. He uses the silence to make eye contact with every member of his team.

"I can confirm that the post-mortem results show that Tony Golding was dead before he was hanged and, like his brother, the cause of death was a lethal dose of medical insulin. The new civilian workers assigned to the team are asking local pharmacies and hospitals to check whether stocks of the medication have been tampered with. Our priorities are to check footage from all cameras covering the road routes to Leigh and, in particular, Two Tree Island. Complete a thorough background check on the Golding family, including tracing any living relatives, and contact rowing clubs or hire firms to ask if they are or have been missing one of their boats."

Kane is convinced that the killer was in the rowing boat seen heading away from the island in the direction of Southend minutes before Tony Golding's body was found. But every possibility must be checked.

"You all know what you're doing and I need you to do it to the best of your ability. Any questions or suggestions?"

DS Scott shifts in his seat. "According to the local drugs squad, Tony Golding was making waves, trying to expand his little empire, and in the process was stepping on the toes of some very nasty people. I think it's worth following that up."

"I agree, Alex. Sounds like an interesting line of inquiry. Surely Tony Golding would have needed some seed money. Some cash to get rolling. Maybe he had a secret backer. Get Weaver to help you with that."

Detective Constable Kush is next to speak. "Are we assuming that the killer is unlikely to target anyone outside the Golding family?"

Kane has been asking himself the same question. "We can't assume anything. Until we know for sure the motive for the murders, we work on the basis that the killer poses a risk to every person he meets. In the next couple of days a forensic psychologist will be drawing up a criminal profile based on the killer's modus operandi. That is supposed to give us more of an idea of the type of person we are looking for and the threat he poses."

DC Brown clears his throat.

"You want to say something, Dec?"

"Just a theory. I've been thinking."

"That's good. Thinking is important when you're a detective."

"Well, I'd say that if Ruth Golding did pay someone to kill her husband because they were going to get divorced and she'd be disinherited, then maybe she got him to kill his brother too."

"Why would she do that?"

"It's possible she feared Tony Golding would contest the will. Especially as he claimed he was robbed of his share of inheritance from his mother."

The same thought had occurred to Kane but he'd dismissed it. If Ruth Golding had hired someone to murder her husband, she'd have wanted it done without fuss. The smart thing to do was to have it look like a suicide or at least have the body disposed of discreetly, not put on public display.

"Ruth Golding is definitely still a suspect," Kane says. "Bring her in and question her again. We've got a lot to do. We need to move quickly, no letting up until this killer is off the streets."

As the detectives file out, Kane beckons Weaver over to the whiteboard.

The police constable approaches tentatively.

"How have you found working with the team?"

"Interesting. I mean, I'm enjoying it. I'm learning a lot."

"Good. I've been thinking about seconding you officially to the investigation as a detective. That means you'll have to abandon the uniform for a while. How does that sound?"

"Well, yes. If you think I'm up to it."

Weaver has made himself useful and feedback from the rest of the team has been positive. Kane remembers his own big break came when he was seconded on to a team investigating a stabbing in a nightclub in east London fifteen years ago. He loved the thrill of the chase, found the pressure to perform addictive and never returned to uniform duty.

"I wouldn't be giving you this opportunity if I didn't think you have what it takes. Is there a problem?"

Weaver shakes his head. "No, I'm loving this experience. It's great. It's just that since I found that body hanging under the pier, I've had a lot of trouble sleeping."

Kane studies the constable's face. His complexion is fresh and there are no signs of fatigue or stress. "You've seen dead bodies before, you said."

"That's right. It's bound to happen in this job. I can't explain it. This one is different. The bloated face, the noose around the neck. I keep getting flashbacks. It's pretty disturbing."

Kane knows that the sooner Weaver sorts this out with some kind of trauma counselling, the better. Pretending to yourself and others that there's nothing wrong usually ends in disaster. "Do you need to stand down from the team and take some leave?"

"No. That's not what I want. I'm good."

"That's fine by me. Just remember this problem probably isn't going to go away on its own. You're going to have to address it sometime."

Weaver nods a silent thanks and leaves the room. Kane puts his hands on his hips. If Weaver doesn't work out a way to build resilience and deal with the worst side of human nature, his police career is going to be short and not very sweet.

He steps closer to the whiteboard and studies the headshots of Adam and Tony Golding. By all accounts, neither of the brothers could be described as pleasant characters. One an inheritance stealer and a cheating husband, the other a drug dealer. The world may be a better place without them in it, but even bad people are owed justice.

Kane turns at the sound of the incident room door opening. Granger walks in. She's wearing a tailored black trouser suit and flat-soled ankle boots. He's hoping she's dressed for work.

"Please tell me you're back on the case."

"I'm back on the case."

CHAPTER 25

The Victoria pub smells of greasy French fries. On the table next to Granger, a man in a grey puffer jacket reads a newspaper while wolfing down chips and fried chicken.

Kane weaves his way from the bar through the rowdy lunchtime crowd, carrying their drinks on a plastic tray. "You should have seen the look on the barman's face when I stopped him putting whisky in the coffees. He says they don't like serving non-alcoholic beverages. Gives the pub a bad name."

Granger picks up a spoon and stirs her coffee slowly. "I don't know why we didn't go to the Starbucks in the high street."

"I wanted to buy you a 'welcome back' lunch. Get a decent meal inside you. You look like you could use one. Anyway, this is nearer to the station and I've a meeting in twenty minutes."

Granger scans the room. The only other woman she can see is serving behind the bar. The pub is a magnet for problem drinkers and petty villains. "The place stinks."

Kane doesn't deny it. He takes a sip of his coffee. "How's Naomi doing?"

"Much better. She still needs to take it easy."

"How come you're back already?"

Granger doesn't want to go into detail. Even though she knows she can trust Kane, she's never liked the idea of discussing personal troubles with colleagues. "My brother Marcus is helping out."

Kane gets the message. She doesn't want to talk about this now. He'll be ready when she does. He changes tack. "I want to talk about the psychological profile of the killer. I've been thinking about how best we can use it."

The eager expression on Kane's face makes Granger uneasy. Criminal profiles are used to give detectives an idea of the suspect's likely social and mental characteristics based on a psychological analysis of the murders. "What are you thinking? Nothing dodgy, I hope."

"I'm a Detective Inspector. I don't do dodgy." He rests his elbows on the table and leans forward. "I reckon we should take the opportunity to rattle the killer's cage. Stir him up a bit in the hope that he gets careless and makes a mistake. Because up to now, I don't think he's made any."

"Are you serious?"

"Deadly."

Granger knows Kane well enough to accept that even though he's asked for her opinion he's already made his mind up. Still, it's her duty to warn him of the risks. See if she can rein him in.

"If it turns out that the killer was, for whatever reason, genuinely focused on wiping out the Golding brothers, it's possible that the killings could stop now. He's done what he set out to do. If you deliberately provoke him, you could push him into committing another murder."

Kane shakes his head. "Whatever the motive is for killing the Goldings — whether financial or a simple drug gang power struggle — this monster isn't going to stop. Maybe for a while, yes, but you know as well as I do that this type of killing is like a drug. He's tasted blood, and sooner or later he'll want more and find another reason to kill again. I'm not going to let this trail go cold. I'll take care to make sure that his mind is focused and nobody else is put in danger."

Granger understands now. He wants to put himself out there as bait. "Have you considered trying to get Superintendent Dean's approval before you do this? She's not going to like it if you go rogue."

"I've thought about it. She'll block it because part of her job description is to be cautious. I'll deal with her the best I can once the shit hits the fan."

Granger sighs. There's no point wasting her time and energy. Anyway, she has a sneaking feeling that it could work, and if it goes wrong, she'll support Kane all the way. "Do you know who's drawing up the profile?"

"Rebecca Baxter. By all accounts she knows what she's doing. She's asked to visit the murder scenes."

Granger pauses to think. "I remember her. The glamorous shrink. Yes, I liked her lot. She's a friend of yours, isn't she?"

Kane screws up his face. "I suppose you could say that." He's never told Granger that during their last case he'd had private therapy sessions with Baxter to help him cope with the trauma of his wife's murder. He decides this isn't the right time to change that. They make a great team. He doesn't want to endanger that.

He checks his watch. "Damn, got to go. I'm meeting her in five minutes."

They both stand. As Granger brushes past the neighbouring table, she notices that the man in the grey jacket has left his copy of the *Southend Herald*. She scoops it up, checks the front page and takes a sharp breath.

She hands the newspaper to Kane. "Take a look at this."

He stares at the main headline, his expression grim.

MURDER POLICE LEFT DANGLING IN HUNT FOR THE HANGMAN.

CHAPTER 26

Kane and Baxter walk briskly along the esplanade. They pass a row of fast-food kiosks, cafés and amusement arcades, all of them shuttered and silenced for the winter.

Kane prefers the seafront like this. Deserted and peaceful, save for the lapping of waves and screeching of seagulls. In a couple of months, the resort will be out of hibernation, the fresh sea air polluted with a cacophony of arcade noise and the odour of burgers and deep-fried doughnuts.

He leads the way down onto the shingle beach. The morning sky is slate grey and pregnant with rain. They follow the curve of the seawall until they reach the crisscrossing of iron columns and steel beams beneath the pier.

The psychologist pulls the fake-fur-trimmed hood of her coat over her head and shivers against the bitter wind blowing off the water.

Kane steps under the pier and points to a steel strut about ten feet off the ground. "The noose was tied to that. It'd take a person with a lot of strength to hoist the dead weight of a corpse up there and somehow hold it in place while tying the rope."

Baxter nods. "This whole area is so bleak. It doesn't just look gloomy, it feels gloomy. I doubt much light gets down here, even in the height of summer."

Kane wonders what she's getting at. But he doesn't ask. He has a feeling he doesn't really want to know.

"There's no vehicle access, which means the killer would've had to carry the body from the promenade. In the centre of town there would always be a risk that somebody would see him. He was clearly prepared to take that chance because it was important to him to leave the body here. I reckon that he would have had to have set it all up a couple of hours before dawn."

Baxter turns and faces the wind, gazing thoughtfully out to where the sky falls into the sea.

Kane checks his watch impatiently. Has she even been listening? He has a feeling this is a waste of time. He needs to get on with proper detective work. He decides to get things moving.

"It may be that the killer chose this place because he knew that once the town woke up, the body would be found quickly. He wanted his work to be seen and appreciated as soon as possible."

He looks at Baxter hoping for confirmation of his theory. She doesn't appear convinced.

"What are you thinking?"

Baxter shrugs. "I believe there may be some truth in what you say. But something about this place makes me think there's a lot more to it. It's murky, cold and damp down here. There's a real sense of foreboding. Above us, the pier is located right at the centre of the shiny — some might say superficial — seaside town. This is like a shadowy decaying underworld. The dark underbelly."

Kane frowns. This is one of the things that irritates him most about criminal profiling. A tendency to speculate too much about the feelings of the twisted people who murder without remorse. He doesn't give a damn about their blunted emotions. "How does any of that help us solve this case?"

Baxter looks surprised by the question. "I'm not sure it does. It's not my job to solve the murder. That's on you. My task is to try to solve the mystery of what's going on inside the killer's mind. I'm simply wondering what factors drew him to this spot. The killer will have his own underworld. On the surface he'll be one of us. If it turns out that he is a homicidal psychopath, then he'll be hiding his psychopathy behind a mask of normality. Seemingly happy, content and probably successful in his chosen career. Underneath, well, that's where the darkness and decay will dominate. You know, there's always a trigger. Some kind of trauma. What interests me is how it all started for him."

Kane is more interested in how and when it's all going to end. "What about the victims of murder and their loved ones? What about their feelings? How are they supposed to move on with their lives?"

As soon as the words leave his mouth, Kane realises it sounds as if he's talking about himself. His loss. The expression on Baxter's face suggests that's exactly what she's thinking.

"That's not my responsibility," she says. "Right now, my priority is to focus on drawing up a profile of the killer the newspapers are calling the Hangman. To do that I need to do everything possible to get inside his mind. Even empathise with him."

"There can never be an excuse for taking someone's life."

"No, but there can be an explanation."

The two of them walk back to the car in silence. Kane takes the coast road west toward Leigh-on-Sea. He's regretting not giving one of his team the job of taking Baxter to the crime scenes. His time could have been better spent preparing for tomorrow's press conference.

"When can I expect to see your psychological profile?" he asks.

"Checking out the murder scenes is the last thing I need to do. Most of the profile is already written. I should be able to email it to you before the end of the day."

Kane nods. "Good. Thanks. Two Tree Island is ten minutes away. Not a lot to see there. Miles of mudflats, marshland, shrubs and scrawny trees. Oh, and wintering birds that get the twitchers excited."

Baxter is deep in thought again, staring out of the passenger window watching the deserted Westcliff beach roll by.

"Oh, I forgot to ask," she says suddenly. "Who was it who found the body hanging under the pier?"

"Actually, it was one of our own. PC Mark Weaver. This isn't his first dead body but this one seems to be troubling him, and he's not sure how to handle it."

"Sounds to me like he needs some trauma counselling."

"Is your therapy practice still open?"

"Yes, of course. I couldn't survive on the money I earn from this type of work."

"He's more likely to talk to someone independent of the force. I was wondering about recommending you."

Baxter gives Kane a sideways look. "You'd recommend me?"

"Maybe."

CHAPTER 27

Sam Hunter is nervous and it worries her. If she's going to prove the doubters wrong and make it as a reporter, she's going to have to toughen up.

She checks the time on her phone. Ten past five. Her contact is late. The sun is already hovering on the horizon and she doesn't want to be meeting a stranger in the middle of nowhere when darkness falls.

She's lost count of how many times she's made sure that the car doors are locked. Five more minutes and then she's off.

Her contact, who'd only give her the name Digger, sent her directions for the rendezvous. Sam had expected to meet in a café or a pub but found herself parked in an overgrown lane on the northern border of a remote caravan site, fifteen minutes north of Southend.

She pulls her seat belt across her body and clips it in, thinking she should never have agreed to come out here alone. She let her desire to prove to her news editor that she can use her initiative in pursuit of a story override common sense. Now, she's in danger of showing just how foolish she can be.

As she moves to start the engine, a loud rap on the front passenger window makes her jump. A pair of small round eyes set in a face peppered with heavy stubble peers at her through the glass. The man, who seemed to have emerged from the undergrowth, gestures impatiently for her to open the car door.

Sam lowers the window a couple of inches. "What do you want? Who are you?"

The man shoves his fingers through the gap and grasps the edge of the glass pane to stop her closing it.

"I'm Digger. Spoke to you on the phone. Come on, woman, get this thing open."

Sam hesitates. Does she risk letting a strange-looking man she's never met before into her car? If not, then she's going back to the office empty handed. An unmitigated failure. Bereft of even a sniff of a story to keep Brady happy.

She takes a sharp breath, reaches for the dashboard and unlocks the doors. Digger slides in, sits down, rubbing his hands and blowing on his fingers.

"It's colder than polar bear shit out there. That lazy wind was freezing me tits right off."

Sam edges a few inches closer to the door and rests her fingers on the handle, ready for a quick exit.

"Lazy wind?"

"Yeah, yer know — instead of going round yer, it goes right through yer."

Sam nods and takes a moment to study her contact. He's no taller than her but gangly. In need of a good feed. He's also dressed for a warm summer's day. Trainers, knee-length shorts and a baggy T-shirt.

Her first impression of Digger is that he's definitely weird. Eccentric would be a kinder word. Maybe he's harmless but the way he's eyeing her up makes her uneasy.

"How about we get on with business?" she says with a cautious smile. "You said you have some information about the murder on Two Tree Island."

Digger tilts his head to one side and gazes at her, stroking the stubble on his chin.

Sam makes a determined effort not to look intimidated. "Let's not waste time," she says. "I don't know about you but I haven't got all day. I can't be sitting here chatting. Have you got something for me or not? I don't even know who you are. What sort of name is Digger anyway?"

"That's what everyone calls me. I got something for yer, don't worry 'bout that." He narrows his piggy eyes and smirks. "Have you got what I want? I think yer have."

Sam knows she can be naive sometimes. One thing she isn't is foolish. "I've not brought any cash with me, if that's what you mean. I'm not that stupid. I'd be setting myself up to be robbed. If you're genuine and have good information for me then I'll make sure you're paid well for it. You can trust me."

Digger scratches an armpit while he thinks. "Can I though? Don't know you from Adam. That other reporter, Jack something, he knew what he was doing. I tipped him off 'bout a few things and he paid up pronto. No questions asked. Yer a lot prettier than him, I'll give yer that. A pretty face can be deceiving, can't it? Jack never told no one 'bout me. Not his boss, not the coppers. That's how it's gotta be."

Sam shifts in her seat. The light is fading fast and this strange man is making her uncomfortable. She swallows hard and tries her best to hide her nerves.

"You can trust me. A good reporter never reveals their sources. You have the right to remain anonymous if that's what you want. Up to now, you haven't told me anything about this secret information you have. I don't know who you are or what you do. I'm starting to think you're a time waster. If you've nothing to say to me, get out of my car now."

She spits out those final words with as much venom as she can muster, trying to assert control, and she's gratified to see Digger flinch.

He stares at her, blinking rapidly, his mouth gaping. "There's no need to be like that. I'm Digger and that's all yer getting. I walk up and down the beaches all day every day and it's surprising what yer can find. Gold rings, earrings, coins, even the odd watch. Soon as I could, I got me own metal detector. That makes my life a lot easier. One time I found a bank card and made a couple of withdrawals before it got cancelled. Hardly any drunken day-trippers on the beaches in winter, though. That's why I started keeping me eye out for other stuff. Stuff I could sell to the paper."

Though Sam is finding this moderately interesting, she's desperate for him to get to the point. She wasn't expecting him to spill his life story. The misadventures of a dodgy beachcomber aren't going get the *Herald*'s readers excited.

"What's this got to do with what you told me on the phone? You said you had information about the Two Tree Island murder."

Digger pulls a hurt face. "You said you wanted to know more about me."

Sam wants to point out that she actually said she didn't know anything about his so-called secret information. She pulls her phone from her jacket pocket, puts it on record and points it in Digger's direction. "Can we cut to the chase, please? It's getting late and I've arranged to meet a friend."

Digger eyes the phone suspiciously. "What yer doing? I didn't agree to that. This has to be off the record."

"I need to record you. I'll need some quotes, from an anonymous source. If it's good, I guarantee you'll be paid handsomely."

Sam is gambling that greed will triumph over caution. She'll find the cash herself if it comes to it. Brady's old-fashioned journalistic ethics mean she'd never sanction paying for a story, even an exclusive about the Hangman. What she doesn't know won't hurt her.

Digger's chews on his bottom lip as he weighs up his options. "Right then, like I was saying before, I'm a beachcomber. I like to get an early start, see. I walk five or six miles a day. The day before they found the body—"

"The one on the island, not under the pier?"

"Yeah. 'Course. I was going down on to Thorpe Bay beach when I saw him."

"Saw who?"

"Him. The man who stole the rowing boat. It was about 6.50 a.m., just starting to get light. I don't sleep much because the hostel bed sags like an overripe banana. He was there, concentrating on cutting through the chain with his bolt cutters. I slipped between two beach huts and watched. Only took him a few seconds to break the chain, then he hauled the boat over the seawall, across the pavement and into the back of the van. He must be a strong guy."

Sam's heart is beating fast and she can't hold her tongue. "The police say they're looking for a white van."

"This one was blue. Dark blue. He didn't hang about. Once the boat was in the back, he climbed in the van and drove off. When I heard the police were appealing for information about missing rowing boats in connection with the murder, I thought, this has to be worth something. I was right, wasn't I?"

"Did you make a note of the van's registration plate?"

"I did better than that. I took a photo of it with my phone."

"You got the reg plate?"

"Even better. I took a photo of him. The boat thief."

"You what?"

Digger grins. "You heard me."

"Can you see his face?"

"Clear as day. Young. Brawny. Quite a looker too."

Sam tries hard to keep her expression calm, knowing the more excited she looks, the more she's going to have to pay. Inside her ribcage, her heart flutters wildly, like a panicked bird.

"Can I see the photo of him now? Show me."

Digger's eyes narrow to sly slits. "Yer not seeing anything until I see a big wad of notes in yer hand. Reckon five hundred should do it."

Sam hides her surprise. She'd willingly pay at least double that for a photo of the Hangman. She wonders whether he's lying about how clear the face is. The light wouldn't have been great that early in the morning. Either way, that photo and the story that would go with it would launch her career into the stratosphere. Prove everybody wrong.

"Let me have a look at it now. Just let me see the image."

Sam's cheeks redden. She sounds like she's begging.

"No way. Yer ain't seeing nothing until the deal is done."

"I'll be able to get you two hundred and fifty. Take it or leave it."

Digger snorts. "I can tell yer hot for it. Let's make it three hundred. I want it tomorrow."

Sam can't say no. "It's a deal. I'll let you know when and where. Right now, I've got to get back to Southend."

Digger gets out of the car and she accelerates away. In her rearview mirror she can see him standing in the middle of the lane.

Her heart is thumping hard. She's landed the scoop of the year.

CHAPTER 28

Granger walks into the kitchen to find Marcus pouring milk into Daisy's coco flakes.

"This is her second bowl. I reckon this niece of mine must be growing. She'll be as tall as me soon."

Daisy looks up from the breakfast table and gives Granger a gap-toothed smile. "I am growing, aren't I, Mum? I might get even bigger than Uncle Marcus."

"I doubt it but I suppose it's possible."

Granger walks to the sink, fills a glass tumbler with water and takes a long drink. "Now you're sure you know where school is?"

Marcus pulls back a chair and sits opposite Daisy and gives her a wink. "Of course I do. I looked it up. But me and Daisy have decided to give it a miss today. We're going to scout out that park around the corner. Then go to a café for lemonade and cakes."

"Is that right, Daisy?"

"No, Mummy. He's only joking."

Granger picks her phone off the table and checks the time. "I've got to get going. I can't be late."

Marcus follows her out to the door.

"There's no need to worry. We'll be fine."

"Please make sure you're at the school gates on time to pick her up. And, thanks for this, Marcus. I really do appreciate it, you know."

She wants him to understand how good it feels to have her big brother back in her life. Their mum isn't the only person who needs him.

Marcus smiles. "I said don't worry. Everything is under control."

The drive to Southend is uneventful and she uses the thirty minutes to clear her head and concentrate on her role in the upcoming press conference. This will be the first time she and Kane will be facing the media together. He has a tendency to get prickly when dealing with reporters. It's not surprising considering the way the media ganged up on him last year, claiming that he was unfit to lead the hunt for the See No Evil killer because he was still grieving his wife. That wasn't fair, and in the end, he proved he's still one of the best when it comes to solving murders.

She pulls up in the station car park and before she gets out, she checks her face and hair in the rearview mirror. She'll do.

She goes straight to the media office, where Kane is nodding thoughtfully while being briefed by one of the force's pinstripe-suited press officers. She's doesn't know why they bother. He must have done this dozens of times.

Granger leaves them to it and sits at one of the desks on her own. She pulls her tablet out of her jacket pocket, powers it up and opens her copy of Baxter's criminal profile of the killer. She's read it before but wants a refresher before the press conference. She skims the opening paragraphs and goes straight to the meat of the report.

> *The offender, almost certainly male, will be capable of meticulous planning and have the patience to wait until the time is right to execute the plan.*

Granger nods. This is certainly the case with both brothers' murders. She reads on.

The offender is likely to be between the ages of twenty-five and thirty-five. The chances are that he will be tall and physically robust. He will live or work in the Southend area. Maybe both. The way that the offender kills his victims is significant. A fatal insulin injection is cold, precise and bloodless. He prefers to keep the act of murder clinical. This is in stark contrast to the decision to hang his victims despite him knowing that they are already dead. This is a deliberate choice to put the bodies on display. Hanging as a method of punishment has always had an element of public humiliation.

Granger recalls the distorted faces and lolling tongues of Adam and Tony Golding. At least they were both oblivious to their final fate. She skims the rest of the profile until she reaches Baxter's conclusion.

Undoubtedly the offender has psychopathic traits. At this point it is not possible to diagnose him as a full-blown psychopath but I suspect that is the case. He's almost certain to have had a troubled childhood and to have suffered trauma. On the surface he will appear to be what society describes as normal. He may have a good, professional career and be well-liked and respected. Beneath that facade lies the darkness. What I am certain of is that he will murder again. Now that he has experienced the thrill of the kill, he will be unable to stop. He poses a danger to everyone he comes into contact with — people who consider him a friend, as well as strangers he's never met before.

Granger switches her tablet off and looks across the room at Kane. He's sitting, head bent, reading a copy of the press release handed to the reporters when they arrived at the press conference. In her opinion, the criminal profile is first class.

She knows how Kane is planning to use it and wishes he'd discussed it with Baxter first.

She walks over to him. "Are you ready for this?"

Kane gets up. "The conference room is already packed with journalists. The national newspapers have descended on us now, for God's sake. They are the worst."

Granger can see he's already resenting having to spend time talking to the press and the conference has yet to begin. She flashes him a reassuring smile. "I don't know what you're worrying about. You're an old hand at this. You know what you're doing."

"Doesn't mean I have to like doing it though."

The suited press officer, who's been listening silently, sweeps back his greying hair and buttons up his jacket. "If you're ready, we should get going. Everything is set."

Kane stands up and gestures for Granger to lead the way. The press officer scurries ahead and opens the door to the conference room. They walk in and the volume of chattering increases as the excitement level rises.

Kane and Granger walk to the centre of a long table set on a podium in front of the journalists and sit down. Granger waits a few seconds for the noise to die down. She takes a couple of slow breaths to steady her nerves. This is a big moment. For her and for the investigation.

"I want to thank you all for attending this morning. I am Detective Sergeant Bailey Granger, part of the team hunting the killer some of you have dubbed the Hangman."

Kane is sitting beside her and she senses him bristle disapprovingly at her use of the killer's nickname. All the national tabloids now chasing the story have adopted it.

"We're doing everything possible to solve this case, including increasing the size of the team and, as always, we value your cooperation."

She glances quickly at Kane, hoping he'll nod in agreement. He stares straight ahead, keeping his expression stony.

Granger was trying in vain to use his contempt for the press to dissuade him from taking a swing at the killer's ego. She's still hoping that he'll change his mind.

"I can reveal today that both Adam and Tony Golding were dead before they were hanged."

The room is filled with murmurs of astonishment. A salvo of camera flashes illuminates the detectives' faces.

"The cause of death in both cases was an overdose of insulin administered by injection. We've decided to reveal these details now in the hope that a member of the public will link them to an individual they are working with, or even living with. I urge anyone who is aware of a person acting suspiciously who might have access to medical insulin to contact us immediately."

Granger pauses to take a breath. A reporter in the front row jumps in with a question.

"Julie Hartley, the *Daily News*. The Hangman has so far only killed members of the Golding family. Is there any reason to believe that he might prey on random members of the public?"

"That's a question that will be addressed by Detective Inspector Kane. He's going to talk about some of the possible characteristics of the killer highlighted in a criminal profile drawn up by a forensic psychologist."

Kane glances down at his notes and clears his throat before looking up at the journalists. He takes a deep breath and exhales noisily in an effort to release tension from his body.

"Criminal profiling is not a substitute for skilled detective work but it can be a useful tool for us. I'm hoping that the information I'm about to give will help someone out there identify the killer. What kind of mind could inject someone with a lethal substance and hang their corpse by the neck on public display? A twisted, tortured mind."

An enraptured hush falls over the room and Granger slides Kane a sideways look. She read Rebecca Baxter's profile carefully and is certain the psychologist never once described the killer's mind as being 'twisted' or 'tortured'.

"As you might imagine," Kane continues, "the nature of the murders suggest they would have required detailed forward planning. It's likely that the killer even kept his victims under surveillance for some time. According to our profiler, the killer is probably aged between twenty-five and thirty-five. He would likely have an above-average level of intelligence and be holding down a professional job. The use of insulin as his weapon of choice suggests he could have a medical qualification or even suffer from diabetes himself. On the surface he will appear to be a perfectly balanced, high-functioning human being. Beneath that mask lurks the real monster."

Granger scans the room. All eyes are firmly on Kane, every single journalist captivated by this glimpse into of the mind of a secret psychopath.

Standing at the back is Rebecca Baxter. The psychologist's arms are crossed, her lips pressed together in a tight line. Superintendent Dean isn't the only person Kane is going to have to explain this performance to.

"A classic phrase used in psychology literature is that homicidal psychopaths wear 'a mask of sanity'. The man you are calling the Hangman is leading a double life. He probably appears charming and articulate. He may well be in public service or in his spare time do charity work. Inevitably there are going to be times when this mask will slip. I want to appeal to the public, to everyone out there to be on their guard. To look carefully at their colleagues, friends, even their partners."

Kane takes a breather to consult his notes, his audience still hanging on his every word.

"Going back to the earlier question about the victims. We are trying to trace any relations of the Golding brothers and are investigating why they were targeted. Our psychological profiler believes that whatever the reason, the killer is unlikely to stop now. He murdered two men and put their dead bodies on display. He wanted the world to see what he did to them.

He's an evil exhibitionist. I agree that he's unlikely to stop. He's sampled the thrill of fulfilling his murderous fantasy and will want more. He poses a serious threat to anyone he meets, or even people in his social circle."

A young woman in the second row stands. Granger recognises the local crime reporter.

"Sam Hunter for the *Southend Herald*. Can you tell us if you still believe that the Hangman used a rowing boat to take the body of Tony Golding to Two Tree Island?"

Kane looks surprised to be asked a question not connected to the criminal profile.

"We still think that is the case. We have looked extensively at footage from cameras tracking traffic to and from the island and haven't found anything to suggest he used a vehicle."

The reporter moves to sit back down, hesitates, and rises again. "You've made an appeal to the public for help but have you got anything to say to the Hangman?"

Granger doesn't need to look at Kane to know that a smile is tugging at the corners of his mouth. This is the question he's been hoping for.

"I won't speak directly to him because he doesn't have the right to be spoken to like a normal human being. He has taken two lives and there is never any justification for murder. Maybe he was born with a brain that makes it hard for him to empathise, to feel guilt. Maybe he had a terrible, traumatic childhood. In my book, none of those is an excuse for becoming a cold-hearted murderer. I'm confident that he'll be behind bars soon because he's not the genius he thinks he is."

Kane pauses and Granger takes the opportunity to hold up a hand to prevent any more questions. She's worried he's gone too far.

"This press conference is over," she says. "Thank you all for your support."

She gets up and Kane follows her out of the room.

They walk side by side along the corridor. Granger is unsure whether Kane wants to know what she really thinks about what just happened. She decides to tell him anyway.

"You went too far. I knew what you were going to do but, shit, that was way over the top."

Kane doesn't break stride. "What's the point in pussyfooting around? Once I'd made my mind up I had to go for it. It wasn't that bad, was it?"

"It was bad."

As they near Kane's office his mobile starts ringing. They exchange knowing glances. It's going to be Superintendent Dean.

Kane doesn't bother taking his phone out of his pocket. He lets it go to voicemail. Granger opens the office door and the phone on Kane's desk starts ringing.

Kane takes the receiver off the hook. "It'll give her time to cool down."

Granger shakes her head in despair. "What are you going to tell her?"

"I'll think of something."

At that moment, the door swings open and Rebecca Baxter storms in. The psychologist's cheeks are red, her eyes blazing.

Granger wonders whether she should leave the two of them to it.

Kane gives her a glance. She stays.

Baxter steps closer to Kane. "That was a disgrace."

"I'm sorry you see it that way."

"There's no other way to see it. It was all so obvious. You clearly intended to poke the killer's ego, get under his skin, and you sexed up my profile to do it. You spiced it up with words I would never use, made me sound judgemental, unprofessional."

"You haven't been named as the profiler."

"That's not the point."

Kane's mobile rings again. He pulls it out of his pocket and puts it on silent.

"You're right. I used your profile to stir up the killer, draw him out into the open, make him do something careless. But I did my best to make it clear that my personal thoughts were not part of your profile."

Baxter's eyes narrow. She clenches and unclenches her fists. Granger understands her anger. She'd be furious too.

When she does speak, her voice is surprisingly calm, if a little cold. "I don't think it was clear at all. I'm disappointed in you. I thought that we were . . . You should have told me what you intended to do. We could have talked it over. Worked out together what you should say."

Kane looks at Granger, inviting moral support. She stays silent.

"You're right again. Maybe I should have told you what I planned to do. I should have asked you what you thought and trusted your opinion."

Baxter opens her mouth, closes it, turns and slams the door behind her.

Kane lets out a long breath and sits down.

"Do you think she was angry with me?"

Granger smiles. "Very. I think she likes you too."

CHAPTER 29

Sam Hunter stares intently at the screen of her laptop reading through her report on that morning's police press conference. It's good stuff. The readers will lap up the sneaky psychological peek into the mind of a double killer. Whether it turns out to be accurate or not.

Sam is a novice but even she can tell that Detective Kane has to grit his teeth when dealing with the media. She kind of likes him for it. Still, he certainly tossed the wolf pack some raw meat with his hostile, almost taunting remarks about the Hangman. He'd know full well that the papers will lap it up.

She presses send and the story wings its way invisibly across the newsroom to the news editor. She slumps back in her chair and sighs, confident she's done a competent job. What will really impress Brady is a big exclusive and she's on the brink of getting one. To clinch it she needs to meet Digger tonight and the mere thought of that makes her anxious. Adding to her dilemma is the fact that she's uneasy about not telling the police she's stumbled on a witness who potentially has a photograph of the Hangman's face.

That thought alone makes Sam catch her breath. A story like that would do wonders for her career. Brady would be desperate to get her on a permanent contract. Maybe even some of the London newspapers would be interested.

It wouldn't be right, though, would it? Keeping this from Kane and his team until they read about it in the *Herald* could help the killer avoid capture. Even worse, it could give him time to find another victim.

Sam looks around the newsroom. Her fellow reporters are either typing frantically on their laptops or on the phone chasing news, hunting glory.

She's told herself a thousand times that she has to be more ruthless. Even if she doesn't feel it, fake it. She swallows hard, grabs her phone and sends Digger a text with the meeting place and time. He replies instantly with two emojis. A thumbs up and a money bag stamped with a dollar sign.

That done, she crosses the newsroom and steps into the corridor to hunt down the drinks machine. Her mind is spinning. She still has doubts. She'd love to find a way to involve the police without losing her exclusive. By the time her cardboard cup is full of coffee, she has made up her mind.

Sam walks quickly back to her desk, puts her coffee down and picks up her phone. She dials the police station and asks to be put through to the Golding murders incident room.

After a short wait, she hears a click. A male voice answers. "Hello, can I help?"

"I hope so. This is Sam Hunter, the *Herald*'s crime reporter. Is it possible to have a word with Detective Inspector Kane? It's urgent."

"All press enquiries have to go through our media centre."

"No, this isn't a media thing. Not really. I've some information for DI Kane about the Tony Golding murder. It's important."

An extended silence followed by another loud click.

"I'm afraid DI Kane isn't available."

"This is really urgent."

"Can I help?"

Sam is reluctant to pass on what she knows to anyone except Kane. She checks the time on her phone. She's supposed to be meeting Digger in two hours.

"Who am I speaking to?"

"This is Police Constable Mark Weaver. I'm working as part of the team investigating both murders."

Sam takes a moment to think, wondering whether she should ask to be passed to a higher-ranking officer. She decides not to waste any more time.

"You probably need to take notes," she says.

An hour later, she steps out of the *Herald*'s offices into the icy gloom of a February evening. A car parked at the kerb nearby flashes its headlights twice and she hurries along the pavement. The front passenger door flips open and a friendly voice calls for her to get in.

She hesitates, bends and peers at the driver. "Constable Weaver?" The man smiles. He's in his mid-to-late twenties, dark-haired.

He shows her his warrant card. "That's right. It's me. Get in."

This time, Sam slides into the seat. As soon as the door is shut, Weaver pulls into the traffic and heads south.

"Remember," he says, "you introduce me to this Digger character as a colleague — a photographer will do. Be careful. If he figures out that I'm police, he could panic and disappear."

Sam nods. It feels good to be doing this with a police officer. She's made the right decision. She gets to keep her exclusive and the police get the information they need.

Weaver slows as they approach a busy junction and turns east onto the coastal road.

CHAPTER 30

Fifteen minutes later, they pull into the car park of the Crown Inn in the village of Little Wakering. A string of flashing-coloured lights hangs across the low-slung building's whitewashed facade.

Inside, the pub is all white walls, stained oak beams and antique clutter. At the end of the room a roaring fire chucks out waves of smoky heat. One thing the place is missing is customers. There's not a single person in sight. Not even bar staff.

Sam turns to Weaver. "This is creepy. Where the hell is everybody?"

"You chose this place, didn't you?" Weaver replies.

"Yeah. One of my colleagues said it was a nice country pub."

An old wooden door creaks open and Digger swaggers out, zipping up his flies. He's wearing the same shorts and T-shirt, even though it's icy outside.

He sees Sam first, stops dead and backs away when he realises Weaver is with her.

"Hey, no girl, no, no, no way. I said just you. No coppers. I ain't interested in talking to no coppers."

"He's not the police. This is Mark. He works with me. He's a photographer."

Sam thinks about using the phrase "I promise" but decides that would be going too far.

Digger eyes them both suspiciously. "He looks like a damn copper to me. I can spot the bastards a mile off. They all think they're something special."

Weaver steps forward and offers his hand. "Hi there. Don't worry. Sam's telling the truth. If we're going to be paying the money you want, then I'd like to check the authenticity of the image and its quality. We trust you but our boss reckons you could have copied a random face off the internet."

"I didn't. Yer calling me a liar?"

Weaver shrugs. "Of course not. We're just following orders. We have to be a bit cautious."

Digger turns to Sam. "Yer got the money with you?"

She pats her handbag.

"It's all here."

She can hear a quiver in her voice and she can tell by the doubt in Digger's eyes that he's unconvinced. Weaver had insisted that she wouldn't need to bring any cash, that he'd be able to sort it out.

Digger grunts. "Come on then, let's go sit by the fire. Me whatsits are freezing."

They do as he suggests, taking seats around a circular wooden table. Digger picks the chair closest to the crackling flames.

"Do you want a beer?" Weaver asks.

Digger looks over at the bar. He leans close to Weaver and squints right at him for a few seconds.

Weaver stretches his open hand out over the table. "Are we going to do this deal?"

Digger flinches and shakes his head. "Not yet, hold on a minute, I'm still thinking about this. Yer weren't supposed to be here. Don't push me. I'm not going to be rushed into nothing. Go get me a pint like you offered. Me brain needs lubricating. Get the girl a white wine while yer at it."

Weaver stands up slowly, his chair scraping the uneven stone floor.

Sam watches him make his way to the bar. She needs to do something.

Digger has whipped out his phone and is studying the screen intently. When he glances up at her she smiles. "Would you like to show me the photograph while Mark's not here? I can tell he's making you nervous."

Digger drags his chair around the table to get closer to her. She can smell the smoke from the fire on his clothes. He sneaks a look over her shoulder to make sure Weaver's still at bar.

"Come on, girl. Who is he, really? He ain't no newspaper snapper. They're always scruffy bastards. Are you sure he's not a copper?"

Sam feels her cheeks redden. She doesn't know what to say.

Digger leans in closer. "Listen to me, girl. I've changed my mind. No deal. I ain't got nothing to sell."

Before Sam can say anything, he scurries across the room and out of the door. Weaver comes back from the bar carrying the drinks.

"Where is he?"

Sam fails to hide her embarrassment. Thank God she brought a police officer along. Who knows what would have happened if she'd come alone.

"He's gone. Doesn't want to do any deal. I don't think he had a photo at all. He was probably trying to scam me for some money."

Weaver raises his eyebrows. "Just as well I came then. I think I scared him off. Do you want this wine?"

Sam shakes her head.

"Right. I'll drop you home on my way back to the station."

CHAPTER 31

Kane stands outside Superintendent Helen Dean's office and hesitates before knocking. He knows what's coming — a lecture about improper use of a criminal profile at yesterday's press conference.

He doesn't see it that way. His job is to catch a killer and he'll do anything and everything necessary. As long as it's legal. He'd never break the law to solve a murder. Unless he was certain that he could get away with it.

He knocks lightly and Dean calls him in. She is sitting at her desk, her arms folded across her chest. Her hair is even shorter and a touch greyer than when he saw her last. He tries a smile. Her expression stays solemn.

"Sit down, Edison," she says. "Please tell me what the hell you're playing at? Press conferences are to impart information and hopefully get some in return. Not to whip up an already deranged killer. What were you thinking?"

Kane and Dean were a good team when they were younger. He valued her logic. She used to trust his instincts.

"I'm thinking outside the box. And I still believe this is a tactic that might work. It doesn't look like our victims have any close living relatives. The killer has wiped out the Golding family. Apart from the first victim's wife, Ruth. If that was his intention it doesn't mean he's going to stop. Now he's tasted blood he's going to hunt that high again. That's what Rebecca Baxter believes and I agree. Once a killer, always a killer."

Dean drums the fingers of her right hand on the top of her desk while she takes a moment to think. Kane reckons that with each promotion she gets harder to read.

"This is why you've decided to bait the so-called Hangman. Make yourself a target. Because you fear he's going to strike again?"

Kane doesn't need to answer. It's not really a question. It's an accurate summary of the situation. He locks eyes with Dean and steels himself for whatever's coming next.

"Have you considered that taunting the killer might stir him up to the point where he kills again just to prove to you that he can and that, at the same time, you may well have put yourself in danger?"

"I've thought this through and I think it can help us solve the case before anyone else gets hurt. This killer is clever and meticulous. I want to force him into making a mistake."

Dean takes a thin blue folder out of a desk drawer, places it in front of her and flips it open. She takes a few seconds to read the handwritten notes before looking up.

"Baxter isn't happy with the way you used her psychological profile either. I don't blame her. She has grounds for a formal complaint."

"Has she complained?"

"Not formally. Not yet."

She drums her fingers again. "Do I need to tell you what I think about all this?"

Kane shrugs. He knows she's going to tell him anyway.

"I think that of all the senior investigating officers under my command, I seem to spend an inordinate amount of my time dealing with you."

"Isn't that because I get assigned the complicated cases?"

Dean remains stern. "Do I have to spell out what I want from you?"

Kane takes a good guess at this one. He knows how the game works. How the top brass think. "You want results."

"Spot on, Edison. Catch this Hangman and nobody is going to worry too much about how you did it, including me. Now get on with it."

Kane stands up and hurries to the door, eager to vanish before Dean changes her mind. She's always been a stickler for rules and regulations. He's guessing she's feeling serious pressure from above if she's willing to bend with the wind.

He's about to close the door behind him when Dean calls for him to wait. He holds the handle and pops his head back into the office.

"One last thing," she says. "Don't do anything you might end up regretting."

It takes Kane forty-five minutes to drive from the Major Investigations Team headquarters in Brentwood back to Southend police station. Daylight is already fading as he pulls up in the car park. Before he gets out, he flicks through his phone contacts and stops when he sees the name Rebecca Baxter. She has every right to resent him. He should at least have warned her about what he was going to do.

If they can bring the killer to justice soon, then maybe she'll give him some credit and forgive him. His finger hovers over the call symbol. There's probably no point in saying sorry again. Give her a bit more time.

He scrolls further down and calls Granger. She answers straight away, her voice tinged with urgency. "I was just about to call you."

"What's happened?"

"Martin Carter wants you down at the mortuary."

"Did he say anything else?"

"Just that it's urgent."

"Okay, call him and tell him I'm on my way."

The rush-hour traffic crawls at a snail's pace. What should've been a five-minute journey takes him fifteen. It would've been quicker to walk.

Carter is waiting for him in the mortuary office, his hands in the pockets of his crisp white coat, his protective mask pulled down under his chin.

"Ah, there you are, Inspector. I was beginning to worry that you'd got lost."

Kane can't be bothered to humour the pathologist. "What's so important, Martin?"

"Come and see for yourself."

Kane follows Carter through a door into the post-mortem room. It's identical to every one he's been in: gleaming white tiles, stainless-steel sinks and dazzling fluorescent lights. A covered cadaver is laid out on an examination table. Carter pulls the sheet down, uncovering the torso.

"Say hello to the late Mr David Dines. Apparently, he liked to be known as Digger."

Kane takes a long look. The eyes are closed. The craggy face serene. Y-shaped stitching extends across the shoulders and down to the pubic bone, where he's been opened to examine his organs and sewn back up again.

"What happened to him?"

"The pulled him out of a river last night. It seems Inspector Munro has already decided it's either suicide or an accident."

Kane is regretting answering Carter's summons. Mortuary examination rooms have never been his favourite places to visit.

"Why am I here and not Munro? It's his case, not mine."

"Patience, Edison. Patience. When I examined the poor man's lungs they contained very little water, which suggests that he didn't drown and that he was dead before he went into the water. Intrigued, I carried out another painstaking examination of the whole body, and guess what I found?"

"Just tell me, Martin, for God's sake."

Carter bends his head close to the dead man's stomach and beckons for Kane to do the same.

"Right there," he says, relishing the moment, pointing to a tiny red mark close to the navel. What about that, my friend?"

Kane's chest and hands tingle as adrenaline surges through his veins. He knows what the mark is and what it means.

He may not have been strung up by the neck on public display, but David "Digger" Dines is the Hangman's third victim.

CHAPTER 32

Sam Hunter takes a bite out of her second slice of toast and jam and washes it down with a gulp of fresh orange juice. She has half an hour before she's due in the office and she's dreading it.

Brady will want to know what she's working on and she's going to have to admit that's she's failed to come up with a new angle on the Hangman murders.

She picks her phone up off the breakfast bar and ponders calling Digger. He's had a day to reconsider backing out of their deal. Maybe there's still a chance she can turn things around. She presses the call button. It goes straight to voicemail.

"Um, hi, Digger. It's Sam Hunter. Sorry about last night. I've been thinking that maybe we should meet again. Just us this time. Try to sort things out. Please call me back."

Sam puts her phone down and finishes the last of her orange juice. It was worth a try. She grabs the TV remote and puts on a local news channel. It's so cold in her rented studio flat, she can see her breath curling into tiny clouds. She's already left two messages on her landlord's phone demanding that the boiler be fixed.

On the TV screen, a grey-haired newsreader beams inappropriately as he announces that the body of a man has been pulled out of the River Roach, north of the village of Barling.

"The naked body was spotted floating face down in the river last night by a local woman walking her dog. The police say that the death is not being treated as suspicious."

Sam switches the TV off, slips her jacket on and wraps a scarf around her neck. Time to face the music. Her flat is on the first floor and she takes the stairs. Halfway down she tries calling Digger again. It goes to voicemail. This time she doesn't bother leaving a message.

She steps out on to the icy pavement into a thick February mist. The newspaper office is a mere ten minutes from her flat and even though she's forced to tread carefully, she still moves faster than the bumper-to-bumper traffic.

By the time she arrives in the newsroom, her fingers and toes are numb with cold. Before she can remove her jacket and get herself a warming coffee, Brady approaches her desk. As usual, the news editor skips the social niceties and gets straight to business.

"We've got a report of a drowning near Barling. Don't know yet whether it's an accident or suicide. A man in his forties, apparently. Stripped off and jumped or fell in. I think there's a good chance the police will have identified the body by now. Chase it up for me and write five hundred words for the website as soon as possible."

Sam unwraps her scarf slowly while she considers how she should react. She's still holding on to the hope that Digger will call her back and she can land her big exclusive.

"Is there a problem?" Brady asks.

Sam swallows hard. "This drowning. I saw it reported on TV before coming in. Police say they're not treating it as a suspicious death. It's not really a crime story, is it?"

Sam holds her breath waiting for the news editor to let loose with one of her legendary bollockings.

Brady puts her hands on her hips and glares at her. "Are you busy working on something else right now? A brilliant exclusive for my front page? Maybe you've got a fantastic new angle on the Hangman killings?"

"Er, no. Not exactly working on it. Not yet. I'm waiting to hear from a contact, though. I called him earlier and he could have something interesting for me soon."

Brady smiles and nods her approval. "That's great. I'm glad to hear it. Can't wait. I'd like the drowning story in my inbox before noon, please."

Sam watches her stride across the room to her desk. If she's going to land a permanent role on the *Herald*, then she's got to make sure Brady gets what Brady wants.

She picks up her desk phone and puts a call into the police media office. It's answered by Dana Steen, an affable press officer she's met a few times.

"Hi, Dana, it's Sam Hunter, on the *Herald*. I was wondering if you have a name for the man who drowned in the Roach last night. I'm writing a piece for our website and an ID would make it so much better."

"Hi there, Sam. It must be your lucky day. We've just been authorised to release the name of the dead man. He's David Dines, aged forty-three. Lives in a hostel near Thorpe Bay beach. He's a bit of a local character, actually. People in the town know him as Digger."

CHAPTER 33

Sam runs out of the newsroom and along the corridor until she reaches an alcove housing the office coffee machine and a water cooler. She rests both hands on the wall, hangs her head and takes slow, deep breaths.

Her heart is thumping, her stomach churning like a washing machine. Two nights ago she sat in a pub next to Digger. Now he's dead.

She hears footsteps and looks up. Brady strides purposefully toward her. Sam quickly busies herself with the coffee machine, hoping the news editor will pass by and leave her to it.

Brady stops. "Is everything all right, Sam? You're looking seriously pale."

Sam resists the temptation to tell Brady everything there and then. She's not ready to confess to letting a big exclusive slip through her fingers. She needs to find out more about how Digger died first. It's possible she can still get a big scoop out of this — *HANGMAN WITNESS DROWNS AFTER SECRET MEETING WITH HERALD REPORTER*. Or is she somehow to blame for Digger's death? If so, she's managed to sabotage her career in journalism before it's properly started — *BUNGLING REPORTER LINKED TO DEATH OF HANGMAN WITNESS.*

"I'm feeling a little nauseous, that's all. It's probably because I skipped breakfast this morning."

Brady frowns. "Are you sure? If you're too sick to work, then go home. I mean it. Take the day off. I can assign the drowning story to someone else. You really don't look too good."

Sam manages a feeble smile. She's starting to realise that Brady is softer than she makes out. "Well, if it's okay with you, I think I will go home for a lie down. I'm feeling a little dizzy as well as sick."

"You do that. Go and put your feet up. Take tomorrow off if you need it. I've got to get moving. I've a meeting with the editor."

Brady makes her way down the corridor. Sam waits until she disappears into the editor's office at the end.

She digs her phone out of her coat pocket and calls PC Weaver, her hand shaking as she holds her phone to her ear.

When he answers, she doesn't give him a chance to speak. "I've just heard Digger's dead," she gushes. "I can't believe it. They found his body floating in the river. I saw it on the TV news. What is going on?"

"Calm down, Sam. I don't know much more than you do. I'll ask around and let you know. He probably got drunk after he left us and fell in."

Sam feels bad for feeling relieved. The poor fool. He was a strange and slightly scary character but she had found herself starting to warm to him.

"What should I do now? I suppose I ought to go to the police station and make a statement."

Weaver is silent for a few seconds before replying. "I think we have no choice. We have to make everything official. Speak to the officer on the case and tell them that we met with Dines in a pub the night before he drowned and explain the purpose of the meeting."

Sam's heart sinks. It means she's going to have to give a full account to Brady of her failure to get hold of the photograph on Digger's phone. She'll have to admit her lack of experience meant she missed a golden opportunity to get one over on their rivals. The thought tightens her throat. "Okay then. It'll take me about twenty minutes to walk to the station."

"No need for that. I'm not sure I can get away right now. If I can't I'll send another officer over to pick you up outside your office in five. Detective Constable Dec Brown. He's nice."

Sam walks tentatively down the staircase to the ground floor, her legs shaky, her mind racing. Perhaps her family and friends were right all along. She's not cut out for this.

She considers turning around, finding Brady and telling her she's had enough. Take the easy way out. Quit before the axe falls.

Sam dismisses the idea quickly. She's not ready to give up. Not yet. She zips up her jacket and coils her scarf around her neck before stepping outside. The cold takes her breath away. She spots a car parked nearby. The figure behind the wheel beckons her over.

She hurries along the pavement, tears pricking her eyes. *What an idiot.* She's supposed to be a professional.

CHAPTER 34

Granger pulls the car up outside an end-of-terrace house. A rusty washing machine adds character to an otherwise bare patch of grass outside the front door.

Kane turns to Granger as he rings the bell. "Maybe it's best if you do the talking."

The door opens to reveal a woman wearing jeans and a beige roll-neck sweater. Her feet are bare, the toenails freshly painted ruby red.

"Mrs Amy Dines?" Granger holds up her warrant card.

The woman leans forward to take a better look. "Yeah, that's me."

"Right. This is Detective Inspector Kane. May we come inside?"

The woman glances over her shoulder, her brow creasing. "It's a terrible mess in there. I'm in the middle of cleaning up and I've got to pick my son up from school in half an hour."

Kane estimates she's ten years younger than her deceased estranged husband.

He steps forward. "It won't take long. It's important we speak."

Dines lets out a long sigh of exasperation, turns and marches inside. The detectives follow her in. The door opens straight into a sparsely furnished living area. Next to the two-seater sofa is a plastic washing basket piled high with dirty clothes. An open bottle of nail varnish sits on the edge of a black coffee table.

Dines sits down. "Well, go on then. Get on with it. I had you lot in here yesterday telling me my husband had drowned. What can be so important? Has he come back to life or something?"

Granger sits beside her. "How long have you been separated?"

Dines throws up her hand. "I've been through all this. I told that Inspector Munro yesterday."

"Yes, I'm sorry to have to put you through this again but we have new information. The situation has changed."

Dines frowns. "I threw him out two years ago. Couldn't put up with his obsession any longer."

"His obsession?"

"Yeah, his beachcombing, his metal detecting. Every spare moment he was marching up and down the beaches, digging up soda cans and rusty nails. That's why everybody started calling him Digger. When he gave up his job at the superstore warehouse claiming he could make more on the beaches, I gave him an ultimatum. He went and did it anyway. I wanted a divorce but we couldn't afford it. Now the silly old fool's gone and got himself drowned. He was a good swimmer too."

Granger throws Kane a glance. "That's why we're here," she says. "I'm afraid we are now sure that your husband's death wasn't an accident. He was murdered."

Dines jumps forward in her seat. Her right knee knocks the table and the bottle of nail varnish rolls on to the floor, thick red liquid oozing onto the threadbare grey carpet.

"Murdered? You're not serious. I don't believe this. Who on earth would want to kill David? He could be a real pain in the neck sometimes but he was harmless. Everyone who got to know him liked him. I don't think he had a single enemy."

She kneels down and picks up the nail varnish bottle. "This carpet is ruined. I'll never be able to get this stuff off.

More money we haven't got." She levers herself back on to the sofa. "How am I going to explain this to Tommy? I've had to tell him that his dad drowned. He's already devastated. Now this. What happened? Why would anybody want to murder David?"

Granger stands and Kane sits in her place. "How old is your boy?"

"Nine. He and his dad were close. Despite everything, David was a good father. After he moved out into the hostel near the seafront, he always came back to see Tommy. Regular as clockwork. Whenever he got hold of money, he'd give me some to help pay the rent. I can't believe anyone would want to kill him."

Kane decides it's not the right moment to tell her that her husband was injected with an overdose of insulin and thrown into the river. He'll leave that to the experts in sensitivity.

"As soon as we can, we'll send round an officer who specialises in looking after the families of murder victims. They'll stay around for as long as you need them. You can ask him or her anything you want. I'd suggest you don't say anything more to Tommy just yet. It'd be best if you wait until you both have the support of the family liaison officer."

Dines sobs loudly, her shoulders heaving. "We're going to lose this place and we've nowhere else to go. I'm behind with the rent and the landlord's already given me a warning."

Kane looks across to Granger, hoping she'll know the right thing to say. She shrugs. "The landlord can't kick you out just like that, can he?"

Dines wipes her eyes with her sleeve, smudging her mascara. "He can and he will. I'm hundreds of pounds in arrears. David told me not to worry. Said he'd struck lucky and had a big pile of cash coming his way. He said he'd be able to pay off a big chunk of what I owe. Now he's gone. We've got no hope."

"When was this? When did he promise you that money?"

"The last time he popped in to see Tommy. Four or five days ago, I think."

"Did he explain how he would be getting this windfall?"

"I don't think so. No, wait a minute. He did say something about having got hold of something to sell to the newspaper. The *Herald*. Said he'd hit the jackpot, and I believed him, because I knew he'd sold a couple of stories to the paper's crime reporter a while ago. He was crazy happy. Happier than I'd seen him for a long time."

CHAPTER 35

Rebecca Baxter studies the young policeman fidgeting nervously on his seat. His hair is dark, his skin pale.

"Welcome, Mark. If you're ready, let's start with you explaining to me why you're here."

Weaver smiles. His teeth are straight and white. "My boss recommended you. I believe you know him. Detective Inspector Kane."

That isn't what Baxter meant and she strongly suspects that Weaver knows that.

"I'm curious why you've chosen to come to me rather than see one of your police service counsellors. They are specially trained to help officers suffering from trauma."

Weaver shakes his head slowly. "I don't want any of this on my work record. I know they say everything is kept confidential. It's hard to believe. I'd be worried that it would scupper any chance of promotion. I reckon DI Kane feared the same. I'm guessing you helped him after his wife was murdered."

Baxter decides not to waste time trying to convince him otherwise. "Everything you say in this room is totally confidential, unless you give me reason to believe that you could harm yourself or another person. I take it you've booked this session because there's something you want to talk about. Something that's bothering you."

Weaver leans back in his chair and crosses his arms. "Yeah, sorry. This isn't easy, is it? I'm finding it hard to get any decent sleep and that's making concentration difficult. It's affecting my work."

"How long has this been going on?"

"I'd say . . . twelve days, maybe."

"Your sleep's being disturbed by what, exactly?"

"Nightmares, bad dreams. You know the sort of thing. Images and thoughts I can't get out of my head. All sorts of stuff."

Baxter knows exactly when and why Weaver's problem started. She needs him to spell it out for her. In his own words. He needs to hear himself say it.

"Do you think you know what triggered all this? Was it something you did, or something that happened to you?"

Weaver leans back and stares at the ceiling. It's the first time he's broken eye contact. Shown any sign of nervousness.

"Yeah. I can tell you exactly what started it. It was the body I found. When I was out on a morning run."

"The man you found under the pier?"

He looks directly at Baxter. "Yeah, that's the man. Noose tight around his neck. Face blown up like a football. Distorted."

Baxter pauses. Weaver is trying to sound matter-of-fact but his breathing is ragged. She needs to slow the tempo. Ease the tension.

"How long have you been a police officer?"

The change of tack catches Weaver off balance. He tilts his head and gives her a curious look. "Almost four years."

"I'm assuming you like what you do? Protecting the public. Enforcing the law."

"More than like. I love it."

Baxter offers a smile of encouragement. "I guess in those four years you've had to deal with a few dead bodies."

"I have. A suicide. A nasty road traffic accident. An old guy who died in his armchair and rotted for weeks before a neighbour complained about the smell."

"Why do you think finding the body hanging under the pier has affected you so badly?"

Weaver looks up at the ceiling again. He doesn't answer.

Baxter prompts him. "Maybe it's because you were off duty. Out running, minding your own business. It would have been more of a shock because you hadn't been called out to an incident."

"Maybe. I suppose it's possible."

"You don't sound convinced. It could be that you were more affected by the other things you've seen than you let yourself believe. This latest body could have been a trigger."

Weaver bows his head and clasps his hands tight.

Baxter has a feeing he knows the real reason and is struggling to spit it out. She throws out another thought. "Is it the way this person died? If you've never seen a hanging before, I can imagine it would be pretty traumatic. Difficult to come to terms with."

Weaver sighs, long and heavy. To Baxter, the sound is a mixture of despair and relief.

"It's the opposite." His tone is flat, emotionless. "You've got it the wrong way round."

"What do you mean?"

"The body under the pier wasn't the first time I'd seen a hanging. The first dead body I ever saw was someone with a noose around their neck, hanging from a banister. I remember the eyes most of all. Bloodshot and bulging."

Baxter suppresses a strong urge to clench a fist and wave it in triumph. That wouldn't be professional. This feeling is one of the reasons she'll never give up offering therapy sessions, no matter how deep she delves into criminal psychology. She'll never get tired of helping people. It's how she helps herself.

"How old were you when this happened to you? Would you like to tell me who the deceased was? Was it someone you knew?"

Weaver lifts a hand and rubs his eyes with his thumb and forefinger. "Can we leave it for now please? I don't feel ready to talk about this. I'm sorry."

Baxter responds with a sympathetic smile. She can't help but admire the young police officer's courage. Admitting you're struggling and need help is never easy.

"Of course, Mark. Let's end this session. This is an important first step. When you feel ready, I'll be here."

CHAPTER 36

Kane stares at the whiteboard in the incident room. Three victims stare back at him now. His mind is whirring after this morning's visit to Amy Dines, his thoughts a heady mixture of excitement and worry.

Both his gut and his experience are telling him that the killing of Digger Dines is the key to solving this case. He doesn't seem to have any connection to the Goldings. This means the Hangman didn't plan to murder him. His hand was forced.

Granger enters the room carrying two coffees. She joins Kane and hands him one. "What are you thinking?"

"That we heard this morning that this Digger was trying to sell a story to the *Herald* before he was killed by insulin injection. Why would the Hangman murder this guy and try to make it look like a suicide or accidental drowning?"

"To stop him speaking to the newspaper?"

"Exactly. Because the information he had would somehow expose the Hangman. We need to speak to the reporter Digger was dealing with as soon as possible. Could you ask the media office for a number for Sam Hunter? Something tells me she's involved in this. She's the crime reporter. She's new, ambitious and probably out to make a name for herself."

While Granger puts the call in, Kane takes a swig of his coffee and pulls a face. It's gone cold.

He recalls meeting Hunter on the seafront, their chat about cooperation, her fresh face, and her youthful enthusiasm. His stomach churns at the thought that she could be in peril. If the Hangman suspects Digger spoke to her, she could become his next victim.

Granger terminates the call. "One of the press officers will be here in a minute. Dana Steen. Says she spoke to Hunter early yesterday."

Kane paces across the room and back again. The next few hours are going to be crucial. This third, unplanned killing will give them a glimpse of an opportunity to solve this case. They must be ready to take it.

A slender woman in a black trouser suit strides confidently into the room. Her dyed blonde hair is short, almost cropped, and she's holding a tablet.

Kane goes to meet her. He doesn't wait to be introduced.

"Hi, Dana. Do you have a contact number for Sam Hunter?"

Steen nods, unfazed by the urgency of his manner. "I do. I've called her a couple of times on my way down here and the calls went straight to voicemail."

"You said she called you yesterday?"

Steen switches her tablet on and studies the screen. "That's right, she did. I logged it here. She called at 9.20 a.m. Wanted to know if the man found dead in the River Roach had been identified and his name released."

Kane exchanges a quick glance with Granger.

"I gave her the details and that was it."

"How did she react when you told her the dead man's name?"

"She didn't react at all really. I thought it a bit strange because she ended the call immediately. See didn't thank me or anything, which isn't like her. She's usually very polite and chatty—"

Kane is on the move, beckoning Granger to follow, before Steen finishes speaking.

"Thanks, Dana. You've been extremely helpful."

* * *

"What's so urgent? I've a newspaper to produce and the first deadline is less than an hour away."

Kane and Granger follow Dawn Brady out of the chaos of the newsroom into a glass-walled office. They sit around an oval conference table.

Kane has always assumed that newspapers like the *Herald* must be run by psychologically dysfunctional egomaniacs. He's hoping Dawn Brady is going to prove him wrong. On the surface she appears perfectly sane, if a little under pressure.

"I am Detective Inspector Kane and this is Detective Sergeant Granger. I'm investigating the Hangman killings and need to speak with Sam Hunter. We believe she may have important information for us."

Brady gives him a long, hard look. "Information about what exactly?"

"It's important that we interview her as soon as possible."

"Well, I'm afraid she's not here. She wasn't feeling well and I sent her home."

"When was this?"

"Yesterday, at about 9.30 a.m. She was supposed to be writing a small piece for me about the man found dead in a river near Barling."

"We need her home address. We've called her several times and she's not answering."

Brady hesitates again. "I can get you that. I believe the place she rents is a short walk from here. But I'd like to know what this is all about first?"

"We're investigating the death of a man who we believe recently contacted your crime reporter offering to sell information regarding a serious offence. We urgently need to find out what he had to sell."

"It'd probably help if I knew the dead man's name."

"His name is David Dines. Known locally as Digger."

"The man in the river? Accidental drowning or suicide we were told. Are you saying he was murdered? By the Hangman?"

Kane sighs. "This is off the record. Nothing can be made public yet. But yes. Now, get me Sam Hunter's home address, we haven't got time to waste."

Brady gets up quickly to leave, then stops. "How is Sam involved in all this?"

"We believe she knows something that may help us find the Hangman."

"That sounds like you think she's in danger. Is she?"

Kane and Granger exchange a worried look.

"We hope not. At this stage she's a person of interest. A possible witness."

* * *

Ten minutes later, the detectives walk up to a shabby-looking redbrick terraced house. Hunter's flat is on the top floor. Granger presses the video intercom buzzer. No response.

She tries again, this time holding the button down for a good ten seconds. Still nothing.

Kane steps forward and presses the buzzer for the ground floor flat. After a few seconds, a woman answers. "Who is it? What do you want?"

Kane holds his identification up to the camera lens. "It's the police. I need to talk to you about the tenant living upstairs."

The intercom buzzes, then falls silent. They hear footsteps approaching the door. It opens slowly. A blonde woman in her thirties pokes her head through the gap, peering at Kane through gold-rimmed spectacles. "What's this all about?"

"I'm Detective Inspector Kane. This is Detective Sergeant Granger. We're trying to contact Sam Hunter."

The woman appears reassured by Granger's presence. She steps back and opens the door fully. She's wearing a fluffy knee-length pink dressing gown. Nothing on her feet.

"Excuse the outfit. I don't usually look like this. I'm just about to hop into bed. I'm a nurse, see. I'm working nights. Desperately need a snooze. What's up with Sam? She doesn't seem the type to get in trouble with the police. Lovely girl. Very prim and proper, she is."

"She's not in any trouble. We need her to help us with a criminal investigation. She's not at work and she's not answering her phone."

The nurse takes her glasses off, exhales noisily on the lenses, and rubs them with a screwed-up tissue. "If she's not at work I don't know where she is. She loves that job of hers. I heard her moving around up there last night. I remember thinking she probably had a visitor because it was noisier than usual. The walls are paper thin and the floors and ceilings aren't soundproofed. I haven't heard a thing today though."

"What exactly did you hear?"

"A bit of banging, raised voices. Didn't last long though."

"In that case we're going to have to go up and take a look," Kane says. "If there's a chance she is up there, I'd like to make sure she's okay."

The woman nods and flattens her back against the wall to let them pass.

The detectives fly up the narrow wooden staircase. Kane raps hard on the door. "Sam. It's the police. Please come to the door. It's important we speak to you."

Silence. Kane turns to Granger. "I'm going to have to force entry. We don't need a warrant if we think someone inside might be at risk."

Granger eyes the door. "It looks pretty sturdy. Do you think you're up to it? Maybe I should give it a go."

Kane glares at her for a few seconds, then takes a couple of steps back.

The nurse runs up the staircase, waving her arms, her face flushed with exertion.

"Hey, hang on a minute. No need to break it down. You'll get Sam in bother with the landlord. I've got a key. Sam gave me a spare one. For emergencies. I reckon this counts as one."

As soon as they walk into the flat, Kane and Granger smell bleach. Kane checks the bedroom first. No sign of the young reporter. The bed is made, the room spotless. Hunter's neighbour is sure she heard banging but there's no sign of a scuffle.

On the bedside table is a framed photograph of Hunter, her arms around the shoulders of a smiling couple in their sixties. Happy parents with their pride and joy.

Kane joins Granger in the living area. Small green cushions are arranged neatly on the grey sofa and single armchair. On the coffee table lies an impressively thick paperback: *The Investigative Reporter's Handbook*.

The mini kitchen is spotless. Granger runs her fingers along a wooden worktop and crosses the room to check out the bathroom. Before going in, she bends and sniffs at the brass door handle.

"This has definitely been wiped with a strong bleach solution. And recently."

She pushes the door open and disappears inside.

After a few moments, the door reopens.

"Quickly, you need to see this."

Kane strides over and steps in. The bathroom is tiny. Granger's back is flat against the rectangular sink. She grabs Kane's arm and pulls him to her side. Reaching for the door, she shuts them in.

Written in red lipstick on the middle door panel are two words. The handwriting is shaky, the capital letters irregular in size.

HELP ME

CHAPTER 37

"The focus of this investigation has changed. Right now, our primary objective is to find Sam Hunter. The longer it takes, the less likely it is that she'll be alive."

Kane puts everything he can into projecting the demeanour of a leader. Calm, confident, decisive. A seeker of justice. Protector of the innocent.

He scans the faces of his team. Every single one of his officers looks both determined and tired. Maybe he's not the only one struggling with sleep.

The incident room whiteboard has been updated. A photograph of the missing reporter is pinned above the headshots of the killer's three victims.

Kane points at her smiling face. "We have good reason to believe that she has been taken by the man who killed the Golding brothers. The post-mortem on Digger Dines has confirmed that he died as a result of an insulin overdose injected before he was dumped into the River Roach. We're now sure that he is the so-called Hangman's third victim."

DC Meera Kush clears her throat. "But he chose not to hang the body because this time he wanted to hide the fact that it was him?"

"Exactly that," Kane says. "It's looking like the information this Digger was offering to Sam Hunter would have identified the killer. Somehow the killer knew this."

Kane pauses, hoping to encourage another of his team to speak. He's a firm believer in the power of questions. The right ones.

DS Alex Scott stands up. "Why would the killer take the reporter? If he suspects she poses a danger to him, why not just kill her too?"

This is something Kane has asked himself. The scary answer is that he has killed her and her body is already lying in some dark place. He failed to protect his wife, then failed to find her murderer. He can't change any of that. But saving Sam Hunter might ease his pain. If he believed in God he'd happily ask his team to kneel down and pray that she'll be found safe and well. That's not an option. He's always considered prayer an excuse for inaction.

"Until a body turns up, we proceed on the basis that she is alive. Based on everything we've seen so far, I don't believe this killer has any conscience at all. If he's holding her prisoner, keeping her alive, then it's because he feels it's to his advantage."

Kane shoots a look at Granger. She steps up to the whiteboard, clutching her tablet.

"Sam Hunter's network provider has been unable to locate her phone. The chances are it is switched off, or has been destroyed. They have, using triangulation, been able to establish that on the evening of the eleventh of February she was in the village of Little Wakering before returning home to her flat. That's roughly forty-eight hours before she disappeared. No phone signal since then."

Granger checks her notes on the tablet and turns to DC Kush. "Meera, I know you've had experience with misper public appeals. Liaise with the media office to get Hunter's photo out on every news website and TV channel. We may have to consider getting the parents to make an appeal."

"Hunter doesn't have any siblings," says DC Brown. "She might have spoken to friends or colleagues about what she was doing."

"I agree, Dec. That's on my list too. You can start with the nurse who lives in the flat below Hunter's. Tracy Dunn. She says they were close."

Kane eyes the two officers waiting for their tasks: DS Scott and the uniform, PC Weaver. The detective sergeant is wearing a scowl. He knows what's coming and is certain he's getting dumped on because he's a local.

Granger smiles. "Alex. You're on video footage again. You know the streets around Hunter's flat and the *Herald*'s office like the back of your hand and exactly where the cameras are. It's important work. Mark will work with you on that."

DS Scott grunts something unintelligible. He's not happy with his role in the investigation but Kane trusts him to do his job properly.

Granger checks her tablet one more time.

"I'll be sending a family liaison officer to Sam's parents' home. They will need reassuring that we're doing all we can. That's it. Let's get going. The next few hours are vital."

CHAPTER 38

PC Mark Weaver climbs the stairs to the waiting area outside Rebecca Baxter's consulting room. The psychologist sounded excited that he'd called, begging for an appointment. People like her love it when a client is desperate to spill their guts. It's a power trip.

The door opens and Baxter appears, all glammed up as usual. She gives him a double take. Weaver gets it. It's the first time she's seen him in his work clothes.

One of the main reasons Weaver joined the police was the uniform. It's like having a superpower. Every morning when he dresses for duty it's like pulling on a new skin. People stare at you, mostly in admiration. Your mere presence makes them feel safe. Law-abiding citizens do what you want them to do. Those who don't trust you, fear you.

"Good morning," Baxter says. "Come on in. I'm squeezing you between two clients because you said it was urgent. I can't give you the full fifty minutes, though. We have half an hour."

Weaver gives her his grateful smile. She can't wait to hear what he's got to say. He's dealt with several shrinks as a teenager and they're all the same.

Baxter ushers him to his seat, closes the door and sits down herself, smoothing her skirt with her hands.

"Would you like to start where we left off last time? Can you remember what you told me?"

Weaver keeps his expression blank. She's trying hard not to sound like she's pushing him but she can't wait to get to the juicy bits.

"You mean that since finding that body hanging under the pier, I've been having flashbacks and stuff?"

Baxter nods thoughtfully. Weaver can tell she's trying to work out whether he really can't remember how their last session ended, or whether he's being obstructive.

"We can, yes, of course, we can talk about the day you found that body, if that is what you feel like doing."

"It didn't really hit me straight away. I probably went into policing mode. I'd seen other dead bodies before, like I said. It wasn't until a few days later that I started having nightmares. Seeing swollen, distorted faces, with bulging bloodshot eyes."

He sees uncertainty flicker across Baxter's face. She pauses and smooths her skirt again.

"Do you remember that you told me before that the first dead person you ever saw had been hanged?"

Weaver drops his gaze to the floor. "That's true. Is it important? Is that why this is taking such a toll on me?"

"It could be. Unhealed childhood trauma must eventually be addressed. You were young then?"

Weaver looks up and nods. "Fourteen. My birthday was three days before."

Baxter waits, letting the silence between them thicken. An old psychologist's trick. Weaver doesn't fall for it, doesn't elaborate. Eventually, Baxter caves.

"Are you ready to tell me who this person was? You said you sometimes see their face, I think. I'm guessing this person was someone very close to you?"

Weaver is surprised by the feeling welling in his chest. This is supposed to be a game. The taunting of a psychologist who foolishly believes she can see inside tortured minds.

He fights a sudden urge to get up and leave. To put a halt to this nonsense. His breath is coming faster. He's struggling to control it. *There's no going back now. No choice.*

"I walked home from school. Ran the last half-mile because I wanted to break my record. I did. By two minutes. I unlocked the front door. Had my own key. I was hungry and hot. I called out but there was nobody home. That wasn't unusual. I went into the kitchen and opened the fridge. Nothing worth eating. I picked up a carton of milk, took the top off and swigged it down. It tasted good."

Weaver pauses. The memory is so vivid he needs a moment to catch his breath. He looks across at Baxter to make sure she's paying attention. She smiles and gives him a nod of encouragement.

"Then I, well, I put the empty carton back where I found it and went into the lounge. That's when I saw her. That's the moment I . . . She was dangling from the banister. The noose around her neck fashioned from a twisted sheet. A wooden chair lay on its side beneath her feet. I couldn't believe what I was seeing. I stood there for a while. Frozen to the spot. Fifteen, maybe twenty minutes, staring at her swollen face, a fury burning inside me. How could this happen to me? How could a mother do that to her child?"

Weaver relaxes. Tension seeps from his body. It's the first time he's spoken to anyone about that day. He can't deny it feels good.

"Thank you for sharing that with me. I know how difficult that must have been for you."

CHAPTER 39

"It looks quaint," Kane says as they pull up in the car park of the Crown Inn. "There aren't many of these traditional village pubs left. They're a dying breed."

Granger kills the engine and gives him a sideways grin. "You do realise you sound like a grumpy old man? You'll be telling me next how great being a detective was in the good old days, when men were men and women made the teas."

Kane gets out of the car and slams the door shut. "That's hurtful. Everyone knows I'm a modern man and still in my prime."

Granger grins. "You try, I'll give you that. You just need a bit of help."

Inside the pub, the Saturday lunchtime rush is in full swing, most of the tables occupied by families tucking into fish and chips, pizzas or macaroni cheese.

The detectives walk across the room to the bar. A woman with an unruly mop of dark hair wipes her brow and sighs as she does her best to serve a huddle of thirsty customers. Watching her work, but not lifting a finger to help, is a rotund, grey-haired man leaning against a chiller fridge.

Kane catches his eye and beckons him over. The man shakes his head and points at the barmaid.

"You'll have to wait your turn like everybody else, mate."

Kane waves his identification. "Police. I need to speak to whoever is in charge here. And quickly, please."

The man straightens up, steps closer and squints at the warrant card. He looks up at Kane to check the face matches the photograph. "I'm Joe Bell, the landlord here. How can I help you, Detective Inspector?"

"We're investigating the disappearance of a woman. Sam Hunter. According to her phone records, she was here last Thursday, early evening."

Granger steps forward and places a photograph of the reporter on the bar.

"Yeah, she was here all right. Not for long. I remember because she was with Digger. He comes in here a lot in the winter. Always sits by the fire. What's the old rascal done now?"

Kane picks up the photograph and hands it back to Granger. "Did you speak to him or the woman?"

"No. They seemed to be having quite a heated conversation."

"About what?"

"Dunno. I don't eavesdrop on my customers."

Kane's phone rings. He checks the screen. It's Rebecca Baxter. He declines the call. Too busy. Also, he's not in the mood for another earful about how he let her down.

"Did Digger and the woman leave together?" Granger asks.

Bell rubs his double chins. "Don't think so. No. Digger went off on his own. The other two left together."

Granger shoots Kane a look. "Do you know who the other person was?"

Bell shrugs. "No idea. Tallish guy. Darkish hair. He bought the drinks. Bit cocky for my liking. Reckon he thought a lot of himself."

Kane quickly scans the ceiling and walls. "Have you any security cameras in this place? Or outside in the car park?"

"Nah, we don't need them. Not a lot a crime in this village. It's quiet. Everybody minds their own business."

Kane doubts Bell is as naive as he sounds. He's just too mean to fork out for a security system.

"I'm going to arrange for one of my officers to take you to the station to give a detailed description of the man with Sam Hunter to one of our E-FIT operators."

Bell frowns. "I've got a pub to run. Can you make it tomorrow morning?"

"This can't wait."

Kane eyes Granger. "Can you call Weaver? Get him to bring an E-FIT expert out here as soon as possible."

Granger gets on the phone and turns away from the bar while she waits for Weaver to answer.

"How about that? You don't even have to leave your pub."

Bell still doesn't look happy. "Why can't you just have a word with Digger? He'll be able to tell you the guy's name, won't he?"

"Digger is dead. Murdered."

The colour drains from Bell's face. "God no. Not Digger. You're joking."

"Do I look like I think this is funny?"

"And the missing woman. You think she's been murdered too?"

The honest answer is that she almost certainly has. Kane can't bring himself to accept that yet. "We won't give up until we find her."

Back in the car, Kane's phone rings again. He gives Granger an apologetic grimace. "It's Baxter."

"Why don't you take it? It might be important."

"I haven't got time to debate the rights and wrongs of what I did with her criminal profile. My focus is on finding Sam Hunter and we need to speak to her parents."

CHAPTER 40

The shivering is getting worse. Uncontrollable. Cold in her bones. Fear in her heart. Behind the blindfold the darkness deepens by the minute. The oily cloth filling her mouth makes her want to vomit. If she does, she'll choke.

Sam Hunter lies curled on her side, the dirt floor cold and damp against her right cheek. She draws her knees up into the foetal position. The bindings on her wrists and ankles cut deep into her skin with every movement.

"They will find me." She repeats the phrase over and over in her head like a desperate prayer. Hope is all she has left. Brady or her parents will report her missing. They must come for her soon. While she can still breathe. While her heart still beats. Before he returns.

When he does come back, he'll kill her. She knows that to be the truth. He has no choice.

Sam reaches down, wraps her fingers around the rope tied around her ankles and yanks it, one, two, three times. Blood trickles down her wrists, the gag stifling her cries of agony. She rolls on to her back, her breathing ragged. She's no action hero. She has no training she can call on. She's a novice reporter and not a particularly good one.

A car passes by. Close enough for her to hear the engine revving. Sam hears shouting, then laughter. She inhales deeply through her nose and tries with all her might to scream. The sound is muffled and she swallows back the bile rising in her throat.

Life goes on around her while she lies helpless in the dark. She can only wait. When he comes for her, she'll ask for mercy. Beg for her life. She'll plead with him not to inject her with a fatal dose of insulin, then hang her corpse for all the world to see.

CHAPTER 41

The Hunters' home is a rectangular, detached house tucked away in a cul-de-sac in the affluent Southend suburb of Thorpe Bay.

Hands in pockets, coat collars turned up, Kane and Granger walk along the garden path to the wooden front door. It's a cold, grey winter's day, the sky obscured by a blanket of menacing clouds.

Before either of them can ring the bell, the door opens. Judy Hunter waves them in.

"Come on, get inside," she says, her voice quivering with a forced cheerfulness. "You must be freezing. Come quickly, I'm letting all the heat out."

Her shoulder-length greying hair is unkempt, her face haggard with worry. Still, she manages a half-smile of welcome. The detectives step inside and she leads them into a small living room. Her husband is sitting on the sofa, his balding head bowed, his eyes fixed on the grey patterned carpet. She sits beside him and places a hand gently on his knee. "It's the police, dear. They've come to talk to us about Sam."

Alan Hunter raises his head slowly and stares at them, solemn-eyed. He doesn't speak. After a few seconds, he drops his gaze back to the carpet.

"I'm Detective Inspector Kane. This is Detective Sergeant Granger. We're here to ask you a few questions about your daughter, if you feel up to it."

Judy Hunter nods. "Don't mind Alan. He's struggling. We both are, really. Sitting here waiting for news is hard. You feel so helpless."

"Of course, I understand how you must be feeling."

It's true. Kane knows exactly how it feels to fear for a loved one. To cling on to hope. Right now, he wants nothing more than to save them from the clutches of unimaginable grief.

"Can you remember when you last saw or spoke to Sam?"

"Well, we haven't seen her in person since she started working for the *Herald*. That must have been about three, maybe four months ago. I suppose she's been busy. Trying to make a good impression. She does call quite regularly though. I think we last spoke to her a few days ago. That's right, isn't it, Alan?"

Her husband stays silent, his eyes fixed firmly on the floor.

"How did she seem?"

"She sounded happy. Full of beans as usual. She's always cheerful, our Sam."

"Did she say anything about being excited about a big story she was working on?"

"Oh no. She never discusses her work with us, and we never ask her about it. To be honest with you, we never wanted her to go into journalism. We don't think she's cut out for it. She's a clever girl, she really is. But she's too nice for that world. Too gentle."

From what he's seen of the reporter, Kane reckons their daughter is probably a lot tougher and even smarter than they think she is. He decides it's time to leave. They're not gaining any useful information here and every second counts. He looks across at Granger and gives her a nod.

She takes a step closer to the sofa and crouches down on one knee, to look Sam's mother in the eye.

"We're going to go now but we'll be sending a family liaison officer over later today. They are specially trained to help families in your situation. If something occurs to you that you think might be important then you must tell them."

To Kane's surprise, Alan Hunter lifts his head and fixes Granger with a glare. "What do you think has happened to our Sam? Is she dead? Tell me the truth. Is she? She's a good person. A kind person. We told her not to take that job."

He drops his head and hides his face in his hands. His wife moves to comfort him. He shrugs her off.

"I wish we had answers for you," Granger says gently. "What I can tell you is that we are doing all we can to bring you daughter back safely. We certainly haven't given up hope and neither should you. Every available officer we have is on the streets looking for Sam. Everything that can be done is being done."

Alan sits up straight, his eyes red, his cheeks damp. "We can't lose her. Not our Sam."

Judy stands. She's flustered, even a little embarrassed, by her husband's sudden show of emotion.

"I'm sure everyone's doing their best," she says.

Kane moves to leave. He hesitates and turns back. Alan Hunter's anger and fear has got to him. The sadness in those eyes touched a nerve.

"I can assure you both that we are doing everything possible to find your daughter. We won't stop until we have. I promise you that."

CHAPTER 42

Granger unlocks her front door and steps gingerly inside. It's the third day in a row that she's hasn't made it home until after midnight. Although she hates letting her mum and Daisy down, she has no choice. Murder victims deserve justice and Sam Hunter's life may be in the balance.

She takes off her shoes and creeps softly along the hall to the staircase. Her bed is calling and she can't wait to crash out.

Passing the living room, she notices that the light is on. She opens the door to find her brother sprawled in an armchair, a stern expression on his face.

"Why are you still here? Are Daisy and Mum okay?"

"They're fine. What about you? You look terrible."

"Thanks. You don't look that wonderful yourself."

Marcus sits up straight. "I don't see how you're going to be able to make this work, Bailey."

"What do you mean?"

"You're always coming home this late, way after Daisy is in bed. Leaving in the morning before she's even awake. You've hardly seen her for days straight. I'm worried for Daisy, and to be honest, for you too."

Granger's head rocks back, as though she's been slapped hard in the face. If her brother wants an argument then he's going to get one. Her bed will have to wait.

"I'm working a murder investigation. Have you any idea what that involves? Three people have been killed. A young woman is missing. We're trying to find her before she becomes the fourth victim."

Marcus holds up his hands. "I get it. I really do. You've misunderstood me, or more likely I've not explained properly. What you do is important. A matter of life and death. I never realised how dedicated you need to be. How long and hard your working days are."

Granger's brain is telling her that he means well. The sensible thing to do is to take a deep breath, stay calm and walk away.

Her heart is telling her something different. Marcus has to accept that his little sister is all grown up. She's in charge of her life. She makes the decisions.

"You and Sterling hated me joining the police. But I love being a detective. Everything about it. It's because I do what I do that I know for sure who and what I am. That can only be good for Daisy. I want her to see that her mother is doing something that matters to her."

Marcus gets to his feet. He gives her a sheepish smile. "I didn't intend to upset you. I'm sorry. I'm just suggesting you need to have a rethink about how we can make this work for you, that's all. I'm happy to help out for another week. Then I'm back at work. I know chemical engineering's not as glamorous as hunting murderers. Still, I need to earn a living."

Granger wasn't expecting him to give in so easily. He always used to have to have the last word.

"Don't think I don't appreciate you helping us out. I do. When you go back to work, we'll manage. Don't worry yourself about that. Mum's getting stronger by the day."

Marcus zips up his jacket.

"Mum's also getting older by the day and we have to accept that. We've had a scare with what's happened and I know we all don't want to lose her. If I can help out again, I will. If you want me to, that is. I'll show myself out. I'll be back in time to take Daisy to school as usual."

Granger waits until she hears the door close before crashing onto the sofa. She leans back and lets out a long breath. Was she too hard on him? Maybe. He sounded like he actually cared about her. She closes her eyes and starts to feel herself sliding into the arms of sleep.

Her phone rings in her pocket and she jerks awake. She checks the screen. It's Kane. Her first impulse is to let it ring out and take herself to bed. Then she reasons he wouldn't be ringing at this hour if it wasn't urgent. Curiosity and a sense of duty gets the better of her.

"Don't you ever sleep?" she says.

"Sleeping is overrated."

"I need my bed right now."

"Listen a minute. What happened about the E-FIT?"

Granger struggles to clear her head. "Er, we sent an E-FIT operator out to the Crown pub to compile an image of the man seen with Digger and Sam Hunter."

"That's right. You called PC Weaver. Asked him to organise it. I've not seen it."

"Me neither."

Kane falls silent. Granger can sense that he's struggling to stay calm.

"I've called him a dozen times. He's not picking up. Can you get in as early as possible tomorrow? Have a word with him. Sort this mess out."

Granger had hoped to have breakfast with Daisy before she left for school. No chance of that happening now.

"I'll see to it first thing."

CHAPTER 43

She's too exhausted to shiver now. Her muscles too weak to contract. The red raw soreness of her ankles and wrists has eased, her torn flesh numbed by the cold. The darkness is impenetrable. Timeless. She can't tell whether it's day or night. The only thing that she knows for sure is that she's dying.

Her mind wanders. She sees a black sky crammed with stars. Hears the hypnotic lapping of waves on a pebble beach. She's looking down, free of the blindfold, and can see herself lying on her side, like a broken doll. Her face glows, almost translucent, in the darkness. Fear shoots through her like an electric current and in an instant she's back. She moves her head from side to side to reassure herself that she's not dead yet.

She hasn't given up. It's just that she knows her fate. He won't be coming back. He's abandoned her. Left her to die. A slow, lingering death. She wants to cry. Tears won't come. She's too tired, too numb, too sad to weep.

She'll never see her mum and dad again. This will tear their lives apart. Her foolishness has condemned them to an endless grief. She'll never achieve anything. Never make her mark in the world. Remembered only as a victim.

What has she done to deserve this? She's never harmed anyone. She's tried to be a good person.

Her parents did their best to dissuade her from becoming a reporter. You're not exactly streetwise, darling. You're too kind-hearted to be cunning. If you swim with sharks, you'll get eaten alive. She knew they were right but couldn't wait to prove them wrong.

Sam closes her eyes. She has a sudden urge to sleep. To drift away from the horror. After a few seconds, her eyes flutter open. She forces herself to stare into the blackness of the blindfold. If she sleeps, she tells herself, she might not wake up.

Metal grinds on metal. Her heart leaps. Someone's coming. They've found her. She tries to shout for help, chokes on the gag, splutters and groans.

Light footsteps. She catches a waft of citrus aftershave. This isn't her saviour. It's her Angel of Death. From the moment she'd climbed into the car she knew something was wrong.

Fingers untie her blindfold, then the strip of cloth around her mouth. He removes the gag, taking care not to hurt her. She coughs, spits and splutters.

"Don't shout or I'll gag you again. Nobody will hear you anyway, it's the middle of the night."

Sam blinks, staring up at her captor's silhouette. He turns away. Perhaps he's ashamed to look her in the eyes. Her prison is small and damp. Dirty brick walls, a muddy floor.

"Please let me go. I'll do anything you want me to. Please don't hurt me."

"Stop it. Stop whining."

Her instinct is to keep pleading until he relents. She clamps her lips tight. Making him angry won't help. She needs to keep him sweet. Appeal to his sane side. If he has one.

He walks around her, puts his hands under her arms and lifts her into a sitting position.

"It'll be easier for both of us if you accept what's happening to you. There's no way out of this."

"You don't need to kill me. I'm not a threat. I don't have to tell the police anything if you don't want me to."

Sam's throat is dry. Her brain is so scrambled it hurts to think. She's sure this is the only chance she's going to get to save herself.

"Even though I don't understand why you've done what you've done, I know you must have your reasons."

The man who holds her life in his hands gives her a killer smile, his eyes shining with amusement. If you didn't know you'd never guess that behind the charm lurks a cold-hearted monster.

"I'm surprised you're still alive," he says. "To be honest, it's been so cold I thought I'd find a corpse."

The tone of his voice is matter-of-fact. Sam shudders with fear. If he leaves her again, she won't last another night.

"I'm cold, hungry and thirsty. Please don't do this. I'm begging you."

He picks the gag up off the floor and tries to tie it around Sam's face. She resists, shaking her head desperately back and forth. He stands up, hands on hips and glares down at her.

"You know, I can end this for you now. It would be for the best. No drawn-out death. No pain. No suffering. All this will be over. What do you think? Would you like me to do that for you?"

Sam's mind is spinning. He's talking to her and she thinks that's a good thing. If she can get to him, engage with him, convince him that she's no threat, maybe there's still hope.

"I don't know why you're doing this, but whatever I've done, I'm sorry. I really am. I've always been a good judge of people and I know that deep down you're not a bad person. Please don't hurt me."

She looks him in the eye as her tears flow. He watches her silently, a curious smile on his face.

"Don't you understand that I'm offering to do something nice for you? End your suffering quickly."

Sam can't believe what she's hearing. "You think killing me is something I should be grateful for?"

He gives a nonchalant shrug. "You're scared of dying. I get that. There's no reason to be. You'll simply cease to exist. I've watched people die. Stared into their eyes until they slipped away. They all looked so peaceful. Surprisingly beautiful."

Sam shudders again. She realises trying to talk him into untying her and letting her walk away is futile. Her best option is to play for time and pray that the police will find her.

"Please leave me alone. Just go. I'd rather be left alone."

"Face it — if I leave you here, you're going to die anyway."

She knows it. But she's not ready to give in. She takes a deep breath and summons all the courage she can find. "I'm not scared of dying. I'm not. I'm scared of not living."

"Let's see, shall we?"

A muscular arm wraps around her throat and squeezes just tight enough to make it hard to breathe. Her heart flutters inside her chest like a butterfly trapped in a jar.

Sam feels herself slipping away. Doubt and fear flood her mind. She fights to stay conscious. An endless blackness beckons.

CHAPTER 44

Kane had woken up that morning with a fresh surge of determination. Sam Hunter vanished three days ago. His gut is telling him that if they are to have any hope of saving her they have to find her, or at least track down the Hangman, in the next forty-eight hours.

DC Kush enters his office. "Everything is ready for Hunter's parents to make their public appeal. They are both terrified at the prospect, but they're willing to do anything if there's a chance it'll get their daughter back."

Kane wishes there was a way to avoid putting the couple through the ordeal of appearing on TV. The plan is for them to make a general appeal for information and possible sightings. Then, they'll speak directly to the killer in the hope that he's watching. They'll plead for their daughter's return. Beg him for mercy, even though Kane suspects he doesn't have a single merciful cell in his body.

"We're at the stage where we have to throw everything we've got at this. If they're ready, let's go now. There's no time to waste. Get the media office to alert the press and have them here as soon as possible."

* * *

Judy Hunter takes her husband's hand in hers, squeezes it tightly and looks straight down the lens of the television camera. She lifts her chin, her lower lip quivering.

"Our Sam is precious. Always has been, always will be. We can't imagine living our lives without her."

Kane is watching, just out of shot, his back against the wall, his arms crossed. He's decided to let Granger handle the press this time. He's happy to observe.

Sam's mother lifts her free hand to sweep a stray lock of grey hair off her forehead. She glances nervously at Granger beside her, and down at her script, before carrying on.

"We want our Sam back safe and sound. We are ordinary people. We usually don't like being the centre of attention. But we're doing this today because we're desperate. We'd do anything for our daughter. That's why I'm asking anyone who knows anything about Sam's whereabouts or what has happened to her to come forward and contact the police. Even the tiniest bit of information could help us find her. Something that might seem insignificant could turn out to be an important clue."

She pauses and looks to her husband. Kane knows that Alan Hunter has been briefed that this is his moment to take over and make his own plea. He bows his head and refuses to look at the camera.

His wife leans in and whispers urgently in his ear. He looks up, his haggard face as grey as his hair, his eyes haunted.

"I just can't do it. I'm sorry," he mumbles.

Judy Hunter reaches across and picks up her husband's script. She scans it quickly. Takes a long, deep breath.

"Alan isn't feeling up to this right now, so I'm going to do his bit for him."

She forces a half-smile. Kane's heart goes out to her. She's more resilient than she looks. He hopes Sam has inherited some of her mother's strength.

"Our beautiful girl has been missing for three days now. She'd never leave without telling us where she was going. The police believe she was taken against her will. The thought terrifies us. We can't sleep. We can't eat. If the person who took Sam is watching this, please let her go, or tell us where we can find her. Please, please, whatever you do, don't harm her. She's kind, an innocent soul, who's just starting out in life. I beg you with all my heart. Send her back to us."

She drops the script onto the table and rubs her eyes with her hands. An awed hush falls over the room. Kane knows they've all witnessed TV gold and that the footage will be featured in full on every prime-time news bulletin.

The Hunters stand up and fall into each other's arms. Dana Steen steps from the sidelines and leads them away to a sympathetic burst of applause from the assembled journalists.

After a few seconds, Granger holds up a hand for silence. "We have time for a couple of questions. No more."

A balding journalist wearing a crumpled linen jacket and thick-framed designer glasses stands up and identifies himself. "Tom Wallis, of the *Daily Chronicle*. We all know that Sam Hunter is a local journalist and was covering the hunt for the Hangman. Can you confirm that her abduction is connected to the recent murders?"

Granger pauses and looks quickly across at Kane. He knew this question would be asked. That's why he arranged for the Hunters to be taken out after they finished. It's crucial to keep the focus on their appeal for information that might help find their daughter.

"This press conference is about bringing Sam Hunter home safely. That's all. We are still treating her disappearance as a missing person investigation. We have no evidence that she has been harmed. We will continue to do everything within our power, use every resource available, to bring her back safe and sound."

A dark-haired woman in a bright red jacket sitting in the front row, jumps in with another question. "Anita Shar, *Daily Post*. Given that Sam has been missing for three days, is there really any chance that she's still alive? That strikes me as being overly optimistic."

A murmur of excitement ripples around the room.

Kane catches Granger's eye again and gives her a nod, their prearranged signal for her to end the conference.

"As I explained a few moments ago, this case is still a missing person inquiry. If anybody has any information about this young woman's whereabouts, please contact us immediately. Thank you for attending on such short notice this morning."

Kane watches the reporters file out of the room, his expression grim. Anita Shar is right. Every hour that passes reduces the odds of them finding Sam Hunter alive.

CHAPTER 45

Kane leaves the conference room, striding purposefully along the narrow corridor, glad to be able to get back to proper police work.

Appeals to the public for information are important. He accepts that. But at the core of every murder investigation is the incident room.

As soon as Kane steps inside, DS Alex Scott waves him over to his desk.

"Come take a look at this. We've found a good CCTV image of Sam Hunter getting into a car, a dark blue Ford Focus, a few hundred yards from her office."

He waits for Kane to pull up a chair before pressing the play button.

Although the footage is grainy, Kane can make out Hunter running along the pavement in the rain. She peers through the front passenger window and appears to speak to someone before getting inside.

"What about the driver? Do we get to see his face?"

Scott shakes his head. "No such luck, I'm afraid. The angle of the camera is all wrong."

Kane watches the car pull off the kerb and into the traffic. The rear number plate is clearly visible.

"We've checked the registration number. No matches. The plates must be false."

Kane isn't surprised. A traceable plate would be too much to ask for.

"Have you been able to pick the car up on camera anywhere else? A sighting that might give us an idea where it might be heading?"

"Not yet. I've requested the data from the area's Automatic Number-Plate Recognition cameras. Should have it in a couple of hours."

"Good work, Alex. Let me know right away if you get anything new."

Kane walks across the room, hesitates and turns back.

"Where's PC Weaver, Alex? He was supposed to organise an E-FIT for me and I thought he was helping you view CCTV footage."

Scott grimaces. "He's called in sick this morning. Won't be in today."

"What's wrong with him?"

"Didn't say exactly. Just said he's struggling. I reckon he's a bit of a delicate flower."

Kane shakes his head in despair and moves on to the whiteboard. He takes a moment to look at the photographs of the murder victims. The Golding brothers and David "Digger" Dines seem to return his gaze. At the top of the board, on its own, is the larger headshot of a smiling Sam Hunter.

He liked her from their first meeting. Her irrepressible innocence and excitement for life.

Kane needs his team to believe that she could still be alive. The truth is her fate was probably sealed the moment she decided to get into that car. He shakes his head to push the thought away. She's still officially a missing person, not a murder victim. While there's no body, there's still hope.

Kane leaves the incident room and walks briskly along the corridor. As he reaches the door to his office, he hears someone running behind him.

Granger pulls up, breathing heavily. "It's the E-FIT," she says. "I sent an operator out to the pub. Told him it was urgent. You need to see it."

They enter the office, Granger still puffing. She dashes to Kane's desk and taps frantically at the keyboard of his computer.

"There. Come on. Take a look at this."

Kane bends and peers at the screen.

"This is the man the landlord of the Crown saw that night with Digger and Sam Hunter?"

Granger nods. "Do you see who I see?"

Kane stares at the electronically constructed image. The perfectly symmetrical oval face of a young man stares back at him. High cheekbones. Deep-set eyes, a long, straight nose. Short, dark hair, slightly wavy. Thin lips and a strong jawline.

It's a face Kane has seen before but he doesn't want to accept it. Not yet. He exchanges glances with Granger and takes another long look at the face on the screen. This time he's looking frantically for a reason to doubt what his eyes are telling him.

Maybe the nose is the wrong shape. And the lips too. They should be a lot fuller, shouldn't they?

Granger points a finger impatiently at the screen. "It's him, isn't it? It's got to be him. I knew it the first time I saw it."

Kane sits down. He struggling to take it in. He looks at the face one more time.

"I agree. It does look a lot like him."

"No. I'm telling you. It's not a lookalike. It is him. It's got to be."

Kane still doesn't want to believe his eyes. At last, they have the breakthrough that's going to solve the case. They have the face of the killer the press have dubbed the Hangman.

He should be punching the air in celebration. Instead, the image on the screen is his worst nightmare.

"Fuck. You're right. Let's bring Weaver in right now."

CHAPTER 46

Kane bangs hard on the door of Weaver's flat. "This is DI Kane. Open up."

He waits for a response. Nothing.

"You know the score," he shouts. "The neighbouring flats have been evacuated and armed officers have sealed off the block. This is your last chance to give yourself up or we're coming in."

Kane presses an ear to the door. Nothing. He steps back and beckons a burly uniformed constable carrying the 'big red key'.

The officer, wearing a visored helmet and full body armour, jogs forward. Kane gives him a nod and, with a loud grunt, he swings the steel battering ram at the door.

The lock shatters, and the wooden door crashes open. The constable's momentum takes him running into the flat. He's followed swiftly by two more uniforms.

Kane steps inside. The door opens straight into what is supposed to be a living area. It doesn't look as if anyone has been doing much living there. Bare floorboards. Not a single piece of furniture. No television. At the far end of the room is an alcove built for a mini kitchen. It's empty, except for a fridge.

One of the uniforms pokes his head around a door. "In here," he says.

Kane walks across and enters the room. It's small and square. Unlike the living room, it is carpeted. An unfurled grey sleeping bag lies along the wall under the window. Beside it, a large backpack.

"Make sure nobody touches anything," Kane says. He returns to the living area as Granger arrives.

"The firearms unit is standing down," she says. "Do you think he knew we were coming?"

Kane shrugs. "Who knows? How long has he been living here?"

"This is the address he gave Human Resources when he transferred from the Metropolitan Police to the Essex force a year ago."

"It doesn't look like he's into interior design, does it? Get this place sealed off and call Forensics. I've got to break the bad news to Helen Dean."

Granger walks slowly over to the fridge. "You know what you have to keep refrigerated, don't you?"

Kane joins her. "Yeah. Beer. Milk. Cheese."

"And insulin."

Granger bends and opens the fridge door. "Oh, shit."

On the drive back to the station Kane decides to try a mind trick he's used with some success before. Reverse engineering the facts of the case. Weaver took Sam Hunter because she knew of his connection to Digger Dines. He killed Digger because he had taken a photograph of him stealing the rowing boat he used to transport Tony Golding's body to Two Tree Island. He murdered Tony Golding and hung him from a tree because he was Adam Golding's brother. He killed Adam Golding and strung him up under the pier because... he was Adam Golding.

Granger pulls up in the car park and kills the engine. "Is everything all right? You've been very quiet."

"Everything's fine. I've been going over the investigation. Trying to work out the link between Weaver and the

Goldings. We'll have Weaver's DNA on the Essex force's elimination database, won't we?"

"That's right. All officers and staff must give a sample."

"Good. I want that run through all our databases and checked against the DNA of Adam and Tony Golding, first thing."

"I'll sort it."

CHAPTER 47

"Whatever you do, do not name the suspect. Not yet. The last thing we want is the press to know that the man we're hunting is a police officer."

Detective Superintendent Helen Dean is adamant. Kane understands why.

"I'm uncomfortable holding back on this. We're going to have him locked up soon and it's all going to have to come out anyway."

Dean shakes her head. "That's not the point and you know it, Edison. I need time to brief my superiors and prepare for the inevitable media onslaught. This case will damage public confidence in the police and cause widespread questioning of the integrity of our officers."

Kane checks the wall clock above Dean's head. He doesn't want to be wasting time talking force politics. He wants to be out on the streets finding out what happened to Sam Hunter and catching the killer cop who has betrayed the trust of the public and his colleagues.

"That's not really my concern. I need to get on with putting that evil bastard behind bars." He starts to rise.

Dean holds up a hand for him to stay put. "Sit down until I dismiss you."

Kane hesitates before deciding to get all the drama over in one go. He knows Dean will only summon him back to her office within the hour.

He sits down and she gives him the silent stare treatment for a few seconds. "How certain are we that PC Mark Weaver is the Hangman?"

"I'd like to say there's room for doubt. There isn't. The E-FIT is the spitting image of him and we found syringes and several vials of medical insulin in his fridge. The batch numbers match those stolen in a break-in at a pharmacy in east London when Weaver was still a Met officer."

Dean opens a beige folder on the desk in front of her and scribbles a note.

"And you seconded Weaver on to your team at the start of the investigation, didn't you?"

Kane smiles grimly. He knows what's going on. Dean has always been a good planner. That includes having all the information necessary to point the finger and provide the top brass and the press with a scapegoat.

"I did that, yes. Weaver found the first body while on an early morning run."

"Of course he did."

Dean makes another note. When she finishes, she puts the pen down, closes the file and drops it into a drawer.

"There's another reason it makes sense to keep the killer's identity a secret at this stage," she says. "You know as well as I do that once the media get hold of this it'll become their main focus. The big story. Bigger than the actual murders. A huge, unwanted distraction. Put an appeal for sightings out with the E-FIT but no other details. Not yet."

Kane wishes it was that simple. If someone works out that the killer is a police officer before it's officially announced, all hell will break loose. On top of everything else, they'll have to deal with accusations of a cover-up.

He gets to his feet. "Can I leave and get on with the job I'm paid to do now?"

Dean responds with a glare. Kane gives her a curt nod and walks out.

He slides behind the wheel of his car and pulls out his phone. He needs to fill Baxter in. She needs to be warned that the police officer claiming to be traumatised by the sight of Adam Golding hanging by the neck is the monster who murdered him and strung him up.

The call goes to voicemail.

"Hi, Rebecca, it's Kane. Could you call me back when you can? It's about PC Weaver and it's urgent."

CHAPTER 48

Rebecca Baxter's phone vibrates loudly on her desk. Her client stops talking and narrows his eyes in displeasure at the interruption.

"Ignore it," she says. "Please carry on."

Mark Weaver folds his arms across his chest and waits until the buzzing stops. He looks different. Scruffier than usual. His black tracksuit trousers and grey hoodie hang loosely on his frame and heavy stubble darkens his complexion.

"As I was saying, my mother was an extremely troubled woman. To tell you the truth, I can't remember a single day when she seemed happy with her life."

Baxter is surprised that Weaver is already willing to dive into the traumas of his childhood. It usually takes longer than a few sessions to reach this level of trust.

"I take it she had mental health problems?"

"Oh yeah, mental and physical. Even though I was a child I became her carer. Before school I'd get her ready for the day. After school I'd cook then get her ready for bed."

Baxter shifts in her seat, an uneasy flutter in her stomach. Something isn't quite right. Weaver is unnaturally eager to spit out details. Almost desperate.

"Why don't we slow things down a little? Let's talk about how you've been feeling since we last spoke. Are you sleeping any better?"

"I'm sleeping like a baby. The sleep of the guiltless. Satisfied? Now I'm going to talk about my mother."

Baxter frowns. Weaver is no longer the personable, polite young man who walked into the room. His face is slack, his gaze dead-eyed and his voice monotone. The session has taken an unexpected turn. She needs to tread carefully.

"All right, Mark. If you feel ready, then go for it. What would you like to tell me about her?"

"My mother was clinically depressed. She took antidepressants. They never did her any good. I reckon they made her worse. Suicidal."

"That must have been difficult for you. It would have been for any child. I take it your father wasn't around to help?"

Weaver clenches his fists, his knuckles a bloodless white. "I never met my father. He was never mentioned. All I knew about him was that he wasn't around."

"It sounds like you and your mother had it hard. I think she'd be proud. You've built yourself a life. A career in the police."

"I'm not here to whinge about how difficult life was for me. Pain and suffering can make you stronger if you have the will and the right mindset. Post-traumatic growth, you shrinks call it."

The phone vibrates again. Baxter glances nervously over her shoulder.

"Sorry about that. Let me put it on silent mode."

"Just leave the phone alone. I want you to concentrate on what I've got to say. Why don't you stop asking stupid questions and let me talk?"

Baxter's face flushes. She's never seen this side of Weaver before. Although she's used to dealing with difficult clients, this situation feels different.

"I'm going to have to end this session early if you carry on like this."

Weaver sits up straight and stares at the psychologist, his brown eyes darkening with menace.

"Am I scaring you? I hope not. There are things I need to tell you. Things I know you'll want to hear."

Baxter checks her watch. She's never felt this jittery during a session and there's still forty minutes left.

"We can carry on for a while but this is psychological therapy and I'm your therapist. If I feel that it's necessary to stop, then I will do so and you need to accept my decision."

"I don't have to accept anything people like you say to me. I learned that a long time ago. You shrinks can't control me. Never could."

Baxter jumps up out of her chair. "That's it, we're done. This is over. I want you to leave this minute."

Weaver leans back in his seat, puts his hands behind his head and smirks.

"You know, you need to do find yourself a good therapist to sort out your anger issues. I'm not going anywhere. You're going to listen to what I've got to say whether you like it or not."

Baxter's phone vibrates again. She eyes Weaver warily. His unnatural stillness makes the back of her neck tingle.

She steps quickly to her desk and picks the phone up. She sees it's Kane.

"I'll just take this outside."

Weaver doesn't move. "No. Stay where you are."

"Hello, The Baxter Clinic, how can I help you?"

"At last. I've been trying to get hold of you all afternoon."

She keeps her eyes on Weaver, fighting back an urge to scream down the phone.

"Listen, I'm with a client at the moment and can't talk, can I call you back later today?"

"This is important, Rebecca. Haven't you listened to my voicemails? It's Mark Weaver. He's the killer. He's the one who took the reporter. All this time he's been part of the team investigating the murders, hiding in plain sight."

"Ok then, yes. I understand. Thanks."

"Is everything all right, Rebecca? You sound scared. Is he there? Is Weaver with you? If yes, stay calm and tell me you're fully booked."

"All right then. Just give me a second and I'll check."

Baxter turns to her desk and flips through the pages of her appointment diary.

"I'm sorry. I'm all booked up this week. What about next Monday? I can fit you in at noon. Brilliant. See you then."

Before she can terminate the call, an arm encircles her neck and squeezes. She tries to twist free, frantically jabbing her right elbow into Weaver's ribcage.

He grunts loudly and tightens his grip. Baxter's vision blurs, the room spinning around her, faster and faster.

"I can't breathe," she gasps.

Weaver increases the pressure on the sides of her neck, compressing her carotid arteries, cutting off the supply of blood to her brain.

Baxter's knees give way, her body flopping like a ragdoll. So, she thinks, this is what dying feels like. She has no choice but to surrender as she plummets into the black abyss.

CHAPTER 49

She sits up, gasping for air. Her eyes widen at the sight of Weaver grinning at her. Her heart tries to beat its way out of her chest.

"Take it easy," he says. "Try to relax. The good news is you're not dead. Not yet."

Baxter's breathing is ragged. She looks down. She's handcuffed to the metal arm of her chair. She yanks her right arm as hard as she can. The carbon steel cuts into her wrist and she cries out.

"That was dumb. I thought you psychologists are supposed to be smart."

A thin rivulet of blood trickles from the gash on Baxter's wrist. "I thought you were going to kill me."

"It was close. I reckon if your brain had been deprived of oxygen for another six or seven seconds, you'd be dead. At least severely brain damaged."

"How long was I unconscious for?"

"A minute at the most."

Weaver raises a hand to show her he's holding her phone. "Don't worry yourself. We've got plenty of time before the cavalry get here. At least twenty minutes, I reckon. Maybe more."

Baxter can't fathom how he's staying so calm when he knows the police are on their way. Is he thinking of giving himself up once he's finished with her?

"What exactly do you want from me?"

"I told you. I want you to listen to what I've got to say. Listen carefully."

"Then what?"

"Then I'll decide whether you live or die."

Baxter swallows hard. She needs to focus. Her life depends on figuring out what this cold-hearted killer needs to hear her say. How he wants her to react to his story.

"Go ahead, Mark. Tell me about your relationship with your mother. How did you feel when you found her body after she hanged herself?"

"Shut your mouth. Shut up."

Baxter stops talking. *Best not provoke him. Let him say what he has to say, encourage him even. Stay safe. Stay alive. Hope that Kane gets here soon.*

Weaver grips the arms of his chair. The veins on the backs of his hands bulge and his jaw clenches.

"My mother's name was Rose. She had the worst start to life anyone could imagine. Abandoned as a newborn. No more than two days old. Left in a cardboard box on a stranger's doorstep."

Weaver pauses. Looks at Baxter expectantly. She hesitates, scared to say the wrong thing.

He holds his stare, his eyes flashing. Baxter caves. "That's terribly sad. Tragic. It must be so hard for a person to come to terms with something like that."

"She never did. She spent her childhood in various care homes. When she was nineteen, she had me and life got even worse for her."

Baxter considers reassuring him that his mother wouldn't have thought that way. That he would have been loved. She thinks better of it. Only he knows the truth.

"I suppose hanging herself was the best thing she could do," Weaver says. "The only way out. It ended her suffering. Her miserable existence."

Weaver glances up at the wall clock. Time is running out.

Baxter wants to keep him talking. "I'm sure you did your best for her. You were a child. I'm sure you did all you could."

Weaver tilts his head and frowns. "Did I? I tried, I suppose. I made sure she took her antidepressants every day. She was diabetic too. Born with it. Sometimes I'd have to inject her with insulin because she couldn't be bothered. A fourteen-year-old boy and I had to inject my own mother to keep her alive. Then she goes and hangs herself anyway. After everything I did for her."

He falls silent and Baxter senses she's supposed to react to this revelation. She decides the safest thing is to say nothing.

Weaver slips his right hand into his jacket pocket and pulls out a knife. His fingers caress the black handle as he wipes both sides of the serrated blade on his sleeve.

"Nothing to say all of a sudden? I've never had a shrink go shy on me before. Usually you can't stop them voicing their overrated opinions."

Baxter fixes her gaze on the knife. Cold beads of sweat trickle down the back of her neck. "It's a lot to take in. Your story is unique."

"You should feel honoured, you know. You're the only shrink I've told the truth to."

"Why me?"

"I want to know what you think. I'd like to hear your verdict on why I turned out the way I have. Murderous."

Baxter is struggling to think clearly. Her focus is firmly on the knife in Weaver's hand.

"Do you feel any sympathy for me?" Weaver asks.

"Maybe. A little. You've suffered a lot."

"Do you believe the trauma of finding my mother's hanging body made me a murderer?"

"Er, maybe. It's possible it triggered something inside you. What you saw that day you can never unsee."

Weaver gets up out of the chair, brandishing the knife. "How disappointing. Wrong answer. I know for a fact that isn't true. You're just like the rest of them. Full of bullshit."

Weaver jabs the point of the knife at Baxter's face. She flinches. He grins at her fear.

She needs to get him talking again. Stall him until Kane arrives.

"Why did you murder the Golding brothers? They weren't random killings, were they? They were personal."

He jabs the knife at her again. She jerks her head away. "Please don't do that. What have you done with Sam Hunter? Is she still alive?"

Weaver gives her a knowing smile. "No comment."

He steps closer, slips the knife under her chin and holds the blade against her neck.

"I read on the internet that if someone slits your throat, you'll be dead in thirty seconds."

Baxter swallows back the sour taste in her mouth. She's not ready. All those years studying the human mind and still she's not prepared for this.

Weaver pulls the knife away and steps back. "Don't worry. I won't be cutting your throat. Much too messy."

He puts the knife back in his jacket. "That isn't for killing. I carry it purely for self-defence. You can't be too careful. There are a lot of nasty characters walking the streets. The world is full of bad people."

Weaver digs into his trouser pocket, pulls out a small black case, unzips it and shows Baxter the contents. A syringe and several vials of clear liquid.

"This will do the job nicely. Send you deep into a never-ending sleep. Once the brain stops getting enough glucose, well, that's it. Sweet dreams. It works best in fatty tissue so I usually like to inject into the belly. But I guess you're not going to keep still for me."

Baxter tenses her body and wraps her free arm tightly around her stomach. "You don't have to do this. Why would you want to hurt me?"

"Why not?"

"Because I don't believe I deserve it. I've only ever tried to help you, haven't I? I still can if you let me. When Kane catches up with you, and you know he will, we can carry on with the therapy. It'll help you come to terms with what you've done."

Weaver laughs. "You don't really believe that, do you? What about the criminal profile you did for Kane? According to you, my mind is twisted and tortured. I'm an evil exhibitionist. You warned the public that behind my mask of sanity lurks a monster."

"Those weren't my words. I promise you. Kane embellished the profile for the press conference. He wanted to provoke you. Force you to do something rash."

Weaver eyes her curiously. "If that's true, then it looks like he succeeded."

Baxter watches him line up three vials of insulin on the table. He fills the syringe expertly and checks the needle. Death is a pinprick away.

"Listen to me, Mark. You haven't time for this. You've got to get going now. Kane will be here any second. Please just leave. Don't do this."

Weaver gives her a grim smile and closes in, syringe in hand. He points it at her right shoulder. She twists her torso and grabs at his wrist. She realises his move is a feint too late.

He ducks swiftly, jabs the needle into the fleshy part of her left thigh, and empties the syringe.

CHAPTER 50

On Kane's instructions, the two marked cars clearing the way keep their sirens silent. Racing through the streets, their bright blue lights flicker across the buildings.

Kane follows, his knuckles white on the steering wheel as he fills Granger in.

"Weaver is with Rebecca at her therapy centre. I called her and she sounded terrified. I've called out an armed response unit and I want the roads sealed off. I'm going in the front door. You make sure the back of the building is secure."

"You're not waiting for the armed officers?"

"No time."

The patrol cars screech to a halt outside a modern low-rise building. Kane pulls up behind them. He leaps out of the car and runs straight for the door to Baxter's tiny reception area, sprints upstairs and bursts through the consulting room door, followed swiftly by two uniforms.

Baxter is slumped in her chair, her head bowed, her body shaking uncontrollably. Kane crouches on one knee beside her.

"What's he done to you? Are you hurt?"

She lifts her head slowly. "Help me," she slurs. "In-su-lin."

Kane cradles her face in his hands and slaps her lightly on the cheek.

"Come on, Rebecca. Everything's going to be all right. Just keep those eyes open. Can you do that for me?"

He turns to the uniforms.

"Call an ambulance. Get these handcuffs off her and keep her awake until the medics get here. Do anything you can to stop her falling asleep."

Standing up, he scans the room. The door leading to the back of the building is ajar. Weaver's way out.

Kane rushes down the concrete stairway and barges through the fire door.

Dusk has fallen and the car park is unlit. Kane spots Granger flanked by two uniforms standing by the exit barrier. He jogs over. Granger shakes her head.

"No luck," she says. "We must have just missed him. Probably by no more than a minute or two. What about Rebecca? She okay?"

A siren wails close by, the armed response unit arriving. Kane grimaces in frustration. A minute earlier and they would've had the bastard. One minute. One evil act. One moment of life and death.

"Weaver handcuffed her to her chair and injected her in the thigh. I don't think she's going to make it."

CHAPTER 51

Kane jogs behind the paramedics wheeling the stretcher along the airless, starkly lit hospital corridor.

An emergency doctor in full scrubs and a mask appears from nowhere, firing a barrage of questions about the patient's condition. The quick-fire exchange is too technical for Kane to understand but its urgency confirms they're in a race against time.

He keeps his gaze on Baxter, searching for signs of life. An oxygen mask covers the lower half of her face, her eyes closed. A thin tube feeds clear fluid into a vein in her left arm.

At the end of the corridor, the paramedics steer the stretcher through double doors. The doctor raises a hand to stop Kane.

"That's as far as you go," she says. "Best you stay out here and let us do our jobs. Are you family?"

Kane shakes his head. "Police. She's a crime victim. Is she going to die?"

"She's sinking into a hypoglycaemic coma. We need to act fast, so stop asking stupid questions."

The doctor pushes through the doors and before they swing shut, Kane catches a glimpse of masked emergency staff moving purposefully around the patient, inserting more tubes, hooking her up to an array of flashing devices.

He turns away, walks a short way back along the corridor and sits on the end of a row of red plastic chairs, his back against the wall. He drops his head into his hands and takes a deep breath.

His phone rings. It's Granger.

"Please tell me you've got him."

"Sorry, not yet," she says. "We've got every available officer scouring the streets."

"He must be holed up somewhere."

"We'll get him. He's got to be panicking now. He'll slip up. One of the civilian researchers looking into Weaver's background has found something significant. He was the only child of a single mother who hanged herself when he was fourteen. He spent the next four years in various children's homes. He stayed in the care system until he was eighteen, then as soon as he had the chance, he joined the Met Police. His service record is good."

Kane turns to the sound of footsteps. It's the doctor he spoke to earlier.

"Sorry, I've got to go, I want to check Rebecca is going to be okay before I leave the hospital. I'll be heading back soon but I know you've got everything covered without me for a couple of hours."

He ends the call, slips his phone into his jacket pocket and stands, his heart suddenly pounding.

"How's she doing? Is she going to be all right?"

The doctor is wearing a black knee-length open raincoat over her scrubs. Without the surgical mask, Kane can see she's half his age.

"You said you're police?" she asks.

"I'm a friend, Doctor Joshi," he says, eyeing her name badge, "and a colleague. Detective Inspector Kane. I'm leading the investigation into a series of murders. Rebecca was attacked by the killer and, if she survives, she'll be a vital witness."

"You're talking about the Hangman, aren't you?"

"That's what the tabloids call him."

The doctor pauses to zip up her coat. "Well, Inspector, your friend has survived. We were able to get enough glucagon into her to pull her out of the coma. It's an insulin antidote and works fast if you get it into the patient quickly."

Kane heaves a sigh of relief. "When can I speak to her? Is she awake?"

The doctor hesitates, weighing up the situation. "I suppose you can see her now, but be brief. It's past midnight and she's been through a lot."

Kane pushes the door slowly and enters the room. She's lying on her back, her hair splayed on the crisp white pillow. She's breathing softly, her eyes closed. A vital-signs monitor beeps loudly beside her. She doesn't stir.

He decides to let her sleep and starts to retreat as quietly as he can. She turns her head to look at him. "Don't go."

He hesitates. "I didn't want to wake you, I'm sorry."

"I've done enough sleeping. Why don't you take a seat?"

Kane pulls a grey metal and canvas chair closer to the bed and sits.

"They say you're going to be fine."

Baxter manages a smile. "Apparently so. I was lucky, I guess. If I hadn't been treated so promptly, I'd have, well, you know."

It's Kane's turn to try to summon a smile. He fails miserably. "I'm sorry, Rebecca."

"You're in an unusually apologetic mood. What exactly are you sorry for?"

Kane isn't sure where to start. "I sent Weaver to you. Put you in danger."

"You did. But you couldn't have known."

Baxter closes her eyes for a few seconds. "He's a master deceiver. He deceived us all. Don't beat yourself up."

Kane knows what she's saying is true. It doesn't make it any easier for him to accept.

Baxter raises herself on to her elbows with a grunt and slides up the bed. Kane jumps up and adjusts her pillows, enabling her to sit up.

"Weaver got away, didn't he?"

Kane sits back down. "We missed him. He slipped out the back before we were able to seal the building off. Don't worry. A uniformed officer is on duty outside this room twenty-four seven. There's no way he can get to you here."

Baxter frowns and Kane realises that the thought that Weaver might attempt to finish what he'd started hadn't crossed her mind.

She takes a long deep breath. As she exhales, her body shudders. "Do you really think he could come for me?"

Kane would like to reassure her. "When he hears on the news that he's failed to kill you, who knows how he'll react? How did he seem to you?"

Baxter grimaces in disgust. She reaches for a glass on her bedside table and takes a sip of water.

"I think he's unravelling. To plan the first two murders, carry them out and keep living the life of a police officer must have taken immense control. He's lost that. I believe he knows the game's up. He feels backed into a corner and he's becoming more and more unpredictable."

She leans back against the pillow and shuts her eyes. Kane can tell that dwelling on what happened is draining her energy.

"When you're feeling stronger, I'll need you to give a full official statement about your encounter with Weaver. For now, I've just got one more question for you. If you feel up to it."

Baxter drains the glass of water and places it down.

"Okay. Go ahead."

"Did Weaver say anything about Sam Hunter? Anything at all. Where she might be, whether or not she's still alive?"

Baxter pauses to gather her thoughts, screwing up her face in concentration. "He mainly wanted to tell me what a miserable life his mother had. How she was a foundling. You know, abandoned at birth. Left on a doorstep when she was only a few days old. As an adult she suffered depression and hanged herself when he was fourteen."

Kane stands up. He paces across the room. It sounds to him like Weaver's already started making excuses for what he's done. *Lots of people struggle through terrible childhoods and they don't end up killing people for fun.* He keeps those thoughts to himself.

"So he told you about his past but nothing about the present and Sam?"

"Actually, I brought her up. After he handcuffed me to the chair, I was desperate to keep him talking. I asked him directly what he'd done with her."

"What did he say?"

"He said 'no comment'."

"That was it? Nothing else?"

"That's all he said. I had a feeling that he was tempted to say more. That maybe he hadn't killed her."

"What makes you say that?"

"The self-satisfied smirk on his face. The knowing look in his eyes. He's relishing the power of holding her fate in his hands."

"You mean even if she is still alive, he could decide to kill her at any point?"

"That's exactly what I mean. Now you get yourself home. You look as exhausted as I feel."

Kane doesn't bother telling her that's he's unlikely to see his home until Weaver is behind bars and Sam Hunter is found, dead or alive. If she is still clinging on to life, she'll be waiting, hoping and praying that someone is coming for her. He put Weaver on the case. He can't let her down. He can't let her die.

Kane's phone rings. He snatches it out of his pocket and checks the screen.

"It's Granger. I've got to take it. I'll be back in a second."

He steps outside into the corridor.

"Hi, I'm still at the hospital."

"You need to hear this," Granger blurts. "But you're not going to believe it."

Her breathing is noisy. Like she's just run a four-minute mile.

"Go on then. What have you got."

"I've just taken a call from Forensics. They ran Weaver's DNA through all the databases like you asked and got two matches. Adam and Tony Golding."

Kane frowns. "That can't be right. It doesn't make sense. Weaver knew what he was doing. He was careful. Forensics didn't find anyone else's DNA at the murder scenes."

"They're not the sort of matches I mean."

"What then?"

"They were familial matches."

"Say again."

"Weaver is related to the Goldings. According to the DNA, he murdered his mother's brothers. He killed his uncles."

Kane takes a moment to let this news sink in.

"We're one hundred per cent sure about this?"

"DNA doesn't lie."

* * *

"It's all making some kind of twisted sense now," Baxter says, sitting up straight in the bed. "He told me his mother had been abandoned a few days after she was born."

It strikes Kane that she is more excited than shocked by the news. It's as if she's just discovered the missing piece in Weaver's psychological jigsaw.

"This is the motive we've been looking for," she says. "He killed Adam and Tony Golding because they were the last remaining members of the family that rejected his mother. Total erasure. That rejection was the cause of her depression and ultimately why she committed suicide."

Kane thinks she's probably right. In a way. He still won't accept the idea that Weaver is some kind of victim.

"Whatever happened to his mother. Whatever happened to him as a child. There's no justification for what he's done."

"I agree. There will be an explanation though."

This is one point that they'll never agree on.

"You're lying in that hospital bed, lucky to be alive, because Weaver tried to take your life."

"I don't think that it was personal."

Kane can't believe what he's hearing. Maybe Baxter's still suffering the effects of being in a coma.

"Murder is about as personal as it gets."

"It could be that he sees me as representing all the psychologists who let him down when he was a child."

"Maybe it's not that complicated. Maybe he's just plain bad."

CHAPTER 52

Weaver checks that he's not being watched with a quick glance over both shoulders before slipping the key in the door and stepping quickly inside.

He allows himself a self-satisfied smile as he walks into the kitchen and takes a cold beer out of the fridge. If he could reach, he'd give himself a big pat on the back.

Deciding to hole up in Tony Golding's tenth-floor flat turned out to be a masterstroke. *Who'd expect a murderer to be chilling out in his victim's home?*

Golding had been surprised to see him when he'd knocked on the door insisting that he return to the station to answer a few more questions. But once again the uniform worked its magic.

Even a hardened criminal like Golding didn't baulk when he produced his handcuffs. He'd walked meekly to his death like a lamb to the slaughter. Weaver smiles as he recalls the feeling of power it gave him.

He goes into the living room and slumps on the sofa. The tower block is the perfect place to lie low. The crime scene tape on the front door keeps looters away, and there's still power and running water.

He picks up the remote and puts the TV on, hopping through the channels in search of news about the psychologist. Nothing yet. He guesses he'll have to wait until the morning. The shit is about to hit the fan. He smiles at the thought of the press going crazy when they find out the Hangman is a cop.

Weaver swigs down the last drop of beer and lobs the empty bottle across the room onto the armchair. He swings his feet up and stretches out on the sofa, his hands behind his head.

His mind and body are still buzzing. A surge of serotonin heats his blood. Killing is more addictive than he'd expected. Each murder makes the next one easier. It's just a shame that his plan has been scuppered. It was simple: erase the Goldings from the planet, then see where life as a police officer took him. It could have worked if Digger hadn't stuck his nose in. Weaver's only regret is that he'll never wear the uniform again. He knew becoming a police officer would give him the power he needed. He hadn't thought that he'd enjoy it so much.

He closes his eyes, recalling the sheer terror on Baxter's face as she felt the syringe lancing into her thigh, death flowing into her veins. He considers her death a bonus. Symbolic revenge for all the children's home shrinks that let him down. It was never part of the plan but the opportunity had been too good to resist.

He swings his feet back onto the floor and sits up. He's had a good run. The time has come to look for a way out. Maybe steal a small boat and take a trip across to Belgium or Holland. Simply getting back to London would be a good move. There are plenty of hiding places in the shadowy corners of a sprawling metropolis. Weaver gets off the sofa, walks across to the window and peers through the narrow gap in the curtains. The cold, bright lights of the estate flare in the darkness.

It's always useful if you have something other people want. Something that can give you an edge. Sam Hunter gives him leverage. An element of control.

If you want to survive you must adapt and adjust. The survival of the cruellest. That's always been his approach to life and so far, it's paid off.

Weaver pulls the material of his T-shirt up to his nose and sniffs. He could do with a shower and some fresh clothes. That will have to wait. He has important stuff to do first.

He puts on his jacket, his trainers and his baseball cap before slipping out of the front door. Avoiding the lift, he runs down the concrete staircase, screwing his face up at the smell of urine and weed. The stench of misery and squalor.

It's still dark outside. The streets deserted. A dangerous silence hangs over the estate. Weaver pulls the peak of his cap down and breaks into a jog. He passes the playground, constantly checking that there's no one lurking in the shadows.

His dark blue van is parked on the pavement near Tony Golding's lock-up. He climbs into the driver's seat, starts the engine, pulls away and puts his foot down. Up ahead, he spots three figures emerging into the harsh glow of the street lights.

Weaver curses under his breath and pulls his cap down further over his face. All three youths are dressed in loose-fitting tracksuit trousers and hoodies, despite the temperature being close to freezing.

They turn in unison and shoot him hostile stares, like salivating guard dogs eyeing a trespasser. He guesses they're members of one of the estate's drug gangs.

He accelerates past them, keeping his gaze firmly on the road ahead, doing his best to appear unconcerned. He tells himself he has nothing to worry about. Youths like that live outside the law. They despise the police. They see them as rivals. Just another well-armed violent gang.

The roads are empty and the journey takes him ten minutes. He parks up, takes the torch out of the glove compartment and shuts the van door slowly to keep the noise down.

Treading carefully through the darkness, he keeps the torch off until he is inside. He stands still, waiting for his eyes to adjust to the absence of light. Inside, it's even colder than it is in the open air. The place smells of decay.

On the floor, wedged against the back wall, lies Sam Hunter. She's exactly where he left her, wrapped from head to foot in a slimy plastic sheet. He steps forward, crouches, pulls down the flap of sheeting and shines the torch beam on her face.

Her eyes are closed, her skin pale, with a sickly sheen. Weaver brushes her cheek with the back of his hand. Ice cold. As cold as his heart. He slaps her. Gently at first. Then harder.

"Wake up. Come on now. Time to rise and shine, you lazy little bitch."

He slaps her again. Zero response. Not even a twitch. He places his index and middle finger on the side of her neck under her ear, searching for a pulse.

Weaver folds the plastic sheeting back up over her face. Anger burns in his chest like a splash of acid. Not because he cares. He hates that she's died like this. Without him. Depriving him of the chance to watch her go. The last moments are the sweetest.

Reaching into his pocket, he grabs a small bottle of mineral water. He unscrews the top and pours the liquid on to her lips, then over the rest of her face, in a final desperate attempt at revival. Nothing.

He throws the bottle down beside her. Barely alive or a cold corpse — it makes no difference to him.

CHAPTER 53

The morning arrives with daylight streaming through the blinds on the incident room windows. The place is swarming with detectives, most of them having worked through the night.

Kane pushes his chair back and gets wearily to his feet. He needs a second wind and that means another coffee. He heads down the corridor to find Granger striding toward him. She raises a hand, her expression a mixture of urgency and excitement. "There's a caller on the information hotline claiming he knows where Mark Weaver is hiding out. Says he wants to speak to whoever is in charge. The call handler says he sounds genuine but he's pretty jittery."

Granger looks at Kane. He gives her a nod. "Let's go. You speak to him. I'll listen in."

In the hotline office they sit down at adjoining desks. The call handler puts the call through.

Granger takes a quick breath. "This is Detective Sergeant Bailey Granger."

"I asked to speak to the guy in charge."

The voice is youthful. The tone suspicious.

"I understand. Detective Inspector Kane can't be contacted right now. I'm a senior investigator in the case. You can speak to me."

The line falls silent. Panic flutters in Granger's gut. "If you don't want to give me your name, that's not a problem. My colleague says you claim to know the whereabouts of Mark Weaver."

The silence stretches. Beside her, Kane grips his phone receiver tightly. He gestures frantically for Granger to keep talking.

"Hello. Are you still there? Thank you for calling us. Please don't hang up. This is important. Any information you can give us could help save the life of the missing woman."

"I seen him. The man."

Granger's heart jumps. "Great. That's good. Are you sure it's him? Have you seen the E-FIT image?"

"It's him. No bullshit. I knows it cos I seen his smug face before."

"That's really good. It's great you're sure. Really helpful. Do you know where he is now?"

"The guys a rotten cop. A killer cop. Iced those guys good and proper."

Granger throws Kane a look of surprise. "You know him?"

"I said I seen him, didn't I? You listening, or what? When you lot came to the estate to get Tony. The man was there. Struttin' in his uniform like he owned our streets."

Kane remembers the youths milling around outside the Kingsbury Estate tower block when they brought Tony Golding in. He has a feeling the caller is the tall guy in the hoodie. He led the mob away on Golding's orders.

"Where's the suspect now? Do you know where we can we find him?"

"He's holed up on the estate."

"Tell me where exactly?"

"I seen him sneaking around. He usually waits until it's dark. Wears a baseball cap and it looks like he's trying to grow a beard. I always keep eyes on the block. I saw him last night. I know he's the guy."

This kid thinks he's tough. Street smart. He hasn't got a clue how much danger he's in.

"Make sure it stays that way. He's armed and extremely dangerous."

The caller grunts. "I ain't no stupid kid. No way. This dude needs locking up. We don't want no psycho cop lording it up on our estate."

"Where can we find him?"

The caller falls silent again. Granger knows better than anyone that it goes against the grain for a gang member to give information to the police.

"Just tell us where this man is hiding. We'll sort it out. Nobody needs to know that you made this call."

"He's holed up in Tony Golding's flat. Number seventy-eight. Tenth floor."

Granger pauses to let that sink in. He's hiding in the tower block home of his second victim. She can't decide whether that's clever or arrogant. Either way, it could turn out to be his biggest mistake.

"You're sure about this?"

"I told you, didn't I? The dude's got balls of steel, I'll give him that."

The line falls silent and Granger the slams the phone down.

"He's gone."

Kane stands up. "This is it. We need to move fast. We've got him. Let's get a team together and pull Weaver in as soon as possible."

CHAPTER 54

Kane and Granger sit facing the laptop screen. A grey-haired, solemn-faced Superintendent Dean stares back at them.

"At last. Fantastic news. You know where this police constable turned serial killer is. Now explain why you are wasting time talking to me. Get out there and bring the murderous bastard in."

Kane shifts nervously in his chair. "DS Granger has an idea and I think it's a good one. It's going to be our best chance of finding Sam Hunter alive."

They can both hear Dean's fingers drumming on her desk. Though her expression stays impassive, a slight twitch of the muscle below her right eye reveals the pressure she's feeling.

"Something tells me I'm not going to like this idea one little bit. Come on then. Spit it out. I haven't got all day."

Kane gives Granger a nod of encouragement. She slides her chair a few inches to the side to make sure Dean can see the whole of her face when she speaks.

"We know where Weaver has been staying. The advantage we have is that he doesn't know that we know. If we bring him now, there's a risk he'll shut down completely, refuse to answer questions, and it's likely we'll never find Sam. If we watch him, put him under full surveillance, there's a chance he'll lead us to her."

"That assumes she's still alive. That Weaver is holding her prisoner, and making an effort to keep her alive. If he's already killed her, and has disposed of her body in a shallow grave somewhere, why would he go back there?"

Granger flicks a glance at Kane. He takes it as an invitation to back her up and he accepts. "If Sam Hunter is already dead, there's nothing we can do about that. If she's alive and Weaver refuses to tell us where she is, she'll die of thirst or starve to death. This way, if we let Weaver think he's still in control, there's an outside chance we can save her."

Dean picks up a glass of water and takes a long sip. She puts the glass down slowly. Her bony hand trembles slightly. Kane has never seen her so close to losing her composure.

"I admit this plan has its merits but the risks are high. This killer is a serving police officer and when the shit hits the fan everyone will be ducking. If we let Weaver slip away because we were trying to be too clever, I guarantee we will not survive. Edison, I've known you a long time and, despite everything, I have learned to trust your judgement. What do you really think about letting this suspect stay on the loose?"

"I believe it's worth taking a risk like this if it means a life could be saved. I'm prepared to take full responsibility. If it all goes horribly wrong, I'll take the fall. Say it was my decision. Mine alone. Nobody even needs to know that this conversation took place."

Dean takes a moment to think, her brow creasing in concentration. "Okay then. You've twisted my arm. Let's do it. But make no mistake, Edison, if this does backfire, the three of us will be lucky if we end up scraping a living as supermarket security guards. Make sure you watch the bastard like a hawk. Don't let him out of your sight. I can give you twenty-four hours to try to save Sam Hunter. Not a minute more. After that, pull Weaver in and lock him up."

Dean terminates the call and the laptop screen goes blank. The two detectives sit quietly for a few seconds.

Kane breaks the silence with a clap of his hands. "Right then. We're doing this. Pick your surveillance team. I suggest we bring in some reinforcements. Faces Weaver won't recognise. I want you out there tonight. Get eyes on him, as soon as you can. Confirm it's Weaver."

Granger gets up to leave. She hesitates at the door. "This is the right thing to do, isn't it?"

Kane studies his detective sergeant. She rarely doubts herself. "What's wrong? Something troubling you?"

"What the hell do you think? Yes. I'm worried that Sam is already dead. Maybe she's dying right now."

"Listen to me. Your idea makes sense. It's her only chance and the clock's ticking."

CHAPTER 55

"Psychologist Rebecca Baxter is stable and recovering well in hospital after being brutally attacked at her clinic by the triple killer known as the Hangman, an Essex Police spokesperson revealed earlier today."

The bespectacled anchorman grins like a maniac as he delivers the news. Weaver watches with a horrified anger. The insulin injection has never let him down before. If only he'd slit her throat when he had the chance.

He grabs the remote off the arm of the sofa to hurl it at the TV, pausing when a photograph of Baxter flashes up on the screen. It looks like a promotional picture lifted from her website. She's smiling softly, eyebrows slightly raised in an expression of concern. Weaver is repulsed but can't drag his eyes away from the screen.

"No details of the attack or the injuries suffered by the psychologist have been released."

The grinning newsreader reappears.

"The as-yet unidentified suspect is also wanted in connection with the abduction of Southend Herald *reporter Sam Hunter."*

Weaver turns the TV off quickly. He doesn't want to see a picture of her. Not now. Not ever. She doesn't look like that now. He gets up and puts on his hooded jacket. He doesn't like going outside until it's dark but the place is starting to feel like a prison. He walks into the kitchen and gulps a glass of water before slipping out of the front door.

Stepping outside the tower block's main entrance, he zips up his jacket, pulling the hood over his baseball cap. It's a uniform of sorts. Not the one he's used to. He misses putting on the black peaked cap with chequered band, tilting it a fraction. He misses the buzz of clipping the radio on his lapel, the security of the stab vest and the threat of the handcuffs on his belt. Wearing that uniform felt good. Helped him control the anger inside.

It's a dull, cold day. Prowling the streets of the Kingsbury Estate, he feels wild. Out of control. Like a dangerous dog, unmuzzled. The shrink cheated death and Weaver wants to make someone pay.

He passes the deserted playground and lock-up garages, stays on the main street, shunning the temptations of the alleys and cul-de-sacs. Too easy to get lost or, even worse, trapped.

Two youths speed in his direction on electric scooters. He scowls at them. They pull up abruptly in front of him. Both have the hoods of their grey tops pulled up and bandanas covering the lower halves of their faces.

"Get the hell out of my way," he says.

The tallest boy steps closer. "Not seen you sneaking round our streets before, have we?"

Weaver grins. These kids have got some nerve. They deserve credit for that.

"So what?"

"Well, yer see, anyone who comes on this estate uninvited has gotta pay a special tax. A territory tax. These streets are ours. You gotta pay if you want to walk them. It's only fair. We accept cash. If you ain't got cash we'll take your phone."

Weaver shakes his head slowly. "Listen carefully, kids. Please go now. Get out of my face. I don't want to hurt you, but I will if necessary."

The youths exchange confused glances. This isn't how it usually goes. The tall one grabs his scooter, steps off the pavement, and crosses the road. His friend follows quickly, glancing nervously over his shoulder.

Weaver walks on. If only he was in uniform. He'd bawl them out, threaten to lock them up for the night and confiscate the scooters.

A car passes by and the hairs on the nape of his neck prickle. His instincts tell him that something isn't right. The vehicle approached too slowly and accelerated past him too quickly. He digs his hands into his pockets, turns and walks back to the tower block.

They know he's here. He has no doubt about that.

He knew they'd find him eventually. *Let them come.*

CHAPTER 56

Granger walks down the corridor and bursts into Kane's office. He looks up from his laptop.

"Weaver's been spotted. Dec drove past him a few minutes ago. He was having what seemed like a heated conversation with a couple of youths on a street corner not far from the tower block."

"Did he see Dec?"

"There's no reason to believe he knows we're watching him. He was seen returning to the flat ten minutes later and is still inside. We've got two surveillance cars in the area and four plainclothes officers walking the streets."

Kane slams his laptop shut. "It's possible he's holding Sam Hunter prisoner inside the flat. Maybe we should go in now."

The same thought had occurred to Granger. "If she's not there and Weaver decides not to talk, we'll lose any chance of finding her."

Kane nods. "You're right. If he moves, we follow. We also take the opportunity to enter the flat. Make it clear to the team that if we get a hint that Weaver knows we're on to him then we pull him in and hope that we can get him to tell us where Sam is. The one thing we can't do is allow him to slip out of our grasp."

Granger leaves the office, takes the lift to the ground floor and steps outside into the cold night. The car park is half-empty and poorly lit. A single lamp-post flickers weakly in the darkness.

She checks there's nobody in earshot before making the phone call.

Marcus answers straight away. He doesn't give her a chance to speak. "Don't bother with the bullshit, Bailey. I can guess. You're going to be late again and can I hang on until you get back."

Granger wishes it was that simple. She swallows hard. "Sorry but I'm not going to make it home at all tonight. Can you stay over? I don't think Mum's strong enough to be left alone with Daisy yet."

The silence stretches for so long, she starts to think that her brother has cut her off.

"Marcus. Are you there? Did you hear me?"

"I heard all right. I don't know what to say."

Granger can tell that he's having to work hard to stay calm. "I am sorry. We've got a major surveillance operation going on through the night. I told the team that everyone stays on duty until the job's done. That includes me."

Marcus falls silent again. "I understand what you're saying but this is something that's going to have to be sorted out. I'm willing to help out when I can but you can't go on like this. You have to consider Daisy."

Granger grits her teeth. She doesn't need to be told what's important in her life or what's best for her daughter. She also knows this isn't the right time to pick a fight. "Can I take that as a yes?"

"Of course you can. Remember I'm going back to work next week though."

Granger can't think about that. She's got a serial killer to catch and a missing woman to find.

"Thank you. I'll ring you as soon as I can tomorrow." She terminates the call before Marcus can even think about guilt-tripping her again.

She goes back inside and climbs the stairs to the first floor. As she walks down the corridor, she hears the buzz of excited voices in the incident room.

Kane emerges, running, his face flushed.

"Where have you been? Weaver's left the flat. Looks like he's on the move."

CHAPTER 57

Weaver stands outside the tower block and breathes in the cold night air. He loves fear. The smell of it excites him. The thrill of the hunt is visceral. Even if you're the one being hunted.

He crosses the road and walks straight to Tony Golding's lock-up garage. Before he opens the door, he checks over both shoulders to make sure that no one is watching. The gesture is for show. He has no doubt that eyes are on him.

Once inside, he slips the backpack off his shoulders and unzips it. He takes out a pair of disposable plastic gloves and puts them on. Digging deep into the bag he pulls out a grey trainer and places it sideways against the back wall. Reaching in again, he pulls out a can of black spray paint and gives it a shake.

He takes a moment to think before spraying the stark image carefully on the wall. When he's finished, he steps back to admire his artwork and grins. Kane will get the message. No doubt.

He pulls the gloves off, puts them back in the backpack and leaves the lock-up, slamming the door shut behind him.

It's late. The estate is quiet. Weaver puts his hands on his hips and looks up at the pitch-black sky. He knows how police surveillance works. They're watching and waiting. Ready to pounce. They'll be pumped by adrenaline but they'll be nervous. Probably even scared. Because they know what their prey is capable of.

One factor in his favour is that they want Sam Hunter. Even if the best they can hope for is to bring home her corpse. That's the only reason he's not already locked in a cell. Kane is so desperate to find the girl, he's willing to let the dreaded Hangman run loose.

The Detective Inspector is a tortured soul. He's allowed the murder of his wife to change him. He's lost his edge. Gone soft.

Weaver sets off again, striding toward the row of assorted vehicles parked along the side of the playground. He stops at his van, opens the driver's door and throws his backpack on to the passenger seat. He climbs in and accelerates away.

Checking the rearview mirror, he smiles to himself. He knows what's coming. A few seconds later, in the distance, a pair of headlights appear out of a side road. *Game on.*

CHAPTER 58

Granger pulls up on Thorpe Bay Esplanade behind a row of beach huts, their bright colours shades of grey in the darkness.

Kane grabs his radio for an update. "What's happening, Dec? Where's he heading?"

"He's going south on Royal Artillery Way. Seems to be keeping to the speed limits. Looks to me like he's making for the coastal road. Should hit the junction in about ten minutes. If he goes east, he's either aiming for Shoeburyness or driving deeper into the marshland."

"Okay, keep your distance. I don't want him spooked."

Kane's palms are moist. He wipes them on his trousers. A big decision is coming up. *If Weaver drives through Shoeburyness, should he be allowed to head into the bleak expanse of salt marshes, mudflats and lagoons?* As well as being a perfect place to hide a body, the landscape would make a moving surveillance operation virtually impossible.

He turns to Granger. "I think we're going to have to take him before he reaches the marshland."

She looks disappointed but doesn't comment. Another update comes over the radio. This time it's DC Kush.

"We've got a problem," she says.

"What do you mean?"

"Well, I think there's a chance he's got Sam Hunter with him and that he's taking her somewhere to hang her."

Kane's heart drumrolls in his chest. "Tell me more."

"We've checked the flat. She's not there. We're pretty sure he's been holding her in Golding's lock-up. We found one of her trainers." Kush is gabbling now. She pauses to catch her breath. "And there's a freshly spray-painted Hangman image on the wall — you know, a stick figure hanging from gallows. The figure strung up has long hair. A woman."

Kane curses under his breath. There's no time to waste. He calls DC Brown again.

"Dec, I want you to move in now, take him down now, do you hear me? Backup is on the way."

The radio crackles.

He tries again, shouting this time. "There's a chance she's in the van and in grave danger. Take him now."

Above the crackling, Kane hears an engine revving, the sudden screech of brakes, then Brown's breathless voice.

"I think he's turned off onto the coastal road but I can't see the van anymore. No, wait — I think I can see someone running down onto the beach. Heading back your way."

Kane gets out of the car and sprints across the road to the line of beach huts. The tide is out, the vast expanse of mudflats as dark as the moonless sky.

He turns to see Granger scurrying towards him, radio in hand.

"Dec says the van is empty. He's sure Weaver is heading our way along the beach. He could reach us in minutes."

Kane's heart jackhammers. Weaver knew he was being tailed all along.

"We've an armed response unit on standby nearby. Call them in now. And tell Dec to start organising a search of the area. I want every beach hut checked."

He peers east along the shore, straining his eyes in the darkness. Nothing. *If Sam's not in the van, what has he done with her?*

Weaver is a runner. A fit young man. But Kane can't work out where he might be running to.

He must know that he's hemmed himself in. There's no escape. No exit.

He walks back into the gap between the huts. He squats down and takes a couple of deep breaths.

Footsteps crunch on the shingle behind him. It's Granger.

"Are you all right?" she asks.

"I'm fine. Thinking."

"The armed response unit is a few minutes away."

Kane stands. "Good. Can you make sure we've got uniforms watching the road in case Weaver decides to leave the beach? I'll stay here."

Granger starts to go, then hesitates. "You don't need to do anything. The armed squad will be here soon. And we've deployed other officers further down the beach. No need to take risks."

Kane doesn't respond.

Granger tries again. "We know Weaver has a knife. If he comes, let him pass. There's no way out for him."

Kane grunts this time, his eyes searching the darkness for movement.

"I'm coming back," Granger says before darting away to the esplanade.

Kane hears the roar of an engine, doors slamming. Sounds like the gun guys have arrived. He breathes a sigh of relief.

At that moment, he spots what looks like no more than a shadow moving swiftly along the beach. As the figure comes closer, it's clearly Weaver, his hands gripping the straps of his backpack, his pace relentless and purposeful.

Kane crouches and pulls back into the shadows. He waits until Weaver passes, then stands up and follows. He's calm. No need to panic. The trap has been set and the Hangman is running straight into it. He walks along the beach, his eyes fixed firmly on Weaver's back.

A line of torch beams flashes in the darkness. Kane hears the armed police officers shouting their warnings. Weaver accelerates, swerving to his left, heading straight into the mudflats.

Kane gives chase, lifting his knees high, the mud clawing at his ankles. For a few seconds he closes in, before the gap widens again. It doesn't matter how fast Weaver is. There's nowhere for him to go.

Kane pumps his arms harder, his chest almost bursting with the effort. Weaver stumbles, lurches to one side and falls flat on his back.

Kane slows, sinking to his knees beside him. He grabs the collar of Weaver's jacket with both hands, raises him up and slams him back down into the foul-smelling mud.

"Where is she? Where's Sam? What have you done to her?"

Weaver looks up at him, his dark eyes cold, a sneer on his pale face.

Kane releases his grip and takes a couple of deep breaths.

"Police Constable Mark Weaver, you are under arrest for the murders of Adam Golding, Tony Golding and David Dines, the attempted murder of Rebecca Baxter, and for the abduction of Sam Hunter."

CHAPTER 59

It's almost midnight but Kane doesn't want to wait until the morning to interview Weaver. Every single minute lost could mean the difference between life and death for Sam Hunter.

Granger enters his office carrying two coffees, puts them on Kane's desk and sits down. "He says he wants legal representation, which means we can't talk to him until the duty solicitor arrives."

"How long is that going to take?"

"At least an hour."

Kane picks up his coffee and takes a small sip. "Naturally, I want you with me during the interview. Actually, I think you should start the questioning. Go straight in on Sam. She's top priority right now. He's going to confess to the killings eventually, isn't he? He must know he's got nothing to gain by denying responsibility. He's definitely going down for them. I'll watch Weaver's reactions and join in when I feel the time is right."

Granger nods slowly. Kane can see she has her doubts.

"It's very possible he's not going to say anything," she says. "He knows he doesn't have to. We could let him sweat in the cell until morning. Give him a few hours to consider his situation. It might loosen his tongue."

"No. I don't think so. As soon as the duty solicitor arrives, we let them have a short consultation then haul them into the interview room. We give him the chance to help us save Sam Hunter. If he refuses, we keep the pressure on until he cracks."

It sounds simple. Kane knows it probably won't be. Knowledge is power. Weaver is the only person who knows where the reporter is and whether she's alive, dying or dead.

He's unlikely to relinquish the feeling of control that gives him until he gets bored, or he feels that he'll be getting something in exchange.

* * *

Weaver lies on his back on the cell bed, his hands tucked behind his head, and stares at the ceiling. He knows what's coming his way. A whole life sentence. He'll live and die behind bars.

The knowledge fills him with revulsion and loneliness. This isn't the way his story is supposed to end. His heart thuds at the injustice.

Kane and Granger aren't bad cops. Both are pretty sharp in their own way and together they make a decent team. Still, neither can compare with him when it comes to executing a plan of action, achieving a target. They got lucky. He got unlucky.

The white-tiled walls of the tiny cell press in on him. For the first time in his life, he feels the threat of powerlessness. He raises himself up and sits on the edge of the bed.

This isn't over. He's not ready to surrender. Not yet. He's the only person in this world who knows the truth about himself. Who he really is. What he is.

He starts at the clang of metal on metal. The cell door swings open and a stocky, red-faced uniform steps in.

"Come on, lad. The solicitor's here and he needs to speak to you before your interview."

CHAPTER 60

Kane and Granger stand outside the interview room door and lock eyes. They know this is a big moment. Both for them and for Sam Hunter.

Mark Weaver waits on the other side. A young colleague they both believed had a bright future in law enforcement now revealed to be a police officer infected with the killing sickness.

Kane grasps the chrome handle, pushes the door open and they both step inside. Weaver sits at a table in the centre of the room. The duty lawyer beside him — a rotund, greasy-haired middle-aged man in an ill-fitting suit — looks up at them like a startled rabbit. Weaver doesn't move a muscle.

Granger sits down first, placing a folder containing several pages of her notes on the table. Kane pulls his chair back slowly and locks eyes with Weaver as he sits down.

Granger flicks her folder open. "This interview with Police Constable Mark Weaver is being recorded on film. I am Detective Sergeant Bailey Granger. Also present is Detective Inspector Edison Kane, and . . . ?" She glances at the duty lawyer.

"Erm, Charles Ince, Mr Weaver's legal adviser."

Granger pauses for a second, then goes straight on the attack. "Mark, we need you to tell us what you have done with Sam Hunter."

Weaver looks across the table at her and smiles. "I don't know what you mean, or who you are talking about."

"Sam Hunter. The *Southend Herald* crime reporter. The young woman you snatched off the street outside the paper's offices on the thirteenth of February."

Weaver shrugs. "This isn't making any sense to me. I've never met anyone called Sam Hunter. I think you've got the wrong person."

Kane studies Weaver. He's staring straight across the table at Granger. Not a hint of fear. A chill runs down Kane's spine, knowing the cold-blooded cruelty the man is capable of.

Gone is the affable, eager-to-please, hard-working police constable. This is a different person. Merciless and predatory. Kane has seen this kind of transformation during interviews with other killers. This is the real Mark Weaver. A homicidal psychopath stripped of his mask of normality.

Granger carries on. "Have you killed Sam Hunter? If so, you need to tell us where we can find her body. If not, you have to tell us right now where she is. The longer this goes on, the less chance she has of surviving."

Weaver laughs out loud, as if it's the funniest thing he's heard in a long time.

The duty solicitor touches his client's forearm and shakes his head.

Weaver shrugs Ince off and wipes his lips with the back of his hand. "No comment."

Kane detects a hint of a smirk and clenches his jaw. Weaver is under no obligation to utter a single word if he doesn't want to. Granger closes her folder. She knows they need to try something different.

Kane is ready. He pulls a piece of paper out of his jacket pocket, unfolds it and places it on the table.

"Why don't you begin by telling us how this all started? Why kill Adam Golding? Why murder his brother? You must have had your reasons."

Weaver responds with a flurry of blinks. It's enough of a reaction to encourage Kane to press on and try to touch a nerve.

"Why don't you tell us what they did to you? It must have been bad."

Weaver gives a half-smile and shrugs.

"What can I say? Some people just need killing."

Kane lets that statement hang heavy in the air. The duty lawyer catches Weaver's eye and shakes his head again.

"Do you think your mother killing herself was the trigger that set you on the path to murder?"

Weaver lifts a hand and rubs the bridge of his nose with his thumb and forefinger.

"No comment."

Kane looks down and takes a moment to read the notes typed on the sheet of paper in front of him.

"My team have been doing some research and it makes interesting reading. According to hospital records and newspaper coverage at the time, your mother was left in a carrier bag on the doorstep of a house in Weaver Street, Bethnal Green, East London, on the 7th of October, 1976. The woman who discovered her and took her to hospital was called Rose. They gave your mother her name.

"How old were you when you first decided to wipe out the Goldings because the family abandoned your mother?"

Weaver clenches his jaw. His face flushes. His eyes flame with rage.

"No comment."

Kane presses on. "Tony Golding was born here in Southend four years later. His mother was twenty. That makes her sixteen when she gave birth to Rose. We'll never know the exact circumstances that led to the teenager abandoning her child. One thing we do know for sure is that the DNA proves your mother, Tony Golding and Adam Golding were half-siblings. Different fathers."

Weaver slumps back in his chair, his anger fading as swiftly as it flared.

"This is a waste of time. The Goldings deserved everything they got."

Kane suppresses an urge to punch the air. Weaver's talking again. Not only that, he's virtually confessed to two murders.

"What I can't understand is why you went to the trouble of hanging them. They were already dead. It would have been much easier if you'd just dumped their bodies."

"You can't understand? How disappointing. I had you down as one of the smarter ones."

"You wanted them dead. I get that. Why string them up? Why put them on display?"

"Because taking their lives wasn't enough. I wanted their corpses to be put on show. They deserved to be publicly humiliated. Just like that family humiliated my mother."

Kane swaps a quick glance with Granger. Weaver sounds proud of what he's done. Time to focus on their priority.

"What have you done with Sam Hunter, Mark? If you tell us where she is, that will go in your favour. Is there a chance she is still alive? If there is, then please tell us where we can find her. Think of her parents and what they're going through."

Weaver grins again. "No comment."

Kane can see that Weaver's relishing getting off on a power trip every time they ask about Sam Hunter. He pushes his chair back and stands up. "I think this is a good time to take a short break. Ten minutes."

Kane and Granger step outside, both replaying and analysing Weaver's reaction to their probing, trying to figure out where they go from here.

"The only time he shows signs of cracking is when we talk about his mother," Kane says. "I'm thinking we go for the jugular. Focus on her suicide. Try to break him that way. Maybe that's our only chance of getting him to tell us where Sam is."

Granger nods. "I agree. We're not going to have any luck appealing to his better nature, so let's go for it."

They step back into the interview room to find Weaver sitting upright in his chair with his back to his solicitor, chatting enthusiastically about football with the uniform police constable guarding him.

He acknowledges the detectives with a cold smile. The fresh-faced uniform stands stiffly to attention, blushing like a schoolboy told off for talking in class.

Granger sits down and restarts the recording and filming devices. When she speaks, she doesn't mince her words.

"I reckon the day you found your mother hanging by the neck in your home was when everything changed for you. You must have felt that she abandoned you just like her mother abandoned her. Then you were moved around children's homes and never got the help you needed. You know, I actually feel sorry for you. Pity you, even."

Weaver's smile vanishes. "You don't know anything about me."

"Trust me. I know a lot more about you than you think."

"I don't trust anybody. Not even myself."

Granger pauses. She's deliberately provoking Weaver and it's going well. He's talking at least.

"I imagine your mother's suicide would have left you feeling frightened and alone in the world."

"I think you have a very active imagination. Have you ever imagined what it feels like to die?"

Granger ignores the question, wondering whether it was meant as a genuine threat, or just to unsettle her.

Kane decides it's his turn to turn the screw. "Do you believe your mother killing herself like that, knowing that you would be the one to find her, has contributed to the way you have turned out? I guess that's the sort of thing a psychologist would say."

Weaver looks across the table, his eyes dark slits. He says nothing.

"I guess when your case comes to court your defence will be suggesting that none of this was your fault. That childhood trauma turned you into a murderer. Maybe that's true. Maybe you were born a killer. Maybe your mother knew that all along. Do you know why your mother made the decision to kill herself?"

"I have a pretty good idea."

"And that is?"

"Because she didn't want to go on living."

Kane detects a quiver in Weaver's voice.

"Did Sam Hunter want to die?"

Weaver doesn't answer. He shrugs. He eyes Granger quizzically. Looks across the room at the uniform and then back at Kane.

"Have you harmed her? Is she alive?"

No answer again.

"She was last seen getting into a car close to her work. We have reason to believe you were driving that car. I guess she trusted you because you're a police officer. Did you drive her to her flat? Is that where you attacked her? Did you kill her there and then, because you knew she would eventually work out that you murdered David Dines to shut him up?"

Silence and another icy stare.

Panic creeps slowly up Kane's spine. He senses the last chance of finding Sam slipping out of his grasp. Weaver knows he will spend the rest of his life in prison, his life as a hidden psychopath and his wicked crimes exposed to the world. He seems determined to keep a firm hold on at least one secret.

"Why not take this moment to get everything off your chest? I guarantee you'll feel better for it. Tell me what you did to Sam Hunter and where we can find her."

Weaver's lips curl into a knowing smile. This is the one part of the interview he's enjoying. He holds the power. He's the star of the show.

Kane's not ready to give up.

"This is your chance to do something decent. You can put her mother and father out of their agony. They are desperate for their daughter to come back. They want her home. You can make that happen for them."

CHAPTER 61

Granger sits on the edge of Daisy's bed and watches her daughter sleep, her excitement at being able to fit in a flying visit home tempered by the disappointment of last night's interview.

Weaver is still keeping silent on where he's hidden Sam and the officers trawling the eastern marshes have so far drawn a blank.

She strokes Daisy's cheek. "Time to wake up now, my darling. You've got school."

Daisy stirs lazily, opens one eye for a few seconds and then the other. She throws back her duvet and sits up with a squeal. "Mummy."

Granger lays a hand on her little girl's head and strokes her hair softly. "Hi, darling. Brush your teeth and get dressed. I haven't got long but I'll be getting your breakfast ready."

Daisy frowns.

"What's the matter, darling?"

"I want you to take me to school. I haven't seen you for ages."

Granger leans across and kisses her gently on the cheek. "I know, darling. I'm sorry. I'll make it up to you, I promise. But I've got to get back to work after breakfast. I'm so busy."

Daisy perks up. "Catching bad guys? My friend Lucy says the police chase the nasty guys and put them in prison for ever."

"Does she? Well, she's nearly right. I'll tell you all about what I do at work sometime. Not right now. You need to hurry up and get dressed." Granger plants another kiss on her daughter's cheek. "See you in a minute."

Downstairs, her mother sits at the kitchen table, sipping a cup of tea. Granger takes a carton of orange juice out of the fridge, fills a glass and drinks half of it.

Her mother raises her eyebrows. "How's everything going at work?"

"Could be going better."

"How's your Detective Inspector Kane doing?"

"He's fine. We've been working through the night. He's still at the station. It was his idea that I should take a short break to see Daisy and you."

"He's a decent man. A good one."

"Yes, he is."

"You care about him then?"

Granger does. She stops herself from saying so because she realises what her mother is trying to suggest.

"Don't be ridiculous. We work well together and we respect each other's qualities. That's all. He's still struggling to come to terms with the murder of his wife. Anyway, he's old enough to be my father."

"Your father isn't a decent man."

Granger doesn't disagree. Even so, she wishes her mother hadn't said it out loud. Nobody likes to hear that their father is a waste of space.

Her mother stands up and puts her empty cup in the sink. "Well, I'm proud of you, Bailey. Look what you've achieved. You always work harder than everyone else on every case and you're good at what you do."

Granger appreciates having a mother who always knows the right thing to say and when to say it.

"I could have done a better job last night. I should have. Weaver refused to tell us what he's done with the missing reporter. She's probably lying dead somewhere and her parents will never know what happened to her."

"I'm sure you did your best. You're much too hard on yourself sometimes, my girl."

"I'm not killing it though, am I? Not as a detective and not as a mother."

Granger bows her head, silently praying that Sam Hunter is still alive. If they can save her, it would make all her sacrifices worthwhile.

CHAPTER 62

Weaver opens his eyes and stares at the tiled ceiling of the holding cell. He feels refreshed after a good night's rest. Surprisingly — considering the things he's done while awake — he's never had a problem falling asleep. Never been troubled by nightmares.

Shrugging off the thin blanket, he sits on the edge of the bed. He presses a hand to his chest. As always, he's comforted by the steady beat of his heart. The warming of his blood. The twisting of the poison in his veins.

He's always known exactly what he is and he's never been able to understand why it's been so easy for him to hide it. Even the so-called experts can't see it. Maybe they're too scared to really look.

The cell door clangs open and a uniformed constable places a tray on the floor. "Breakfast is served," he says before slamming the door shut.

Weaver eyes the offering. A sausage, a fried egg and a pile of congealed baked beans. He accepts he'll have to get used to eating prison slop, no matter how much his gut protests. Not yet, though.

He crosses the cell quickly, picks up the tray and hurls it against the wall. The plate shatters. The greasy mess clings to the white tiles for a few seconds, then slides to the floor.

This is going to be a big day. The day that Kane, Granger and the world will see him for what he is. More than a son consumed by hatred and a burning desire for vengeance. More than a psychopathic murderer. So much more than a traumatised child who grew up with a talent for killing.

CHAPTER 63

On her way to Kane's office, Granger stops off in the incident room. Dec Brown gets up from his desk and walks over to meet her. His cheeks are flushed, his eyes bright.

"Morning, Dec. I was expecting to be the first one in. Don't tell me you've been working here all night again."

Brown grins. "I won't. Because I haven't. I do have some news though. I know how Weaver traced his surviving family to Southend."

Granger sits down at a desk near the whiteboard.

"Enlighten me."

Brown perches on the edge of a neighbouring desk.

"It's simple really. DNA again. We know none of the Goldings featured on any of the police national databases. Not until they'd become murder victims. I decided to check out the commercial family history companies. You know, the sites like *Ancestry* and *FamilyTrees*? Well one of them got back to me first thing — *FamilyMystery.com*. Mark Weaver joined two years ago and had his DNA tested. He was quickly pinged with a family match. It seems Adam Golding was looking to trace his ancestors and was happy to spit into a test tube to do it. Bingo. Weaver has a name to trace and a link to the family he blames for his mother's suicide."

Granger nods thoughtfully. She's read about cases in America where police forces used commercial DNA databases to catch serial killers by tracing close relatives. This is the first time she's heard of killers using them to track down victims.

"Great work, Dec. Send me all the details."

"Already sitting in your inbox."

It's a positive start to what Granger is still expecting to be a tough day. Even though Weaver has admitted to the murders, every bit of evidence linking him to the deaths must be carefully collated in case he decides to claim he was coerced into confessing.

She glances up at the photograph of Sam Hunter on the whiteboard. Brown follows her gaze.

"You never know. He might tell us where she is. He's had the night to mull it over. The chance to make amends and end her parents' suffering might appeal to him."

Granger smiles ruefully. She appreciates that the detective constable is trying to lift her spirits.

The door swings open and DC Meera Kush strides in and heads straight for Granger.

"Weaver's having some sort of meltdown in his cell. He's throwing stuff around, pounding on the door and demanding to speak to you. Says he wants to do a deal."

CHAPTER 64

Kane perches on the edge of his desk, thinking hard about what he's just heard.

"Maybe this is our one and only chance of finding Sam. But Mark Weaver has murdered three people. Probably four. You know the CPS will never sanction a sentence reduction for a serial killer."

Granger shakes her head. "That's not the kind of deal Weaver's looking for. He wants a meeting with Rebecca Baxter, nothing more. He says if he's satisfied with the way it goes, he'll tell us where we can find Sam Hunter."

"I'm wondering why he would want to speak to the woman he injected with a lethal dose of insulin."

"He claims he needs a final therapy session with her. He has something important he wants to tell her."

Kane is as desperate as Granger to solve the mystery of what happened to Sam Hunter. But he hates the idea of letting Weaver have any control over the situation. "How do we know that he's being genuine? He could take his chance to say what he wants to Baxter and still refuse to tell us about Sam."

"There's no guarantee. He's saying he'll reveal all if he's happy with Baxter's reaction to what he tells her. We can't control that."

Kane stands. He's made his mind up. "If Rebecca agrees, then we'll go for it. I don't want anyone saying we didn't do everything possible to find Sam."

Granger smiles. "I was hoping you were going to say that. I've already called Rebecca and told her we need her help interviewing Weaver. I said we'd pick her up. I thought you could explain in more detail exactly what we need her to do. She's more likely to agree if you ask her."

* * *

Baxter steps out her front door as soon as their car pulls up outside her modern townhouse close to Southend's Central railway station. Granger jumps out from behind the wheel and ushers the psychologist into the back seat, where Kane greets her with a nervous smile.

Baxter pulls the seat belt across and fumbles a few times before managing to fasten it, clearly flustered by Kane's presence.

Granger starts the engine and pulls out into the heavy afternoon traffic. Kane turns his face to the window and watches a fish and chip bar, a pawnbroker and a Turkish barber shop slide by.

Baxter breaks the awkward silence. "Well, come on then. Are you going to tell me what this is all about?"

Kane gets straight to the point. "Mark Weaver wants to speak to you. He wants some kind of final therapy session before he's hauled off to prison."

Baxter doesn't react for what must be a full minute. Sixty seconds is quite a long time when you're holding your breath.

When she does speak, Kane thinks she sounds remarkably composed, considering everything she's been through.

"This man wanted me dead. He looked directly into my eyes as he injected me."

Granger brakes hard at a set of red traffic lights. She exchanges a glance with Kane in the rearview mirror. "I'm sorry I didn't explain before," she says. "It's all about Sam Hunter.

He's offering to tell us what he's done with her if we can get you to agree to this."

As Granger accelerates away from the lights, Baxter drops her head and covers her face with her hands. When she looks up she turns to Kane. "This is hard. I want to help find that poor girl, of course I do. Her family must be going through hell. What do you honestly think?"

Kane is surprised that Baxter isn't rejecting the idea out of hand. It says a lot about her character that she's even willing to consider helping.

"I think you need to know everything before you decide. Weaver says he has something to tell you and whether he gives up his secret depends on your reaction."

"You mean like some kind of sick test?"

Kane knows that Baxter is teetering on the edge. One clumsy word could push her the wrong way. His best bet is to appeal both to her compassion and professional curiosity.

"I guarantee you won't ever be alone with Weaver, and this time he'll be the one in handcuffs. It'll all be recorded on film as an official interview. He's going to reveal something about himself. You can ask him questions and then you will come up with a verdict, or psychological diagnosis of some kind. If he thinks you're right, he'll tell us what we and Sam Hunter's parents want to know."

Baxter falls silent again. Kane can almost feel her brain fizzing. If she backs away from this, he won't blame her.

Granger turns into the police station car park and pulls up near the back entrance. All three of them release their seat belts and stay where they are, the silence still loud and expectant.

Granger twists around, looks at Kane, then turns to Baxter.

The psychologist lets out a long sigh. "This is crazy. But I'll do it."

CHAPTER 65

Kane pulls a chair up to the main desk in the video observation room. In front of him are two screens, one showing an overall view of the action, the other for zooming in on individuals.

He's happy to have taken the decision to step back from this interview. Weaver seems to be more hostile when he's in the room. As an observer he can keep a close eye on how things are going and switch places with Granger if he deems it necessary.

Kane checks the screens. The interview room is empty, the bare walls sterile and cold. In the centre of the room are two tables, placed several feet apart.

In a few minutes, the door will open and five people will file in. No matter how calm they appear on the outside, at least four of them will be feeling the heat.

He sits down. Baxter's nerves must be in shreds. If she keeps her composure through this, she'll deserve a medal. He'd struggle not to launch himself at the bastard's throat.

He stands up, checks his phone's screen and considers sending Granger a reminder that Weaver must be handcuffed. He dismisses the idea quickly. It wouldn't go down well. She doesn't need to be told.

A movement on the screen catches his eye. A telltale twitch of the door handle. He sits back down, his heart thudding. Here they come.

First in is a shaven-headed, uniformed constable, who clearly spends most of his spare time pumping iron in the gym. Weaver follows, his hands cuffed in front, a swagger in his step as though he's running the show.

Let him think he is. If they get the result they want, it'll be worth it.

A second uniform follows. Tall, wiry, with a close-cropped dark beard.

Weaver sits at one of the tables, the two constables standing a couple of paces behind him. He tilts his head and stares straight at the camera. Kane shifts uneasily in his seat. Weaver knows someone will be watching.

Granger and Baxter enter the room and sit behind the other table, facing Weaver. Baxter, her head down, busies herself placing her notepad and pen in front of her, not yet ready to look Weaver in the eye.

Kane leans closer to the video monitor to check that the audio is on and the volume high. He doesn't want to miss a single word.

Granger speaks first. "Can you confirm that you know this interview is being filmed and that this time you have waived your right to have a solicitor present?"

Weaver drops his cuffed hands onto the table. "That's fine. But are these really necessary? What do you think I'm going to do?"

Baxter lifts her head to look straight into the eyes of the man who tried to kill her. "The handcuffs are non-negotiable. Now, shall we get started? What would you like to tell me?"

Weaver sits back and drags his hands to fall on to his lap. "You're looking well. I'm glad."

"Glad I didn't die?"

"You know, I did enjoy our therapy sessions. Just me and you. This isn't quite so intimate. Before I start, can I just check that the usual rules apply? That anything I say is completely confidential?"

Weaver turns in his chair to grin at the two uniforms. Kane shakes his head. Weaver is enjoying himself too much.

Baxter opens her notepad and picks up her pen. "What is it you want to talk about? About you, I guess. You want to know if you are a pathological misfit, insane or simply a monstrous human being."

Weaver freezes. Kane turns quickly to the other screen and zooms in on his face. He's gazing at Baxter in faint astonishment. "What makes you say that?"

Baxter opens her notepad and scribbles furiously for a few seconds. Kane is impressed. She's staying composed and professional.

"Knowing your true self isn't easy," she says. "We all struggle with that."

"I know exactly who I am. I know what I am and why. What I can't understand is why nobody else can see the truth."

"What do you class as the truth?"

Weaver doesn't hesitate. "I am a killer."

Baxter makes another quick note.

"That is one truth. Nobody can deny that. You have confessed to murdering three people. What about Sam Hunter?"

Weaver shifts his gaze to Granger, then looks up at the camera again. Kane can almost feel his eyes bore into him.

"I have killed four people."

Granger and Baxter exchange glances. Neither of them was expecting a straightforward confession. Kane stands up. He can't understand why they aren't demanding details.

Baxter speaks, her voice soft, coaxing. "I'm listening, Mark. Where is she?"

He sits up straight. When he answers, his voice is flat. Robotic. His lack of remorse sends a shiver down Kane's spine. "She was too much trouble. She kept complaining. Whining all the time. I couldn't bear it any longer. The pressure. The hassle. So I . . ."

Weaver falters and bows his head.

Kane frowns. He's never shown any hint of remorse before.

Baxter gives Weaver a moment to compose himself before pressing on. "I think you were about to tell us something important."

He lifts his head slowly. "I injected her with insulin. Much too much. It didn't take long. She went into a coma. And then I . . . I went upstairs, took a sheet off her bed, twisted it to make a rope and went back down. I dragged her to the stairs, tied one end of the sheet around her neck and pushed the other end through the banisters halfway up. It was easier than I thought it was going to be. I hauled her off the ground and knotted the sheet around the banister rail. She was small and skinny, and I was big for my age. I waited a while to make sure she was dead, then called the police. Told them I found her like that when I came back from school."

Kane slumps forward, closer to the video monitor. Granger shoots a look up at the camera, her eyebrows raised. Baxter stays calm, her expression unchanged.

"You murdered your mother," she says. "Made it look like she killed herself. You were only fourteen."

Despite Baxter's effort to remain professional, a quiver in her voice gives away her shock at what she's just heard.

Weaver sighs loudly. "It was so easy. Nobody suspected a thing. She was depressed. She showed me how to inject, so I could give her the daily shots she needed. The police were only too happy to sign it off as suicide. I'd even go as far as to say it was the perfect murder."

Baxter closes her notebook, sits back and crosses her arms across her chest.

Weaver shakes his head in frustration. "Is that it? Haven't you got anything to say?"

"What do you want from me?"

"I want you to give me your verdict. I know what I am. I'd like your diagnosis. Is it a personality disorder? Am I a psychopath, a narcissist? Or plain crazy?"

All of the above, Kane thinks. *Plus a cold-blooded, murderous bastard.*

"One last question," Baxter says. "Would you say you killed your mother because she asked too much of you? Because you'd had enough of looking after her?"

Weaver takes a moment to think. "Not just that. That was a small part of it. The truth sounds weird, saying it after all these years. I did it because I wanted to know what it feels like to kill someone. So what's your verdict?"

"Okay. You asked for this. Here's my diagnosis. It's something I thought I'd never hear myself say, because I have always believed that human beings are inherently good. That it is environment and childhood trauma that can turn people into beasts. In your case it is my firm belief that you are pure evil. You were born evil. You will die evil."

Weaver stares straight at Baxter, his eyes narrowing to slits.

"Bravo," he says. "At last. Now I'll take you to Sam. To her body."

CHAPTER 66

In the fast-fading light, the police motorcade turns off the coastal road and heads toward the old garrison town of Shoeburyness.

The rear window of the marked patrol car is close enough for Granger to see the back of Weaver's head. Two uniforms sit either side of him.

Kane sits beside her in thoughtful silence. They've been on the road for twenty minutes and he's hardly said a word.

She gets it. After everything, they're too late. They've failed. Weaver said he'd take them to Sam's body. In a matter of minutes, they'll find out what he did to her.

Granger checks her rearview mirror. On her tail is an ambulance and, behind that, a forensics van. She glances to her right, where the land slopes down to the shore. In the distance, the twilight darkens as it settles over the rolling sea.

Weaver has surprised them again, leading them into the centre of the former military barracks. Granger expected to be taken to a remote woodland or an overgrown marshland ditch.

Kane stirs in his seat. "Do you think Rebecca is going to be all right? You know, she told me once that she doesn't believe in evil. Said it was a medieval construct. Totally unscientific."

"I guess that was before she was attacked by Weaver."

Granger switches on her headlights and follows the patrol car into Mess Road, pulling up after a couple of hundred metres. One side of the narrow street is lined by the back gardens of expensive-looking homes. The other side borders an area of lightly wooded parkland.

Kane and Granger get out of the car and cross the road where Weaver is already waiting. He's still handcuffed and flanked by the two uniforms.

Staring across the field into the gloom, he doesn't even glance at the detectives. Granger can't believe how unmoved he appears. For him this moment holds no sorrow. It's nothing more than a tedious chore.

"Where is she?" Kane demands.

Weaver nods into the distance.

"Over there, underground."

The taller of the constables opens the patrol car's boot, takes out a flashlight and a large stainless-steel pointed spade.

Granger takes the torch. "Come on then. Let's get this over with."

She and Kane walk either side of Weaver, the torch beam throwing a path of light on the wet grass. The two constables follow close behind.

After about twenty metres, Weaver stops suddenly. Ahead, the beam of the flashlight picks out a long, low, grass-covered mound. The shape reminds Granger of an ancient burial barrow.

The nape of Granger's neck prickles. "What the hell is this?"

"It's an old World War Two air-raid shelter. There are a few around here. She's in that one."

Granger and Kane approach it slowly. On one side, a metal grid covers a small rectangular entrance. The grid is tied shut by a length of blue nylon rope. Granger guesses Weaver forced the original chain and padlock.

She snatches the shovel off the uniform and uses the sharp edge to chop down frantically on the binding. The clanging of metal on metal resounds in the darkness and Granger strikes harder and harder until the rope splits.

She drops the spade, shoves the metal grid aside and steps down into the shelter. Inside, the air is dank. It smells of mould, sweat and fear. Granger turns, crouching to avoid hitting her head, and lets the torch beam fill the space. The muddy floor is littered with stones and broken bricks. At the far end, a small, fully clothed figure lies unmoving in the foetal position.

Granger kneels beside Sam Hunter and places the fingers of her right hand on her neck under her ear. Kane kneels beside her.

"Can you feel a pulse?"

The only thing Granger can feel is the iciness of Sam's skin. She shakes her head. "No pulse. Nothing."

Kane points to an empty plastic bottle lying close by.

"It looks like Weaver might have left her some water."

Granger wants to weep for this young woman. She's too angry. The world shouldn't be this dangerous.

Kane reaches forward and rolls Sam gently onto her back. She looks peaceful. Her face ashen and gaunt. A heavy dread presses down on his chest. He's going to have to break the news to the parents. Tell them their daughter is gone. It's his duty, his responsibility, his punishment for failure.

He bends down and places his right cheek just above her pale lips. His eyes widen.

"Get the medics in here, quick. I think she's still breathing."

CHAPTER 67

Two Weeks Later

Detective Superintendent Dean smiles broadly. "If you want time off, take it, Edison. As long as you need. This case has been draining for everyone."

This isn't what Kane wants to hear. He'd prefer the top brass to be desperate for him to move straight on to the next case for fear the murder squad falls apart without him. There's also the added bonus that being busy stops him thinking too much about Lizzy.

"Actually, I'm feeling as fit as a fiddle and I'm raring to go again."

Dean drums her fingers on her desk. "You do know that you don't have to carry on at all if you don't want to. You've not done your thirty years yet but because of all you went through, with Lizzy, you'd almost certainly qualify for early retirement on a full pension."

Kane's stomach lurches. This is the last thing he wants and he's disappointed Dean has suggested it. In the past, she's always made a point of stressing the importance of holding on to her most experienced investigators.

"This wouldn't have anything to do with Mark Weaver, by any chance? The media are going to have a field day when he's in court for sentencing in a couple of months. I suppose it would be great for you to have a ready-made scapegoat. You can announce that the senior investigating officer has left the force."

Dean's smile vanishes. Her cheeks redden. "I'm going to ignore that. Because I've known you a long time and know that sometimes you speak before you think things through. Weaver is admitting everything and the reforms of our recruitment and vetting system will deflect press criticism. I'm only thinking of your well-being."

It's Kane's turn to smile. "Well, thank you very much. It's appreciated. I have no intention of handing in my badge just yet."

Dean surrenders with a nod. "The fact that the reporter was found alive will help take the heat out of the Weaver situation. Granger did a fine job too. She'll make a top senior investigating officer one day."

Kane doesn't disagree. He wouldn't hesitate to recommend her as his successor. When the time comes. Before then, he has a lot more killers to catch, including the monster who murdered his wife.

* * *

A thirty-minute drive later, he pulls up outside the home of Sam Hunter's parents. A beaming Judy Hunter opens the front door.

"Come on in, Detective. Sam is upstairs, first room on the left. Tea or coffee?"

"Nothing for me, thanks."

He climbs the stairs and follows the sound of raucous laughter to the open bedroom door. He goes inside. Granger smiles up at him from her chair.

"You're late. We started without you."

"I got held up. Dean was being difficult."

Sam is sitting up in bed, her phone in one hand, a half-eaten chocolate biscuit in the other.

"Detective Kane. So nice to see you. Bailey wasn't sure you were going to turn up. She says you don't like socialising much."

"She said that, did she?"

Alan Hunter enters the room carrying a plate of biscuits. He puts them down on the bedside table.

He turns to Kane. "Thanks for coming. Me and Judy, well, we really want to thank you both for not giving up. For never giving up. We'll never forget what you did."

Kane's not sure how to respond. "We were just doing our job" sounds too crass. Instead, he gives a shrug and smiles awkwardly.

Alan Hunter leaves the room and Sam snaps her laptop shut.

"I want to thank you too. Both of you. I think I only survived that long because Weaver left me that one bottle of water. Don't know why he did. Maybe he didn't really want to kill me."

Kane isn't happy about giving Weaver credit for anything. The doctors said Sam wouldn't have survived another day.

"What have you got planned once you're up and about again?"

Sam casts a quick glance at the open door. "I'm going back to work as a reporter. The *Herald* wants to give me a permanent job. Don't say anything to Mum and Dad though. I haven't told them yet."

Outside, Kane walks with Granger to her car. She climbs in behind the wheel.

"I'll see you next week. Enjoy your few days off with your family."

Granger smiles. "I will."

She shuts the door and starts the engine.

Kane turns and walks away. His phone rings. He pulls it out of his pocket. After listening for a few seconds, he runs back to Granger's car just as she's pulling away. She jams the brakes on with a screech. He opens the passenger door and leans in.

"What's going on?"

Kane doesn't know whether Granger's going to laugh or cry.

"A body's been found in a lane near Hockley Woods. A knife rammed up to the hilt in the victim's right eye. A message written on his skin. Dean wants us there pronto."

Granger stares at him for a few seconds before letting out a loud sigh.

"What are you waiting for, then? Get in, for God's sake."

THE END

THE JOFFE BOOKS STORY

We began in 2014 when Jasper agreed to publish his mum's much-rejected romance novel and it became a bestseller.

Since then we've grown into the largest independent publisher in the UK. We're extremely proud to publish some of the very best writers in the world, including Joy Ellis, Faith Martin, Caro Ramsay, Helen Forrester, Simon Brett and Robert Goddard. Everyone at Joffe Books loves reading and we never forget that it all begins with the magic of an author telling a story.

We are proud to publish talented first-time authors, as well as established writers whose books we love introducing to a new generation of readers.

We won Trade Publisher of the Year at the Independent Publishing Awards in 2023 and Best Publisher Award in 2024 at the People's Book Prize. We have been shortlisted for Independent Publisher of the Year at the British Book Awards for the last five years, and were shortlisted for the Diversity and Inclusivity Award at the 2022 Independent Publishing Awards. In 2023 we were shortlisted for Publisher of the Year at the RNA Industry Awards, and in 2024 we were shortlisted at the CWA Daggers for the Best Crime and Mystery Publisher.

We built this company with your help, and we love to hear from you, so please email us about absolutely anything bookish at feedback@joffebooks.com.

If you want to receive free books every Friday and hear about all our new releases, join our mailing list here: www.joffebooks.com/freebooks.

And when you tell your friends about us, just remember: it's pronounced Joffe as in coffee or toffee!

www.ingramcontent.com/pod-product-compliance
Ingram Content Group UK Ltd.
Pitfield, Milton Keynes, MK11 3LW, UK
UKHW021311270325
5189UKWH00037B/413